BLACK ORCHID GIRLS

BOOKS BY CAROLYN ARNOLD

DETECTIVE AMANDA STEELE

The Little Grave

Stolen Daughters

The Silent Witness

Black Orchid Girls

BRANDON FISHER FBI SERIES

Eleven

Silent Graves

The Defenseless

Blue Baby

Violated

Remnants

On the Count of Three

Past Deeds

One More Kill

DETECTIVE MADISON KNIGHT SERIES

Ties That Bind

Justified

Sacrifice

Found Innocent

Just Cause

Deadly Impulse

In the Line of Duty

Power Struggle

Shades of Justice

What We Bury

Girl on the Run

Life Sentence

MATTHEW CONNOR ADVENTURE SERIES

City of Gold

The Secret of the Lost Pharaoh

The Legend of Gasparilla and His Treasure

STANDALONE

Assassination of a Dignitary

Pearls of Deception

Midlife Psychic

CAROLYN ARNOLD

BLACK ORCHID GIRLS

bookouture

Published by Bookouture in 2022

An imprint of Storyfire Ltd.
Carmelite House
50 Victoria Embankment
London EC4Y oDZ

www.bookouture.com

ISBN: 978-1-80314-215-9
eBook ISBN: 978-1-80314-214-2

ONE

She was going to die. Today.

Restraint had been shown for far too long. Now was the time for action. And the observer was ready.

She'd be easy to find. She loved the trail that cut through the woods and dipped down to the Potomac River, winding alongside it like a twirling ribbon. The observer had followed her there before and watched from a distance. This morning it would just be the two of them—up close and personal.

Privacy, solitude. Exactly what was needed.

Looking on from this vantage point, tucked within a thick copse of trees, she appeared nervous and cautious. But it was much earlier than when she normally came here. The sun had yet to wake up, leaving the woods mostly in darkness but for the fine tendrils of moonlight that reached through the towering canopy like fingers.

The girl kept looking over her shoulder, and she raised her flashlight at every small noise—an animal scurrying in the underbrush, chattering squirrels, squawking blue jays. She would startle, then freeze. Seconds later, she would look around again, sweeping the beam of her flashlight over the area.

Eventually, seemingly satisfied that she was safe, she set her light on the ground with her backpack and crouched down, her hands busy with her findings on the water's edge.

All was still. And calm.

Until the observer started to approach and stepped on a small twig, causing it to snap.

The girl snatched her flashlight, bolted to her feet, and spun around. "Oh." That was all she said as she lowered her light.

The moon's glow put her in a spotlight. Her milky-white complexion, her flawless skin. She knew no enemies and feared no one. She was the princess in the ivory tower who had been handed everything and looked down on others.

The observer stepped toward her, slowly and mindfully, imagining that otherwise the prey might catch a whiff of danger and run off like a jackrabbit. That would be a most undesirable consequence. Running wasn't enjoyable—at all—but it turned out the fear of her fleeing was unnecessary.

She let the observer get close, trusting from a blind ignorance.

In one swift and fluid movement, the observer pulled the blade from a pocket and thrust it into her gut.

She clutched her stomach and stared with bulging eyes. Shock washed over her expression, her mind trying to register what had just happened. Her mouth fell open, and she let out a feral scream as she turned to run.

The observer grabbed her arm and spun her around and proceeded to thrust the knife into her torso repeatedly, counting each stab. One, two, three...

With each penetration, the observer stirred to life. This was right—everything about it. They never should have waited so long to satisfy this craving.

The girl clung to the observer, confusion and disbelief mingling in her eyes. The observer felt nothing but justification and continued stabbing until her screams fell mute and her body collapsed to the ground.

In that moment, all went extremely still. Silent.

The observer took a deep breath and closed their eyes, mentally processing what had taken place. They had taken a life, and it hadn't been that bad at all. In fact, it was rather liberating.

But there was still work to do.

The observer got to work on preparing her body. It had to be presented just so.

TWO

Monday morning, and there was already a murder.

Detective Amanda Steele was aware of every twig she crunched underfoot and the stones on the path that she rolled over, despite the forest floor being plastered with colored leaves. The air was moist and had that clean, crisp smell of fall that made one think of pumpkin-spice lattes and curling up on the couch under a blanket with a book. At least for some people. Amanda didn't have time for that, so even though she was headed to a crime scene, she inhaled deeply, deriving what pleasure she could from her surroundings.

She and her partner, Trent Stenson, were being led through Leesylvania State Park by Officer Leo Brandt with the Prince William County Police Department. The discovery of a young woman had been made earlier that morning, and the call had come in just as Amanda had touched her ass to her chair down at Central Station. The park's official address was in Wood-bridge, putting it squarely within the PWCPD's—and Amanda and Trent's—jurisdiction.

They worked in Homicide and were called in whenever death was deemed suspicious. In this case, foul play was an obvious conclusion—at least based on the briefing that Amanda had received. The victim had been stabbed multiple times and found deep within the park next to the Potomac River. Had the killer specifically chosen this location for its isolation—and was it where the murder had taken place, or had the woman simply been dumped there?

The park opened at six, and though time of death still needed to be confirmed, it was likely the body had been left there before then. It might also mean the killer circumvented or bypassed the normal access points to the park. Currently the park was closed to the public while the investigation took place. The only vehicle that remained in Lot C was a white Honda CR-V that was registered to a Paul and Joni Swanson—the couple who had found the body. Police vehicles and responders had parked out at the road.

"And the Swansons were here because...?" Trent asked.

"Just hiking, far as I know." Brandt spoke as he kept walking and continued to follow the trail toward the river.

"Do they come here regularly, or know the victim?"

Brandt glanced over a shoulder. "You'll need to ask them, but my grasp of the situation is *no* to all the above."

Trent looked over at her, and Amanda pressed her lips and hitched her shoulders.

Did the Swansons have something to do with the girl's fate? Or was it purely happenstance that they'd been the ones to find her? "Where are the Swansons now?"

"Still here. The wife's a mess."

Amanda nodded, not that Brandt could see her. "How much farther now?" She was familiar with the park but not intimate with all its twists and turns, and she was anxious to get to work.

"Just around that there bend"—Brandt pointed to where the path veered right about twenty feet ahead—"and off trail for a bit. So, not long."

Amanda had been able to see the Potomac for a while. With each step she took, voices became clearer. They took the turn off the trail, and as they came closer to the water, a cool breeze gusted around her. Amanda hugged her coat tighter to herself. They were fortunate the weather didn't get as bitter as it did farther north during the fall and winter months, but some days the chill still managed to seep into her bones.

"Right there." Brandt stopped walking and pointed about another twenty feet away toward the riverbank. Not that it was necessary to declare this was the crime scene—the evidence did that for itself.

Crime scene investigators were working around the body, snapping photographs, and yellow markers dotted the area.

From this distance, Amanda caught a glimpse of the victim's head—a halo of blond hair.

Amanda's heart squeezed at the sight. A young woman. Murdered. That part wasn't news, but somehow, being here in this place, the loss was tangible and permeated the air. It entered her with every inhale she took. Not the smell of death so much as the all-encompassing awareness that this was the scene of a horrendous crime. Something told her this wasn't a body dump—even if she didn't have the proof of that yet.

As she and Trent got closer to the body, CSI Emma Blair, who had been taking pictures, stepped back. Amanda recently found out that her father had an extramarital affair with Blair twenty-some years ago, which resulted in a baby. Though she had met her half-brother, she hadn't known who he was at the time. She hadn't confronted the elephant in the room between herself and the CSI yet, but she supposed at some point it would be inevitable.

CSI Donnelly paused her work too and greeted Amanda and Trent. Her tone was somber, succinct. For good reason.

The sight was chilling. Amanda instinctively tugged her coat even tighter to herself, her hands bunching the fabric at the zipper as she stepped around the body—though she did so at a distance to avoid contaminating the scene.

The victim was supine, her eyes fixed blankly on the sky and her feet toward the river. Naked and on display, there was an innocent, ethereal quality that made her more child than woman. Sunlight glistened and danced on tears that had frozen to her eyelashes like tiny diamonds.

She was also pristine. No sign of blood. The killer had taken his time to stage her this way, and he had placed fallen leaves around her, as if tucking her in for the last time.

The girl could have been Sleeping Beauty with a creamy, pale complexion waiting for her prince to kiss her and resurrect her to life—if not for the numerous stab wounds in her torso.

And the black orchid that lay on her chest.

THREE

Amanda turned her gaze away, needing a break from the heartrending scene in front of her. So young. This girl couldn't have been more than twenty, just when life was becoming interesting. Her entire future had lain before her like a buffet of options... until it had been stolen. As if sensing the direness of the situation, everyone around Amanda had entered a reverent moment of silence for the girl. Eventually, Amanda blinked and swallowed the grief and regret that burned up her throat. Time to detach and be objective. Find justice for this victim.

"Were any of her personal belongings found, to provide us with an ID?" She directed the question to the CSIs.

Blair gestured to the body as if to say, *Where would she be hiding it?*

"Nothing yet, Detective," CSI Donnelly said. She was the pleasant one—always had been. "We ran her prints, but no hit in the system."

"Thanks, Isabelle." Naked, shamed, and without a name. The trifecta could topple Amanda's sanity if she allowed it, but she had a job to do, and she was going to do it. She cleared her throat and looked at Trent. He was watching her. "What do you make of it?" She pointed to the woman's body. Trent was in his first year as a homicide detective, and they'd been partnered since January. He'd proven himself an excellent detective, so she'd let him start the theorizing.

Trent took a deep breath, rubbed his brow with the back of his arm, his pen in one hand, his notepad in the other. "I'm guessing you're looking for more than, 'It's not pretty.'"

"Yeah, more would be good." Like her, he was probably busy trying to process everything and make sense of it. She already had a bunch of questions and possibilities running through her mind, but there was one at the forefront. What were they dealing with here—an isolated incident, or evidence of something far worse? The precision, the obvious planning, the lack of fear on the part of the killer... The black orchid. It was left like a signature or a calling card—something that serial killers did. But she talked herself off that ledge. The flower could also be a sign of a remorse. The killer could have known their victim.

Amanda and Trent stepped back, giving the CSIs more room to work. She took in the area. Woods, a dirt path, the river, and a couple talking with a PWCPD officer farther down the trail. She'd guess they were the Swansons, the ones who'd made the discovery. The noise of the woman's sobbing carried in the air, and the man's arm was around her.

"So was she killed here or dumped?" Trent asked. "It's looking rather clean at first glance, so I'd almost think she was dumped here."

Amanda turned her attention to Trent. Though she'd originally leaned the other way—that the girl was killed here— Trent's opinion seemed logical. But by killing her *and* cleaning her elsewhere, the killer would risk trace evidence transfer during transport. Right now, though, it was too early to know exactly what they were looking at. "Maybe once we know who she is, we'll be able to figure out her last movements and what got her to this point. Such as where she was last seen. We might even be able to answer if she came here on her own and ran into her killer, or whether it was someone she knew who she had arranged to meet." She spitballed a few hypotheticals.

"Sick to think someone in her life could have done this to her." Trent flicked his pen toward the body. "Leaving a flower behind, combined with the way she was presented, makes me think her killer may have experienced remorse. That could mean it's personal, just as the number of stab wounds could indicate the murder was ruled by emotion."

"Just not a 'heat of the moment' murder. The killer was prepared. Orchids aren't native around here as far as I know. And the way she's been posed—cleaned and naked—has to be telling us something."

"Which would be?"

"Not sure yet." And that was the truth. While the girl's nakedness was certainly sending a message, Amanda didn't want to jump to a conclusion on what that might be. Had it been to shame her, exploit her, expose her? Had she been sexually assaulted? Amanda pinched her eyes shut briefly, not really wanting to go there unless necessary. She'd faced enough of that ugliness to last her for several lifetimes when she'd uncovered an active sex-trafficking ring in Prince William County earlier in the year. Those involved had since been arrested and the ring shut down, but as her friend Patty Glover from Sex Crimes reminded her, those types had a way of rising back up again.

"And if the killer is about sending messages, why? Are we looking for a serial killer?" Trent pierced her eyes with his. They'd faced one before—not long ago, in fact—and it was safe to say neither of them were ready to go down that path again.

The CSIs both stopped moving and looked at her, stalled on the stark reality of his question.

"Let's not make that leap," Amanda rushed out. "Not yet. Notice how the orchid wasn't placed in her hand but was just set on top of her?" She flicked a finger toward the victim. The girl's arms were at her sides, not clutched around the stem of the flower. "It's almost like it was left there as a last-minute thought, which it couldn't have been. The killer brought it, which indicates planning."

"Uh, just thinking, though... don't they have orchids in the floral sections of grocery stores sometimes?"

"Not usually black ones, and the leaves and flowers on this one look rather large. Thinking this is a stem from a more mature plant." She didn't have a green thumb, but she possessed some basic gardening knowledge.

"Well, I'll take your word for it. I'm not a gardener or botanist."

She held up a hand. "I can't make that claim either."

Trent put his pen in a back pocket of his pants and tucked his notepad under his arm. He pulled out his phone and started tapping away on it.

"What are you doing?"

There was no response as he carried on with whatever it was he was doing.

"Trent?" she prompted.

"Ah, just looking up the symbolism for black orchids. We were just talking about possible messages that the killer intended, right? The flower could very well be a part of that."

"Oh." Impressive. After all, it would make sense that particular flower had been chosen for a reason.

"Here we go," Trent began. "There is actually a duality to the symbolism of this particular flower. It has negative connotations and positive ones."

"Hit me with both."

"Well, it can represent bad luck and death."

"Suitable, considering the circumstances."

"Also black magic." He lifted his gaze from his phone, and she followed the direction of it to the body. "I'm not seeing anything that indicates she was killed in a ritualistic manner or in some way that smacks of the occult," he added.

"Not on the surface anyway." She'd learned from her time as a cop—which was her entire adult life—that first impressions weren't always reliable.

"Fair enough." He put his nose back to his screen. "On a positive note, it can symbolize strength, virility, sexual desires, and success."

"Huh. Was our killer aware of all these associations with the black orchid? Did it factor into their choosing this flower to leave with her body? Is its presence, in fact, a message?"

Trent pocketed his phone. "So it begins."

She angled her head. "Not following."

"The questions. There are just so many of them."

"I'm here. The party can start." Hans Rideout, Amanda's favorite ME, rounded the path and spoke only loud enough for her and Trent to hear him. He worked out of the Office of the Chief Medical Examiner in Manassas. It was about thirty minutes from Woodbridge, and though it was no longer part of Prince William County, their MEs still serviced the area. The forensics lab was there as well.

He passed Amanda and Trent and hustled down the slight incline toward the victim. Rideout could be an acquired taste, and he had morgue humor down pat, but it was his dedication to the job that earned Amanda's respect. He arrived with a male assistant whom Amanda hadn't met before.

She'd give the two of them time to look at the body while she and Trent spoke to the Swansons. She started her way over there, and the officer dipped her head in greeting. Her name tag read *Cochran*. Surprisingly, Amanda hadn't run into her before now.

"Officer Cochran, we're Detectives Amanda Steele"—she pointed to her partner—"and Trent Stenson."

"Traci," the officer said, providing her first name, "and this is Joni and Paul Swanson."

The couple were in their late thirties, not much older than Amanda's thirty-six. Paul had a bushy, dark beard and mustache and a bald head. Joni had a round face and blond straggly long hair. Her eyes were bloodshot, and she was wringing her hands, though they were shaking.

"We heard you two discovered the body. Can you tell us what you're doing in the park today?" Asked to simply establish the groundwork for the conversation and inquiries to follow.

The Swansons looked at Officer Cochran. "We told her everything," Paul said.

"That's good, but now we need to ask you questions, some of which may be repetitive for you. It's procedure," Amanda assured him. "Can you tell us what brought you here today?"

Paul glanced at his wife and answered on their behalf. "Just getting some exercise."

"Of all the days," Joni blurted out, her voice tinged with frustration.

"We can appreciate this wasn't what you imagined when you set out today." It was safe to assume the raw discovery would have been horrid and nothing short of shocking.

"You can say that again." Joni palmed her cheeks, and her chin quivered. "Do you know who she is?"

Amanda shook her head. She had just been about to ask the same question—no need now. "Not yet. Do you normally walk the trails here?"

"No. This exercise thing is just something we were picking up again. Doctor's orders." Joni dug the toe of her hiking boot into the ground, crinkling the leaves and flaking them apart. Everything was so dry out here with the lack of rain in recent weeks.

"What time did you find her?" Trent asked. He had his pen and notepad at the ready.

Amanda had fought like hell against being paired with a partner. She'd never had a good experience with anyone—until Trent. And it was a bonus that he was meticulous about writing things down. It saved her from needing to do it all herself.

"Think it was right around six forty," Paul said as he adjusted his arm around his wife, and she snuggled in closer to him. "Joni wanted to go down to the water to see if she could spot some snails."

"Snails...?" Amanda asked, curious.

"Yeah. They're a type of mystery snail."

"They're pretty neat. They can grow up to three inches long," Joni added.

Amanda had grown up in Prince William County and had never heard of the snails before, but she wasn't a hiker, not even huge into nature. "They sound neat," she offered, hoping to relax the couple. She really didn't get the feeling they were involved with what happened to Jane Doe, and they were being very cooperative, but she still needed to obtain the full picture. "So you spotted the body around six forty, and then what?"

"I called nine-one-one," Paul said. "Well, after calming Joni down some."

Joni tapped a hand over her chest. "It's my heart. It's not in the best of shape. Hence the recommended exercise."

"Sorry to hear that, ma'am," Trent said.

"Thanks." Joni dipped her gaze to the ground, and her body swayed slightly.

"Do you need to sit down?" Amanda stepped forward.

Joni drew back some and shook her head. "I'll be fine."

"As long as you're sure." Amanda studied the couple. Absolutely nothing about them screamed "killer." In fact, the opposite. She imagined they were rather pleasant and down-to-earth people when they weren't forced to deal with something as messy as murder. "Just a few more questions. Did you come across anyone else in the park? They could have just been walking the trails like you?"

The Swansons looked at each other, their lips curled downward, and they shook their heads in unison.

"Anyone in the parking lot? See any other vehicles when you pulled in?" Trent asked.

"The lot we're in was empty," Paul said.

"Actually"—she stared at her husband's profile, then looked at Amanda—"we did run across that ranger in the park, not long after we started on the trail. Remember him?"

Small tingles traipsed across Amanda's shoulders. A park employee would be familiar with the terrain, and that could prove advantageous when executing a murder or even dumping a body. "Did you catch his name? Usually it's noted on a patch on the uniform, like the officer's here." She gestured to Cochran, who pointed at her name, as if showcasing it like a prize up for bid on a TV show.

"Nah, we didn't get that close," Paul said.

"He was on the trail that leads down here, to the water?" she asked.

"That's right."

"And just to confirm, he was headed from the direction of the water, back toward the entrance?"

"Yes."

"Can you tell us what he looked like?" Trent beat her to the question.

"Six feet, give or take?" Paul consulted his wife, and she bobbed her head.

It always bugged Amanda when witnesses sought to verify their stories with another party. It didn't exactly instill confidence, but she understood that stress could toy with the mind and color recollections. She'd experienced that herself when she had to sit with a sketch artist and describe the man who had shot her—*grazed* her arm, more specifically—a couple of months ago. The whole process probably took twice as long as it should have because she second-guessed herself the entire time. "Any distinguishing features? Hair color, eye color, tattoos, build?"

"He had brown hair, cropped short," Joni tossed out, but when she looked at Amanda, she dropped her head and shrugged. She must have realized how generic the description was.

"Age range?" Amanda asked as Trent's pen was coasting over the page in his book.

"Say forties."

Say... Again, not exactly a confidence booster. "Was he carrying anything, a bag or backpack?" She was thinking that the girl's clothing had to be somewhere. If this ranger was the killer, he could have been carrying it out of the park. Then again, he could have stashed the girl's possessions within the park.

"No, nothing."

"Okay. Well, we appreciate all your help. We're just going to need all your information in case we have more questions for you."

"Detective"—Officer Cochran spoke up—"I have that already."

Amanda dipped her head in acknowledgment, having almost forgotten she'd been standing there the entire time. "All right." Back to the Swansons, Amanda said, "You can go home now if you like."

Neither of them moved.

"Would you like to speak with a counselor? I can make arrangements," Amanda offered.

Paul puffed out his chest and tightened his hold on his wife. "No, we'll be all right."

"If you change your mind, or if you think of anything, call me day or night." Amanda handed her card to Paul, and he glanced at it before stuffing it into his coat pocket.

"Will do."

Amanda and Trent left the couple and returned to the body, but stayed back to allow Rideout and his assistant lots of room to work. While Rideout was hunched near the young woman, his assistant stood close and at the ready for any of his boss's requests.

"Here's the Swansons' information, Detective Steele." Officer Cochran stepped up next to Amanda, extending a piece of paper toward her.

Amanda smiled. "Thank you."

"No problem."

A patch of silence fell, and the officer worried her bottom lip and didn't move.

"Something else, Officer?" Amanda asked.

She nudged her head toward the body. "What do you think is going on here? Murder, obviously, but do you think she knew her killer? Is this an isolated incident or something more?"

"Answers I intend to find out."

FOUR

Amanda and Trent approached the ME's assistant and made quick introductions. Liam Baker was new to the Office of the Chief Medical Examiner and looked to be in his mid-twenties, if that. He wore thick-lensed glasses with black, round frames. His eyes were the color of caramel, his mouth was set on an angle, and his full lips stood out as thick worms.

"Cause of death?" Amanda asked, directing the question to Rideout.

He was crouched next to the body, his gloved fingers working over every square inch of flesh—his immediate attention focused on the girl's torso and the multiple wounds. "I'll reserve final comment on that until I have her on a table back in the morgue. It's likely safe to say that one of these did the trick, though." He splayed an opened hand over the victim's torso.

"There would have been a lot of blood..." Amanda glanced around the immediate area again. At first glance, it was clean with no signs that the woman had bled there. Maybe she had been dumped. If not, the killer had done an incredible job of cleaning up.

"There would have been." Rideout stood, groaning as he did so.

Amanda looked at the CSIs who were still working in the area, curious if either of them had found any evidence of this being the actual scene of the crime—versus a crime scene where the body had been left. Blair and Donnelly were still working away, combing the small beach for evidence.

"Looks like she may have been killed elsewhere then brought here," Trent said with more conviction than before.

"It's certainly starting to feel that way." Amanda still wasn't sure, though. How much time had the killer had with the body? The area was isolated, and if the woman was killed here, it was probably early, hours before the park opened. After all, the killer would have needed time to clean her and the area. "Time of death?"

Rideout said, "Preliminarily, I'd say TOD was between three and five this morning."

"The park opens at six," Amanda said. "Regardless of whether she was killed here or dumped, I'd lean more toward your earlier estimate." That would also allow the killer more time to clean up before the park opened.

"I'll let the evidence guide me. Again—"

"You'll know more once you get her back to the morgue," Amanda finished and smiled.

Rideout nodded. "That's right."

Trent pointed his pen toward the body. "Do you know which injury proved fatal?"

Her partner seemed to think he could pry the answer from the ME. She'd expected Rideout to use the "when I get her back to the morgue" defense again, but to her surprise, he didn't.

"There are a total of seven punctures." Rideout paused and pressed his lips into a thin line. "From what I can deduce on scene, they penetrate rather deep. As for weapon type, I'll need to get her back to the morgue. I'd say any of these wounds could have been the fatal blow, as it could have been a collaborative effect. But my experience leads me to this one." He pressed a fingertip to a puncture in her left chest cavity, close to where her heart would be.

"Huh." Trent tapped his pen to his chin, and it had Amanda raising her eyebrows.

"Yes?" she prompted him. It was obvious he'd had an epiphany.

He pointed his pen toward the body again. "In the heart?"

"That would be the right vicinity, yes," Rideout said.

"Huh. Is there something in that? Another message from the killer maybe?" Trent spun to face her. "A jilted lover, unrequited love, jealousy?"

"We'll need to consider all of it until each is ruled out." Her mind drifted some. The remote location and a young, beautiful victim posed naked with one single flower. A black orchid. The dual meanings that Trent had found. Did the flower's symbolism tell them about the victim or the killer? Both? Had this girl been brought out here by a friend or lover and caught unaware, stabbed to death? The ultimate betrayal. The wound to the heart could have been coincidental, the result of an impassioned stabbing that took the weapon all over the girl's torso without rhyme or reason. The multiple wounds also could have been to cover up the fact the killer had gone straight for the heart—because the killer felt betrayed by the victim first? "Do you know in which order the wounds were made?" she asked.

"I'll need to look more closely at her back at the morgue."

She nodded, though disappointed by his seeming go-to response today. "What are the injuries telling you about the killer?"

Rideout popped an eyebrow and smirked. "Isn't that more your area of expertise, Detective?"

"Yes and no. Suppose I should have been more clear. Are you seeing evidence of hesitation on the killer's behalf?" Her brain churned up the words *serial killer* again. She tamped them down.

"None." His facial expression paled while shadows roved in his eyes.

Amanda shivered, and not just from the cold gust encircling her. The question tossing back and forth in her mind, weighing as if in a counterbalance, continued: were they looking at the work of a serial killer, or was this an isolated incident? "Multiple stab wounds, the posing... the flower." She paced a few steps. "Cleaning the skin could indicate remorse, as could leaving the flower. Also it would seem whoever did this wanted her to be found. Otherwise, why here?"

Trent blew out a breath. "Beats me. But posing her naked really doesn't speak of respect to me. So the killer felt remorse but also justified?"

"Could be," she said, then asked Rideout, "Are you seeing any evidence of sexual assault?"

"No."

Stripped and presented naked, but not raped. One small mercy, but why leave her so exposed? To humiliate her in death? Brought on by what motive? And had this girl been living a double life—corresponding with the duality of the black orchid's symbolism? "When can you do the autopsy?"

"I'll get it done this afternoon." Rideout looked at Liam, who pulled out a tablet and started swiping his fingertip across the screen.

"Four o'clock," Liam said.

Despite Liam being a new hire, it was apparent the two of them had mastered unspoken communication.

Rideout faced Amanda and Trent. "Four o'clock."

She smiled at the unnecessary reiteration. The first twenty-four hours of any murder investigation were crucial, but being present for autopsies was also important. "We'll be there."

Rideout dipped his head in acknowledgment and addressed his assistant. "Help me load her up."

Liam put his tablet away and moved into action.

Amanda and Trent stepped back, giving them the needed space. *Her*. The poor girl needed a name. "Any distinguishing markers on her body? Tattoos, scars, piercings?"

The men paused all movement. "Nothing that I've seen. She's not a natural blond, though." Rideout bent down and swept back the hair at her brow. Her roots had grown out about a quarter inch and were dark brown.

"All right. Thanks." She had been hoping for something a little more substantial if they were to hit the missing persons database in search of her.

"That all?" Rideout angled his head, watching her as if he were frozen in place and waiting for her command.

"Yeah. Thanks." She turned to Trent, and they stepped farther away from the ME and his assistant.

"I think she knew her killer," Trent said, tucking his notepad into a pocket of his pants.

"Because...?" She wasn't a fan of unsubstantiated claims, but she was all for brainstorming.

"What got her here so early otherwise? At her age, I slept in every chance I got."

"Huh." She remembered that time of her life, and it felt much longer ago than it actually was. What was sleeping in again? Nothing but a vague memory at this point. "The killer could have also apprehended her elsewhere and brought her here—by force."

"Yeah, I suppose."

"We'll find out soon enough." *Though* not *soon enough*. While the investigators would eventually find blood evidence or something to determine if this was the scene of the murder, there were still so many unanswered questions. But that was the same for the start of every investigation. What was giving her a headache was not knowing exactly what they were dealing with here. No hesitation marks. An experienced killer? Could they expect more victims before all was said and done?

FIVE

There was one piece of the puzzle that could allow the rest to fall more easily into place. "We need that girl's ID," Amanda said to Trent. A throwaway comment, but she still felt better verbalizing it. Not that she put faith in some magical universe to grant her wish. She'd put the necessary work in. If they knew who the victim was, they could dig into her life, track her movements, find out what brought her here. Maybe even find someone in her bubble of friends or acquaintances who could lead them to the killer.

"We can try missing persons, basing it on the area, but we don't have much to go on."

"Running her face through the system might help us—though not in criminal databases as her prints aren't in the system. And all this hinges on the assumption that someone actually filed a missing persons report."

"She looked like she was in decent shape."

"And...?"

Trent stepped back and held up his hands. "Just meant she took care of herself. Her fingernails were polished, and her teeth appeared to be in good health. I wouldn't say she's someone living on the street or with no connections."

"I'll give you that. Still, even if she had people who cared about her, they might not know she was missing."

Trent nodded. "Right. If she just came here this morning, no one might have thought she was."

Amanda's mind was trying to conjure up a way of getting to an identity. "Healthy teeth." She met his gaze. "It's possible she had a dentist take a mold impression to have on file. If so, that could cement ID." That still required them to have a *suspected* ID, though. It wasn't like there was a searchable dental database; dental records were more for verification once identification was suspected. And while they could search them in missing persons, that put them back to the matter of whether she'd even been reported. Amanda's excitement at the epiphany was waning quickly, and Sergeant Malone was striding toward them with a park ranger. The man was equal height and size to the sergeant and even looked similar. It was like Malone was walking next to a mirror. Both men were in their fifties, with receding hairlines, gray beards, and mustaches.

"Detectives," Malone began, "this is Todd Hampton, supervisory state park ranger. He's in charge here during the week."

"Detective Steele." Amanda bobbed her head at him, and Trent introduced himself.

"Ranger Hampton first came down here not long after the Swansons called it in. He's also been helping officers get a feel for the layout of the park," Malone said. "And he can answer any questions you might have."

"The Swansons, who found the girl, never saw any vehicles in Lot C where they parked, but I understand there are several lots that access the premises," she said.

"There are," Todd replied.

Amanda addressed Malone. "We'll need to get officers on

those areas and see if any of them will offer up a lead. Maybe a vehicle or something that ties back to the victim."

Malone smiled subtly. "Already in progress."

"Are any rangers posted to watch the entry points during the off-hours?" Amanda asked.

Todd nodded. "A couple, but they can't be everywhere at once."

"So you have them 'out there' but not at every location?" She just wanted to clarify.

"That's right."

"What about black orchids? Are they native to the park?"

"No, they're not. Whoever did this had to have brought the flower with them."

She *loved* how people liked to step over the line into the territory of detective. He was a peace officer and armed to keep and establish peace and order, but that's about as close as their two jobs came. "Did you see her?" She wanted to read his body language. He'd shown no surprise about the orchid.

"I did. Ghastly sight." His body stiffened, and he hooked a thumb on the waist of his pants.

No obvious signs of guilt. More disgust, fear, and shock at the situation. "Do you know who the girl was?"

"I don't *know* her, but I'm pretty sure I've seen her around."

The skin tightened on the back of Amanda's neck. Could it be too much to wish they'd get her ID sooner than later? "You've seen her around. Does she come to the park often?"

"I'm quite sure she does and has a pass."

That told her three things: one, the girl was likely local; two, she must have visited often; and three, there should be a name on file somewhere in the park offices. "We need to know her name. Could you help us with that?"

Todd's arms flailed about, and he hoisted up on his pants, finally settling his hands on his hips. "I may be able to help with that, but I'll need a warrant." He landed his gaze on Malone, who nodded in understanding.

Amanda didn't quite understand. Sure, it was a state park with rules and regulations, but that didn't stop people from finding loopholes. "It's looking like the girl and her killer gained access to the park when it was technically closed," she put out stiffly. "I suppose it wouldn't look good if it got out that people snuck in after hours. Especially when one of those people became a murder victim." She realized she'd phrased it as if the girl had been killed here, but she was running with that assumption for now. Either way, it put a dead body in the state park.

Todd frowned. "I'm not parting with members' information without a warrant."

"All right. We'll get you one." Amanda met eyes with Malone, who lowered his lids slightly as if to thank her for backing off. Maybe he'd thanked her too soon. "Did the girl make a habit of visiting the park when it was closed?" The unstated implication was that the chief park ranger didn't really have control of what was going on in his park.

Todd clenched his jaw. "There isn't any way I can answer that."

He was going on the defensive, so she had to reel back a bit. She didn't need to make an enemy of him—even if she wanted to impress the seriousness of the situation. "It's a big park," she conceded, stirring in some empathy to soften her previous words.

"It is, and no one can be here twenty-four seven—or cover every square inch."

"For sure. But the fact remains that a young woman was found dead in the park. *Murdered.*" She put that out there and let it percolate. Todd didn't touch it. She went on. "She had a pass, so we can assume she came often?"

"Most likely."

"You don't know for sure?"

"As I said, I've seen her before."

If coming to the park was a routine, then the girl's killer could have known this and lain in wait or followed her here with the intent to kill. "On a regular basis?" she pressed, feeling he may know more than he was admitting.

He shrugged. "To hazard a guess, at least twice a week."

That statement prompted another question. What was so exciting about a state park that brought a young woman, college age, here in the first place? If it was for exercise, she could get that anywhere. "Do you know why she came here?"

"I don't."

"Do you know if she favored one part of the park over another? Did she stick to specific trails?" The more information they could gather about the girl's interests, the greater chance they had of piecing together a trail to follow.

"I don't know. But the computer in the office would tell us at which entrance her pass was swiped. Once I get that warrant."

Lest they forget the blessed warrant... "The Swansons ran into a ranger on one of the trails this morning. Do you have any male rangers who would have been working this morning, six feet tall with short-cropped brown hair? In their forties?"

Todd's brow pressed, then he nodded. "Could be Jamie."

"Last name?"

"Bolton."

"We'll want to speak with him," she said. "He might have seen something or someone." He might also be a person of interest, but Amanda wasn't going to say as much to his boss.

"He's back in the office."

That raised the question of where Jamie Bolton might have parked. The Swansons had said the lot they were in was empty when they'd arrived. Before Amanda could say anything further, a stifled cry interrupted her.

"Oh my God!" A female ranger was walking toward the

four of them, her legs and body swaying like she'd drunk a bottle of booze.

"Ma'am." Amanda rushed over to steady her and keep her back. There were already too many people in the area. At least the Swansons had cleared out.

The female ranger wasn't looking at Amanda but had her head turned toward the water. Amanda followed the direction of the woman's gaze. Rideout and Liam were fitting the girl into a black body bag, a fan of blond hair sticking out, which Liam delicately tucked inside the bag.

"It *is* her." The female ranger lowered herself to the ground.

Amanda placed a hand on the woman's back. "Did you know her, ma'am?"

A loud sniffle and a nod.

Excitement whirled through Amanda. A lead without a warrant?

SIX

"Please, we need to talk. Can you..." Amanda helped the female ranger to her feet and over to a nearby bench.

Malone stayed back with Todd Hampton, and Trent joined Amanda and the woman.

Amanda sat next to her. "I'm Detective Steele, and this is Detective Stenson."

The ranger was sniffling and not looking at them.

"What's your name?" Amanda asked her.

"Helen McCarthy." The woman swiped at her cheeks, which were wet with tears. She stared at Rideout and Liam, who were now making their way from the crime scene toward the trail where a wheeled gurney waited. Amanda had to wonder how much good it would do with the terrain, but she supposed it was still a better option than trying to carry the body. That observation led her to realize that if the killer had brought the body to the scene, he or she would have had a very difficult time.

"Do you know the girl's name?" Amanda was trying not to get too excited.

"No, I don't," the ranger whispered, just when Amanda was starting to wonder if she was going to respond at all.

"But you knew her?" Amanda posed the question as delicately as possible, not wanting to upset the woman further.

"I spoke to her a few times. She was always so... so..." Helen pinched her nose. "You don't have a tissue, do you?"

Amanda shook her head.

Trent whipped one out of his front pants pocket and passed it over. Amanda gave him a wide-eyed look. He was full of surprises.

Helen proceeded to blow her nose loud enough to signal incoming ships to shore in a heavy fog.

"You said 'it *is* her' when you first arrived," Amanda said, "like someone had told you about her. You didn't see the body before now?"

Helen sniffled and shook her head. Her gaze went to Todd Hampton, and Amanda could fill in the rest. He'd come down with the police to talk with the Swansons.

"Did Mr. Hampton tell you about her?" Amanda asked, quite certain she knew the answer.

"Uh-huh. Well, he just described her. Then now"—she waved the used tissue in the air as she gestured toward the crime scene—"when I saw that blond hair, I knew."

"We understand she came here often. Do you know why?"

"She loved the mystery snails."

This was the second time the snails had come up.

Helen dabbed her nose with the now well-used and bunched-up tissue. "The snails are quite common in this area, especially here." She pointed to the shore where the girl had been found.

Their Jane Doe came to the park often and had one destination when she did. The question about whether her killer had been familiar with her or not had been answered with a resounding *yes*. Next... "Why was she so interested in the snails?"

"They're quite fascinating, honestly. They are the largest river snail found in the Potomac River watershed. She had their scientific name, but I can't remember it. Anyway, they can grow up to three inches long."

"Wow," Trent replied, as if they hadn't just heard that from the Swansons.

Amanda noted how talking about a topic other than the girl had helped Helen calm down. But there was something specific Helen had said that really caught her attention. "The girl knew their scientific name?"

"She did. She told me once that she planned to dedicate her life to environmental research."

The victim did appear college age, but it would be a huge leap to act on that assumption and waste investigation hours without a true direction. "Was she in school for it?"

"She went to Geoffrey Michaels University. The science lab..." Helen's face scrunched up. "That doesn't sound quite right."

"The Potomac Center for Science and Environmental Studies? Is that what you mean?" Trent asked.

"Yeah, that's it."

Amanda was aware that was a campus of Geoffrey Michaels University. It was also located right there in Wood-bridge. If they couldn't get the girl's identity through the park membership, they had somewhere else to go.

"Did she ever come here with other people?" Trent asked.

"Uh-huh. Sometimes with her boyfriend. He was a stereo-typical jock. Good-looking and muscled. I got the feeling science and the environment weren't so much his thing. Quite sure he came for her."

Strong and familiar with Jane Doe's love for this park and the snails. He could have held her still while he stabbed her.

She also would have trusted him enough to let him get close to her. "Do you know his name?"

"No. I wish I could give you more."

"Oh, you're doing great, Helen." Amanda gave her a reassuring smile and used the woman's name to set her more at ease. "Can you tell us a little more about what he looked like? Hair color, eyes...?"

"Sandy-colored hair. Can't really remember his eye color."

Amanda nodded while Trent scrawled in his notepad. "Since you ran into the girl several times, what time of day was this normally?"

"I'd check her in pretty much right at opening."

"So around six in the morning?" she asked to clarify.

"That's right."

"And did she come on any sort of regular schedule?" She knew what Todd Hampton had told them, but she wanted to know if Helen could offer more specifics.

"Every Monday and Wednesday. Sometimes on Fridays."

Amanda didn't want to harp on the matter, but it was hard to believe Helen didn't know the girl's name, considering the frequency with which the victim had used her park pass. "And all these times you never noticed her name?"

"You can bet I'll be paying better attention moving forward, but no, I just swiped her pass and off she went. Sometimes I'd see her down at the water and we'd chat. That's how I knew where she went and why she came here."

On second thought, Amanda could understand how the name could be lost to obscurity and the busyness of a day's work. Monday was one of the girl's regular days to visit, but what had dragged her out here before the park opened?

There was chatter going on around where the body had been, and CSI Donnelly was waving Amanda and Trent over. Malone was already there, and Todd Hampton was nowhere to be seen.

"Please call me if you think of anything else." Amanda pulled out her card and handed it to Helen.

"I will."

"You going to be all right?" She didn't want to leave the ranger floundering in the aftermath, but she desperately wanted to see what had Donnelly so excited.

"I will be. Thank you." She winked at Trent, an expression Amanda took as gratitude for the tissue.

They walked over to Malone, who directed their attention to CSI Blair. She was picking up something to put into a bag. "When the body was lifted, there was dried blood on her back, and some soaked into the soil beneath her. CSIs also found some blood spatter and cast-off in the area."

"Obviously I missed seeing any of it," Amanda said.

"On the leaves, just small amounts here and there," Malone replied. "Hard to see unless one's looking very closely."

Amanda nodded and shuffled around to get a better look at what Blair was handling. A large snail. She pointed at it. "And him?" She intended the question for either CSI, but Malone answered.

"He's got some blood spatter." He wasn't looking at her, but at the snail, while he spoke.

A *mystery* snail. Seemingly apt. They certainly had a mystery to solve, but one aspect was now clear: Jane Doe was killed right here. This wasn't a dump site; it was a murder scene.

SEVEN

Amanda pulled her attention from the snail, tearing herself from the craziness of her thoughts. The snail was another victim. It would be taken back to the lab, examined thoroughly, swabbed, possibly dissected. At least its sacrifice would likely be worth it. Unlike the loss of the girl's life. Meaningless.

"Todd Hampton is cueing up the video surveillance they have on the lot," Malone said.

"What about his precious warrants?" Amanda asked.

"I've secured verbal ones through Judge Anderson."

Amanda smiled and bobbed her head. Anderson was a great guy. "Terrific."

"Hold the excitement until we see if it gives us anything."

He didn't need to tell her that. Life had taught her many years ago that nothing was guaranteed. There was no sense counting on a happy ending—they were reserved for fairy tales. She'd had that rude awakening when she lost her husband and daughter in one fell swoop to a drunk driver over six years ago.

"Which way are you leaning with this, Amanda?" Malone asked, no longer standing on formalities since no civilians were around. Also because he was an old family friend—which had both its advantages and disadvantages. One advantage was being able to let down the professional guard every now and then, to shoot straight. The disadvantage could be taking liberties that resulted in hurt feelings.

"Too early to say, in my opinion." He really wouldn't want to hear that she was giving some consideration to a serial killer at work. "Apparently the girl came to the park often, but not before opening."

"That anyone knows about," Malone said.

She chewed on that for a second or two. "I suppose it is possible there were other times she came early. It still raises questions, though. And the way she was posed... Like her killer had remorse. We've been trying to figure out whether it was because the killer knew the girl, followed her here, met her here, or was happy with whomever happened along his path."

"I'd say it's someone who's killed before," Trent interjected. "Rideout said there was no hesitation on the stab wounds. Someone experienced at killing?"

"Oh, here we go again." Malone flailed his arms. "A serial killer?"

Amanda held up a hand. "No one's jumping there yet." But if the evidence did lead them there, it would seem unlikely that remorse was a factor in the posing of the body. Then again, there were some people who had the compulsion to kill, but not the desire. Remorse could come into play in those cases.

"Seems your little buddy is." He jacked a thumb at Trent.

Buddy? That had her going silent for a few beats.

"And correct me if I'm wrong, but wouldn't we be looking at several victims in that case?" Malone asked.

"All we know," she said clearly and pointedly, passing a look at Trent, "is that there was no hesitation. The killer was determined. Possibly an experienced killer, sure, but not necessarily."

"In the least, prepared," Trent pushed out. "This was premeditated."

Amanda nodded. "Now *that* I would give you." She turned to Malone. "The meticulous way in which the killer cleaned the girl's body indicates that. Then there's the black orchid. It's not found in the park."

"Which means the killer brought it with them," Malone said.

"That's right. Also there's the dual symbolism attributed to the flower." She filled him in.

Malone's brow compressed in concentration. "Light and dark. Good and evil."

"Exactly. Considering the flower was brought here, that tells me it was selected, likely picked for its meaning." She felt confident in that assessment. Trent was watching her with a quizzical expression on his face. "What?"

"Just listening to you talk about it, our killer is probably the type of person who would pay credence to such things as symbolism."

The words *black magic* came back to Amanda's mind, but there was a line between that and having an interest in the symbolic meaning of things.

Trent glanced at her as if he had more to say but was hesitant for some reason. She motioned for him to go ahead.

"We also need to consider whether the killer picked it for the full embodiment of its meaning—the dualities—or just one aspect. Does the killer see himself, assuming it's a man, as good and the girl evil? Or the other way around?"

Malone blew out a large breath. "I'll leave that riddle for you to solve."

"So thoughtful." Amanda smirked. "At least one aspect of it is on the way to being solved."

"Oh?" Malone stood taller, stretching out his back.

"From speaking with the ranger"—she butted her head toward the bench where she'd talked with Helen McCarthy—"she said the girl came upwards of three times a week, usually when the park opened at six in the morning. No name yet, but from the sounds of it, the victim attended the Potomac Center for Science and Environmental Studies."

"Geoffrey Michaels University," Malone said.

"That's right. And she was huge into the environment and studying the snails—at least from the sound of it. We could benefit from K-9s coming out, seeing if they can find the girl's clothing, possibly other personal items she had at the time of her murder. If she was here studying the snails, there's probably a phone, tablet, or laptop..."

"I've already made arrangements for a K-9 unit to come in. Officers have already been scouring the parking lots and woods along the trails in this area that lead down to the water."

Officer Brandt was trudging toward them, appearing like a man on a mission and holding up a clear evidence bag. "Found it in Lot C."

Amanda inspected the find. A light-blue coral necklace.

"That's where the Swansons parked," Trent inserted. "They said they didn't see any cars."

"All that means is the killer was gone by then," Amanda said. Had he left in the girl's vehicle, or had the two traveled to the park together? Was there another explanation? "Well, I think it's a good time to follow up with Ranger Hampton."

"Good job." Malone patted the officer on the shoulder, and the three of them headed to the park's office while Brandt took the bag over to the CSIs.

"There's not much to see," Todd told them when they walked into the office. He was seated at a desk behind a counter. He waved a hand toward a computer monitor.

Ranger McCarthy was there too, at another computer, clicking away on a mouse. She met Amanda's gaze, and there was definite sadness in the woman's eyes. Jane Doe had made an impact on her, that much was clear.

"Helen's digging to see if she can find the girl's name," Todd said. "Whenever someone with a pass comes into the park, their card is slid through a reader and timestamped."

Which she'd gathered from talking with Helen, but she nodded as if it were news.

"Here's the video from Lot C, if you wanna take a look." Todd butted his head toward the monitor.

A door in the back opened, and a forty-something man about six foot tall with cropped brown hair emerged.

"Jamie Bolton?" Amanda asked, running with the assumption as she was too far away to read the name on his uniform.

"That's me, ma'am." He tipped his hat.

She was torn between questioning him and watching the video, but it was best to deal with what was standing live and right in front of you. "What time did you get here this morning?"

Jamie's gaze flicked to Todd.

"Go ahead. Answer all their questions."

"I was here at ten after six." He winced as he looked at his boss.

Todd's brow furrowed. "Tardy. Again. Let me get you an alarm clock for Christmas."

Tardy. People actually still used that word? "Where did you park?"

"Oh, my wife just drops me off."

"Why were you late?"

"Technically, I was at the park earlier, but I went for a little walk. I often do before shift. After that, I'm stuck in this cabin checking people in."

"It's your job, Jamie. Jeez." Todd shook his head.

"Did your walk take you anywhere near the river?" Amanda asked.

"No, I didn't go down that far."

All the Swansons had said was the ranger they'd seen was walking up the trail that led to the river. It didn't mean that he'd been to water. There could be offshoots that cut through the woods and didn't go down to the Potomac. "Did you see the dead girl?"

"No, but Helen told me it was the girl who liked the snails?" He said it with the arch of a question, and Helen looked up from her work and nodded at him.

Amanda didn't see any tells that Jamie Bolton was lying. "Thank you for your cooperation." She handed him her card. "Just in case you think of something you feel we should know."

Jamie dropped behind a desk and clicked away on the keyboard. Whatever he was doing, today's shift would feel longer than normal, given the park was closed due to the investigation.

"This is for the time between two and six?" Malone asked Todd, prompting him about the video.

"Yep, just as you asked for. I forwarded until there was some activity. I've got it cued and ready for you. But as I said, there's not much here that I think you can use. We have motion-sensor lights in the lots, but they didn't kick in."

"More foresight and organization on the killer's behalf," Amanda concluded. "He came ahead of time to take out the lights."

Todd squirmed. "Actually, that part is on me. I dropped the ball. Noticed they were out Friday and forgot to mention it to the weekend supervisory ranger so they could get the bulbs replaced."

"Oh." One word, but it got her disapproval across.

"I know." Todd held up his hands. "But, honestly, it's not like anything usually happens here."

"Please just play the video," she said, barely able to suppress her aggravation.

Todd leaned back in his chair. "Here we go."

On screen, the timestamp read 3:30 AM, and the feed was nearly impossible to make out. There was the hint of movement, though, as something silver or metal caught the moonlight. A chrome bumper? The body of the vehicle was probably a dark color, but there was virtually no light to know for sure. Given the height, she'd guess it was a sedan, not an SUV, van, or pickup. A figure emerged from the vehicle, appearing not much more than a black blob.

"See?" Todd pointed at the monitor. "Nothing much to see."

"Keep it playing," Malone directed.

Amanda strained to pick out something helpful, but it was so black. Then a burst of light. The figure had lit a flashlight, its beam shining on the path ahead. The person stopped, and the light bounced somewhat and fell to the ground. *She drop her phone?* The light revealed a fan of blond hair.

"Our Jane Doe," she said. "What's she doing?"

"Looks like picking something up," Trent said as a backpack came into view.

"Hey, pause right there and move in on the bag," she told Todd.

"I'll try. Not exactly a tech wiz." Todd paused the feed, rolled up his sleeves, and proceeded to enlarge the shot.

"A patch with the Warriors logo," Amanda declared rather proudly. "Geoffrey Michaels basketball team."

"I didn't know you were into basketball," Trent said.

"Not really much into any sport, but my brother used to play on the team when he was in school." Her only brother, Kyle, was four years her senior and the eldest of her five siblings. Amanda was the second born and preceded her sisters.

"Good eye." Malone stood back and crossed his arms.

Helen McCarthy had described the girl's boyfriend as a jock. It was possible he played on the basketball team. Then again, Jane Doe could just be a fan. Amanda glanced at her boss. "Something else. She came by herself. I don't see anyone with her."

"Nope," Trent said. "So she was either meeting the person who killed her down by the river, they were there waiting, or they followed her."

"*Or...*" she teased.

"If we just keep watching the video," Todd began, "it might answer some questions."

"Go ahead," Amanda told him, and the video went back to the regular scale and played.

A while after the girl was out of view, headlights from another car appeared. Just like the first vehicle, something refracted moonlight and indicated that a door had been opened. There was another pinprick of light, but rather small. Probably the flashlight feature on a cell phone.

Amanda's chest tightened. It was like watching a horror movie, one in which you knew something horrible was about to happen, but no matter how loudly you shouted at the screen, you were powerless to prevent things from playing out. This person was most likely the girl's killer, but who was it?

The second vehicle reversed out of the lot, its headlights casting light on the new arrival. A black shadow, nothing more.

"Is there any way to get a clearer shot of this person?" She could scream—so close to seeing their potential killer, but so far away.

"I don't see how."

"We'll need to get a copy of this video sent over to someone in Tech," she said. "May I suggest Detective Jacob Briggs with Digital Crimes?"

"Okay," Malone said slowly.

"He knows what he's doing." Amanda shouldn't need to remind him that Briggs had done them a favor with the Parker case a couple of months ago, and his work had greatly advanced the investigation. "He'll probably be able to clean up the image, maybe get us a license plate even." Though that might take a miracle given the darkness of the video, but fingers crossed he could work his magic and make it out.

"Consider it done."

As they spoke, the video continued to move ahead, but there was nothing that helped them identify the mystery figure. When all fell completely black, Todd stopped the playback.

She turned to Malone. "If we can figure out the car type, someone with the proper skill set could approximate this person's height."

"That's if we can determine make and model."

"Someone who knows cars, the spread of headlights..." She stopped talking. She knew just the person. Her brother had been born with a wrench in his hand. Even after all the business schooling their parents had paid for, he'd pursued his love of the automobile and held a job managing a local mechanic shop— only because the owner also let him get his hands dirty.

"Bet Kyle could help," Malone said, as if reading her mind.

She nodded. "I bet he could." Her relationship with her brother was still a little rocky at the moment. Back when Kevin and Lindsey died, Amanda had pulled away from her family thinking it would ease her heartbreak, but in hindsight she'd made things worse for everyone. Her decision, as it turned out, had serious repercussions. Their mother did something that could never be undone—a life and death action. For that Kyle blamed Amanda. And while everything had ended up working out from one perspective, her brother had yet to forgive her for the role he perceived she'd played in the matter.

Malone directed Todd Hampton to get a copy of the video to Amanda immediately.

"Something noteworthy," Trent started. "This person was dropped off."

"So, did the killer take a taxi or some other driving service?"

Amanda's arms pricked with goosebumps. Another lead. "I didn't see any lit sign on the roof or through the front windshield, though." Car services placed signs on the front dash, facing out, to identify themselves.

"Could have been turned off," Trent said. "Either way, we'll need to reach out to cab companies, etcetera. Hopefully something can be made of the plate and headlights."

"Guess we'll see," she said and considered something else. "The girl's car is no longer in the lot, so it's quite likely the killer left in her vehicle. And if he did, where is it now?"

"I'd get an APB out, but we have no idea what kind of car she drove," Malone said.

"This might help." Helen was gesturing emphatically toward her monitor. "Her name was Chloe Somner."

Finally. Their Jane Doe had a real name. But instead of bringing a sense of relief, it only heightened Amanda's determination to find justice for the girl.

EIGHT

Amanda and Trent hustled back to their department car with Malone in tow. Before leaving the office, Amanda had asked Helen about the light-blue coral necklace—in a roundabout way. She'd inquired if Chloe normally wore jewelry, and the ranger had described the necklace perfectly. Helen even added that the girl must have been fond of it because she always wore it. Amanda was also armed with a USB stick containing a copy of the surveillance video.

Trent brought up Chloe's information in the onboard computer. "Chloe Somner, nineteen years old, of Woodbridge. She's the daughter of Mitch and Melissa Somner." A few keystrokes, then, "Also residents of Woodbridge."

Amanda's heart cinched for a moment at the thought of informing them. They'd be going about their day with no idea about the horrible turn it was about to take. "We'll want to make sure it's her."

"Oh, it's her all right." Trent backed out of the car, and Amanda and Malone leaned over and looked at the screen. The girl's driver's license photo.

Blond, blue eyes, small rosebud mouth, and a turned-up nose. Young—her entire life had been ahead of her.

Amanda pulled back and straightened up. "Does she have any vehicles registered to her?"

"Let's see." Trent maneuvered back into the front seat and typed away. "Yep. A Nissan Leaf. Which makes sense."

"Why?"

"She was into the environment, and the Leaf is an electric car."

"I'll get the APB out for it," Malone said. "Color and year, Trent?"

"Red. Last year's model." He also gave Malone the plate number.

"So where does a college student get the money for a new car?" Amanda asked.

"From Mom and Dad." Trent turned from the screen to look at Amanda. Malone had walked away with his phone pressed to his ear. He went on. "Mitch is the CEO of a large medical center in Manassas."

"And the girl's mother?"

"It doesn't look like she's held a job for over nineteen years."

"Around the time Chloe was born. She probably quit to become a full-time, stay-at-home mother."

"Could afford to be."

Malone was walking back to them, his phone in hand. "The APB is being issued as we speak. You guys are heading to see the Somners, yes?"

Sour acid churned in Amanda's gut. Notifications were the worst part of the job. "I guess so. Just keep me posted on anything that might turn up here."

"You know it."

Amanda walked around to the passenger side of the department car, letting Trent take the wheel. Another perk of having a partner—she could be chauffeured around. Not that she was looking forward to the immediate destination.

Amanda handled death notifications with the skill of a seasoned pro, though it was never easy to tell people that their loved one had been murdered. It was always unexpected, blindsiding, and shocking. Unlike an accidental death, a murder typically meant their loved one had an enemy who had detested them enough to snuff them out. This was such a hard thing to accept for those left behind. Somehow death painted with a gentle brush, as if stroking away the deceased's negative traits from life. A slate wiped clean and all forgiven.

Thinking about murder and its aftereffects made her mind go to Zoe Parker, six years old. Her soon-to-be daughter if the adoption went through as planned. Both of Zoe's parents had been murdered a couple of months ago, and Amanda and Trent had been assigned the case. Amanda had fallen in love with the girl and was currently fostering her full-time. Considering all Zoe had been through, including witnessing her father's murder, she was doing well. Amanda had Zoe speaking regularly with a psychiatrist, and that was helping.

Her gaze caught the clock on the dash. Already after eleven. Where had the time gone? Apparently, fun wasn't the only thing that made it fly.

Zoe would be breaking from school for lunch soon and the end of the day would be here fast enough. Amanda needed to make some arrangements for Zoe's care. There was always Amanda's numerous nieces and nephews, but there were two primary options: Libby Dewinter, a schoolteacher who had been a friend of the Parker family and was "Aunt Libby" to Zoe; or Becky Tulson, a police officer with the Dumfries Police Department and also Amanda's best friend since kindergarten. Amanda was grateful she had so much help in caring for the girl, especially with this job that could have her on the go at all hours.

As Trent took them through Woodbridge streets to the Somner residence, Amanda made a call. Becky answered on the second ring.

"Hey there."

"Hey. What's up?"

Normally Becky reserved that type of greeting for times when she was preoccupied. "Is it a bad time?"

"No. It's just— Stop it." Becky was giggling, and there was a muffled voice in the background. A man, and Amanda pieced it together.

"You're with Brandon?" Brandon Fisher was an FBI agent with the Behavioral Analysis Unit, and he and Becky had been seeing each other since they met a couple of years ago during the investigation into a serial killer. They'd just hit it off, and things between them had blossomed from there. Not to say that the road hadn't had its rough patches.

"Yep. Day off, and he's being a— Just stop."

Even Amanda wasn't buying that *stop*. "I won't keep you, but would you mind coming over to watch Zoe after school today?" After asking, a slice of guilt tore through her. Becky didn't get much time with Brandon. His work took him on the road a lot, unexpectedly and for indeterminable lengths of time.

There was nothing but silence.

"You can bring Brandon, of course, but I understand if it's not a good—"

"We'll do it."

"You sure? It's not an imposition?"

"Don't worry about it. How long will you need us to stay?"

Her friend didn't exactly say it *wasn't* an imposition, but she had agreed to mind Zoe. Amanda ran through the day's timeline in her head. The autopsy started at four, and there was a half hour of travel time each way. "Probably until eight or nine. Maybe later."

"Oh."

"You can order dinner in, on me." She hoped that would be enough to sweeten the pot. Becky loved Zoe, and vice versa, but this was an unexpected drop on her friend's agenda.

"Okay. It's a deal."

"There's money in an envelope in the kitchen drawer. You know which one?"

"I do." With that, her friend hung up. No need to hash over logistics. Becky knew the routine and had a key to Amanda's house, as Amanda had one for Becky's place.

Trent pulled onto the Somners' street, located in a nice neighborhood that boasted sizable mansions with long front walkways leading to prestigious double doors—most of them painted black with gaudy brass hardware. He parked in the double-wide driveway for number 3503.

"Here goes," Amanda said as they got out of the car and walked up to the house.

She felt miniature standing next to the large structure and lifted the brass knocker. She was just about to release it when the door opened.

A woman in her late forties with thinly plucked eyebrows stood in the foyer. "Yes?"

Amanda pulled her badge, as did Trent. Melissa Somner looked just like her DMV photo. She was certainly the picture of prim and proper. She even had the "looking down her nose" thing down pat.

"Mrs. Somner, we're Detectives Steele and Stenson. Could we come inside and speak with you for a moment?" Amanda wanted to know if Melissa's husband was home too, but she'd wait to ask once they got in the house. She didn't want to set the woman on edge.

Melissa squinted and laid a hand flat to her chest, her fingers spread, which emphasized her slender digits and the diamonds encrusted around three of them. She also had a French manicure that had unquestionably been done by the hands of a skilled esthetician. She studied Amanda and Trent, peering down that nose like a scientist on an experiment.

"It's about your daughter, Chloe," Amanda added.

Melissa stepped back and gestured for them to enter.

The front area was palatial and something one might expect in the lobby of a fancy hotel. The ceiling stretched above them two stories, and a balcony on the second floor overlooked the marbled entry.

Melissa crossed her arms and stuck out her small chin. "What about Chloe?"

"Is there someplace we could sit?" Amanda was sure to keep her tone neutral and level, not wanting to upset the current emotional balance. It would be toppled like a high rise in an earthquake soon enough.

NINE

Melissa led them to a formal living room. The walls were a soft cream, the furniture white. The only splashes of color were two throw pillows and a vase—all in a shade of teal that resembled the crest of a wave just before it turned over to a whitecap.

Melissa lowered herself onto the couch, and Amanda and Trent picked chairs opposite her.

"Is your husband home?" Amanda asked. Melissa's eyes narrowed. She wasn't taking kindly to the implication that her husband should be present. But once this woman heard of her daughter's murder, she'd be inconsolable. The tough and mighty always fell the hardest, and death was certainly the great equalizer.

"He's not, but I am. Please go ahead with what you've come to say." Melissa still showed no cracks in her demeanor, even though her mind must have been going crazy with curiosity and worry, knowing they were there about Chloe.

"Would you be able to call him now and ask that he come home?" Amanda put it out there as gently and respectfully as possible.

Melissa held Amanda's gaze for a few seconds and then

reached into the pocket of her slacks and pulled out a cell phone. "What should I tell him is the reason for the interruption to his day?"

"Just tell him the police are here." That should be more than sufficient.

Melissa's eyes widened slightly, and in that instant, panic flashed across them. Perhaps it was the worst-case scenario finally playing out in her mind. She placed the call. "You need to come home... Yes, I realize you're busy, but the police are here... Something to do with Chloe. That's all I know. I guess they're waiting for you to be here before they tell me what this is all about?" The last sentence nested a question, and the woman peered at Amanda as if searching for that answer.

Amanda nodded.

A few seconds later, Melissa hung up. "He's in town for a meeting and shouldn't be longer than fifteen minutes. Are you really not going to tell me anything until he arrives?"

"It's best that we wait for him." A preference and a courtesy that wouldn't have the husband hearing the news second-hand from his wife. One convenience for her and Trent was they didn't have to wait for the man to come from his office in Manassas.

Melissa rubbed her arms, indicating that worry was starting to wear on her.

"Could I make you tea or coffee?" Amanda offered.

"Tamara can make it for us." Melissa picked up a small brass bell that sat on the table next to her and jangled it.

"Yes, ma'am." A woman of fifty-something stepped inside the doorway. She was wearing a black and white uniform. The Somner household was certainly one that stood on formality.

"Make some tea, would you?" Melissa splayed a hand over the space as if to indicate Amanda and Trent. "Also, do bring out some cranberry tea biscuits."

"Yes, ma'am." Tamara left the room. The two words were probably the extent of her vocabulary in this household.

Melissa sat back and crossed her legs. "It is puzzling that we need to wait for Mitch." Tenacious and stubborn. Proud. A nudge to have Amanda or Trent explain their reason for being there.

"You should both be present for what we have to say," Amanda said.

"You speak as if something tragic has happened, like someone died." Spoken off the cuff, but as the words came out her chin quivered as if the reality was now sinking in. The woman knew. "My Chloe? She's... ah... she's..."

"Ma'am, please. Let's just wait for your husband."

"Oh my God. She is dead!" She sank into the couch, her body shrinking into itself.

"We'll tell you everything once your hus—"

The front door was thrust open, and Mitch stormed into the room with another man next to him. He barely acknowledged his wife and addressed Amanda and Trent.

"This is my lawyer," he said, gesturing to the man. "Whatever you're here to do or say goes through him. Do we have an understanding?"

Amanda nodded solemnly. It would seem the Somners—or at least Mitch—had something to hide. "I assure you, however, that the lawyer won't be necessary." *Or shouldn't be, unless you killed your daughter.* And did the guy travel around with his lawyer in his backseat? How did he get there so fast? Maybe the attorney was the appointment Mitch had in town.

"Don't tell me what's necessary." Mitch waved a finger in her face.

"Mitch, take a seat." Melissa's voice was small, and she was staring at the area rug.

His brow furrowed, and he did a double take at his wife, as if confused by her timidity.

Tamara entered the room carrying a silver tray loaded with a teapot, teacups, sugar, milk, and cream. There was even a small plate of biscuits, as requested by her employer. Tamara's cheeks blushed, and she backed out of the room with, "I'll get two more teacups, sir."

"Don't bother. They're leaving."

"Dear God, Mitch. Sit." This time, Melissa's tone was firm, and Mitch's shoulders slumped.

He sat down in a chair across the room. The lawyer remained standing and tucked into a corner.

"So, what is this about?" Mitch pushed out.

Amanda let a few seconds pass with only the ticking of a clock. The Somners were watching her, blinking dramatically. It was time. "We're here about your daughter, Chloe," Amanda began.

"Dear God..." Melissa ran her palms over her thighs, appearing to smooth her pant legs, but Amanda read it more as the woman seeking a distraction and bracing herself for what was coming.

"Chloe was found murdered this morning in Leesylvania State Park." Always best to get to the point.

Melissa gasped and covered her mouth. Mitch got up from where he was seated and sat next to his wife on the couch. He took her hand and squeezed it. Melissa leaned in toward her husband.

"I'm going to step outside," the lawyer said and let himself out the front door.

"When did she... ah... die? How? You said she was mur... dered?" Mitch's voice fractured on the last word, a tough one to swallow when it came to a loved one's fate.

"She was stabbed, numerous times." There was no delicate way of putting that.

Melissa gasped out again and pinched the tip of her nose.

Tamara returned to the room with two teacups, her timing

BLACK ORCHID GIRLS   55

terrible. Amanda made solid eye contact with her and shook her head. The woman retreated without leaving the additional cups.

Amanda addressed her next words to Mitch, "As for when, her time of death was early this morning."

Mitch slowly bobbed his head. "Time of death..." His tongue flicked out, and he sniffled. "It's surreal to hear you say this and know you're talking about my daughter."

"*Our* daughter," Melissa corrected in a near whisper.

"Do you know of anyone who might have wanted to hurt Chloe or had something against her?" It was a question no loved one wanted to answer, or even consider, but it was necessary to every investigation.

"No, I have no idea." Mitch turned to his wife.

"Our girl was popular, Detective. Everyone liked her."

Amanda could read between those lines. It might seem those with all the friends were the most liked and untouchable, but reality was often the opposite. Being in the spotlight cast shadows in which enemies were bred. But they clearly weren't going to get the names of Chloe's enemies from her parents. They'd have to rely on Chloe's peers for that information. "We'll need to get a list of her friends from you, if that's possible."

"I can't tell you the names of all her friends, just the important ones," Melissa said. "There's Jayne Russell and Lauren Bennett. She shares a townhouse with them."

The important ones... Melissa was clinging to her self-importance still, probably what she was comfortable with, and the familiarity soothed. No mention of a boyfriend but Amanda would circle back to that. "Do you have their numbers?"

"Yes, of course." But Melissa didn't move to get up or pull out her phone. Amanda would get the details before they left.

"We'll also need an address for the townhouse." The residence on Chloe's file was still listed as her parents' house.

Amanda would wager that she still had a bedroom in this home too.

Melissa nodded but didn't say anything.

"I assume she has a room here," Amanda said. "We'd like to take a look before we leave to see if it offers the investigation any clues."

"Sure," Mitch said and earned a glare from his wife.

Melissa added firmly, "Don't disturb a thing."

"We'll respect her space and things," Amanda assured her.

Melissa nodded.

"Chloe was a student at Geoffrey Michaels?" Trent asked.

"That's correct," Mitch replied. "She's going to make a difference in this world. Save it, if you ask me. She studies at the Potomac Center and is enrolled in environmental science and policy. She wants to make a real change by initiating policies that protect the environment. The degree she's pursuing would qualify her to do just that." He sank his chin to his chest when he'd finished speaking. "I guess all that is actually past tense now. She *was*..."

Amanda let a few minutes of silence pass as a portion of the enormous loss sank in. One small mercy about grief was it didn't hit all at once. It came in waves, though some felt on scale to a tsunami. Those moments were so intense they stole breath and stopped the heart.

TEN

Amanda crossed her legs at the ankles and regarded the heartbroken couple. Human compassion had her wanting to leave them, but there were far more questions to ask. "Was Chloe seeing someone?"

Melissa and Mitch both nodded. "He's a great kid too," Melissa said.

"He's going places," Mitch added, and his face pinched in grief.

Amanda leaned forward. "What's his name?"

"Josh Ryder."

The jock boyfriend that Helen McCarthy had mentioned or someone else?

"Was he into sports?" Trent asked, beating her to a similar question. He must have been thinking along the same lines as her.

"Yes. Basketball. He plays for the Michaels Warriors and is studying bioengineering at the Fairfax campus. Why are you interested in Josh?"

Fairfax was about thirty minutes away, outside of Prince William County. Amanda didn't want to get into the patch on

Chloe's backpack. That would only lead to more questions from the Somners such as when she saw it, etcetera. "Just something we are curious about in relation to the investigation. How did the two of them meet?"

"In elementary school," Melissa said. "He's a little older than our Chloe, but he was held back and had to repeat grade three. That's how they met. The two of them did a lot of growing up together. Still had a lot of growing up to do." She blinked away a fresh batch of tears. "Things didn't get romantic between them until college."

Amanda nodded.

"I thought they'd wind up getting married someday, not that Chloe ever wanted to hear me carry on about that. She called me old-fashioned." Melissa smiled.

The woman was riding a wave of acceptance and nostalgia, but it would be brief and fleeting at best. Amanda smiled back. "She was independent and a forward thinker?"

"Fiercely independent. And definitely." Melissa attempted to hold her expression, but it faltered and didn't reach her eyes.

"We'll need Josh's information too," Amanda said.

"Of course. But he wouldn't have hurt her. Never," Melissa stamped out.

"We'll still need to speak with him," Amanda said firmly.

"They're just doing their job, Mel." Mitch lifted his wife's hand and drew it to his chest where he held it pressed over his heart.

The action was painful to watch. Amanda cleared her throat. "Speaking of, could we have a look at her room now?"

Mitch stood. "I'll take you."

"I'm coming too," Melissa said.

The Somners led them through the expansive home and up to the second floor. Melissa reached for the door handle, and Amanda put out her hand. She was well aware from personal experience how difficult it was to look at the room of a dead child—even after many years had passed. She'd love to protect this couple from that marrow-bone grief. Though she knew that was impossible, the least she could do was postpone the moment.

"Please," Melissa said, appealing to Amanda.

Amanda stepped back—albeit reluctantly—and Melissa opened the door and went inside, Mitch behind her. Trent went next, and Amanda brought up the rear, something she was grateful for as she fought off the sadness of her own memories.

The walls were painted a pale green, and the furniture was white wood. A queen-size sleigh bed, a nightstand, a long dresser with six drawers, a desk and swivel chair, and a large standing mirror. There was a vanity table too, its top and mirror plastered with photographs and flyers.

"When was your daughter last home?" Trent asked.

"End of September? Somewhere around then. Once school got into full swing she hasn't been to stay over, but she was going to—" Melissa left the room, her body heaving with sobs.

"She was coming back for the Thanksgiving long weekend," Mitch finished for his wife and excused himself, stepping into the hall with Melissa.

Amanda turned her back to the doorway, and to Trent, and took a deep breath. She reminded herself that she was tough and built for this job that brought death into people's lives.

"You all right?" Trent asked.

"Absolutely." She squared her shoulders and snapped on some gloves.

The vanity probably held more secrets than elsewhere in the room. There was nothing on the walls telling of the girl's personality, but the pictures... they were personal. She'd guess the guy with the light-brown hair and green eyes was Josh Ryder, but it didn't take a detective to make that leap. They were kissing in some. Leaning against each other, hugging. The smiles were wide and genuine. The pair had something special, if Amanda were any judge of relationships—which she liked to believe she was, since she'd had her once in a lifetime with her husband, Kevin.

"They were happy together," she said, fingering the corner of one photo in which they were facing each other and laughing. "Her death is going to break his heart."

"Unless he's the one behind it."

Trent's comment was a dark cloud but also a jolt back to reality. Murder was messy, and often those closest to the victims were responsible. "Either way, we're going to speak with him."

Trent nodded and opened the closet doors. "Not much in here."

"She probably kept most of her things at her townhouse."

"Maybe, but my sister was a clotheshorse at nineteen. Still is, if you talk to her husband. They have a walk-in closet, and her things take up three-quarters of the realty there."

Amanda was the opposite of Trent's sister. Always had been. She bought clothes to avoid walking around naked. She certainly wasn't a fashionista.

Amanda returned to looking at what was on the vanity. Flyers posted for local events, most of them for causes supporting the environment. There was a logo they all held in common. It was round with the tree of life sprouting from a leaf. No name, as if the image was enough to identify the organization.

They spent a little while looking through the room. The vanity didn't give up any secrets, but Trent discovered a box of journals tucked away in the closet.

"We'll want to bring those with us." She pointed at the journals.

"You think they'll shed light on who killed her?"

"It will shed light on Chloe, and that can help our investigation."

"Okay. We'll run it by her parents."

BLACK ORCHID GIRLS   61

They let themselves out of the room. Amanda slowly closed the door as if shutting it on a sacred space, which it indeed was. A shrine to a life that was no longer.

The Somners were in the formal living room, and Mitch stood when he saw them in the doorway.

"Please, stay seated." Amanda smiled pleasantly.

Melissa's eyes narrowed at the box in Trent's hand. "What are you doing? What is that?"

"Those are your daughter's journals, and we'd like to take them with us to read through, if you'll allow it. I promise we'll treat them with respect and extreme care." Amanda could only imagine being asked the same thing after Lindsey's death, not that a six-year-old kept such things. But if police had wanted her drawings... Her heart ached. "Mrs. Somner, would that be all right?"

"Yes... yes, I suppose so." Melissa sniffled.

"Something else," Amanda began. "I noticed that Chloe had a lot of flyers from one group or company. They have a logo that's a circle and—"

"Planet Rebirth," Mitch said. "They're an environmental group out of Washington."

"Your daughter was a member?"

Mitch nodded. "She dedicated as much time to it as she could."

"I also found diplomas and trophies in her closet," Trent said. "I found it interesting they weren't on display."

Melissa met his gaze. "That was our Chloe. Modest and down-to-earth. She didn't get that from me." Melissa laughed, but it passed quickly. "I tried to put them around the house, and she begged me not to. She said it was embarrassing."

"She didn't do anything for the glory, Detectives. She did it because her heart moved her to," Mitch elaborated.

"It sounds like she was an angel." Grief for the loss of this special girl was burrowing in Amanda's bones.

"She was ours." Mitch was staring at the floor.

This pause in conversation and the dominant feeling of devastation clung to the air, but there was more business to attend to. "Just a couple of things before we go. The guy with Chloe in the photos on her vanity, is that Josh Ryder?"

"Yes, it is," Melissa said.

The next thing was harder to say. "We'll need for the two of you—or at least one of you—to formally ID your daughter." Amanda pulled a business card from her pocket. "The medical examiner will be in touch with you, likely today or tomorrow morning to set up a time."

"Wait... You don't know that it was her?" Melissa snapped. "You could have made a mistake. Mitch, they could have made a mistake."

"If we had a doubt in our mind, we wouldn't have come, Mrs. Somner." Amanda kept her voice calm yet authoritative. "It's just a matter of procedure when there isn't any ID with the body."

"Why wouldn't there be— She didn't have her ID?" Melissa rubbed a hand down the length of her neck.

"No, she did not." Amanda wasn't going so far as to say Chloe had been found naked. The Somners didn't need to know that or drive themselves crazy with wild scenarios of their daughter being sexually assaulted on top of everything else. Unless—or until—it became necessary they know about how Chloe was found, it was best to hold some things back.

"I'm very sorry for your loss," Amanda said as she handed her card to Mitch. "We may be back with more questions, but please get the information on Chloe's roommates and boyfriend over as soon as possible, along with the address of where Chloe was living. Also, if you could supply us with her phone number and service provider. I assume this was something you covered for her?" There hadn't been a phone number associated with Chloe's park membership.

Mitch nodded. "It is... *was*." He rattled off Chloe's number and the provider's name, and Trent scribbled in his notepad. "We'll get the rest to you shortly." He held up Amanda's card as if to indicate he had it under control.

On the way out, she glanced over a shoulder—almost wishing she hadn't. The Somners' pain was palpable. They were hugging and crying onto each other's shoulders. Amanda's gaze dipped to the coffee table and the spread that Tamara had laid out. With everything that had transpired, the tea was forgotten and the biscuits were becoming stale. Amanda would do all in her power not to let that happen with the case.

"Detective!"

Amanda was just getting into the car when Melissa burst out the front door, waving something in her hand. She went over to the woman. "Yes, Mrs. Somner?"

"Take this." Melissa pressed a photo into Amanda's palm. "I want you to remember Chloe the way I will."

Amanda looked down into the eyes of the beautiful young woman, and her heart splintered. So much potential snuffed out. The girl was smiling, the expression genuine and lighting her eyes. "She was very happy here."

"Yes. This summer's family reunion." Melissa sniffled, and her eyes filled with tears. "Find who did this to our Chloe."

"You have my word."

ELEVEN

Amanda was having a hard time shaking the Somners' grief... and even her own. The pain of losing a daughter never left. Not completely. After she lost Kevin and Lindsey, it had taken Amanda a long time to rediscover a purpose to life and a reason to get out of bed in the morning. And now she had Zoe. The blond, bright-eyed six-year-old had made inroads into her heart and healed Amanda in ways she'd never imagined possible. The future looked bright again. She would love nothing more than to drop by Dumfries Elementary this minute and squeeze Zoe, but that wasn't an option.

"That went better than I'd expected." Trent looked over at her from the driver's seat.

"Did it?"

He studied her. "It's never easy when you need to tell parents their kid is dead."

She held eye contact with him, not about to call him out and ask how many times he'd had the burden of conveying that news. That would just be cruel and bitter. "We'll grab a coffee and a bite to eat at Hannah's Diner. Probably by the time we're done, the Somners will have forwarded the other information we're after. We have the autopsy at four, but I'd like to knock some things off our list before then. A visit to the boyfriend, for one. I'd also like to stop by my brother's work to let him see the video before we leave Dumfries. Hopefully, he can ID the car in the park's lot by its headlights."

"I'll be extremely impressed if he can."

"Prepare to be impressed. Kyle lives and breathes cars."

Trent put the car into gear, and Amanda got on the line with Judge Anderson to get a verbal subpoena approved for Chloe's phone history and permission to track the phone. The killer had probably ditched it somewhere, but no stone left unturned, as the saying went. After the call to the judge, she made one to the lab for tracking the phone. She emailed the service provider to request the call history and gave her contact information and Trent's. It usually took a few days to a week for that information to come through. Hopefully it wouldn't take that long this time. All she could think about was that strong woman, Melissa Somner, broken before their eyes, sobbing and fleeing her daughter's bedroom.

The next call she made was to Victim Services to request a counselor go over to the Somners' house.

By the time Amanda finished with the calls and emails, Trent was pulling into Hannah's Diner. Not bad. It was ten minutes from Woodbridge to Dumfries, so she'd made record time with her tasks.

Trent got the door to the diner, and May Byrd was behind the counter. She was in her fifties and had a large bosom and an even larger heart. She was also the pulse of the community. If something was going on—as always seemed to be the case—then May knew about it. Owning the diner, and working it until she was run off her feet at the end of the day, made her privy to a lot of conversations among the locals. But that was a small town for you—everyone knew each other's business. And what May didn't hear at the diner, she heard from the ladies in her book club. May had even once admitted that she remained part of the group more for the gossip and wine than the book pick of the month.

"Hello there, lovelies." May was all smiles when she saw Amanda and Trent. "How are you doin' today?"

"We've been better. We've been worse," Amanda said, not about to get into the fact they just had to serve a death notification.

"That's about all we can really expect. But any day above ground is certainly a good one." The light dimmed in May's eyes as if she'd finally picked up on Amanda's and Trent's energy. "Guess I should mind what I'm saying, given what you do. Coffees all around, then?"

"Oh, please, and make mine super-duper large." Amanda smiled, infusing some levity, desperate to shake the residue of death.

"You got it. And you?" May asked, looking at Trent.

"Same."

May set about getting the coffees, and Trent turned to Amanda. "Super-duper?"

"Hey, you call it Jabba sometimes, so I don't think you can really judge."

"Uh-huh."

When they'd first been partnered, Trent had told Amanda that his younger sister had substituted *Jabba* for *java* as a kid, as if she confused the caffeinated beverage with the blob character from *Star Wars*.

After May returned with their coffees, they both ordered a sandwich and sat in a booth. They started on their coffees while they waited on the food.

"You probably overheard, but I requested a trace on Chloe's phone. I also sent an email asking for her call history. Hopefully either—or both—will give us something to go on and provide some clues."

"Not holding my breath on the trace. I'm sure her killer's not that stupid. He, again assuming our killer is a man, showed organization and planning. I doubt he'd keep her phone."

"You never know, though, and we need to be diligent." She didn't want to consider what it might mean if the killer had held on to Chloe's phone. Would that mean it was a souvenir, like a serial killer would keep? She took a tentative sip of her coffee. Still a little hot for gulping.

"I'm sure we'll get somewhere with her call history. Given Chloe's age, she's probably quite active on social media. That should help us learn about her."

"I'm starting to think we can't make any assumptions about her. You saw her bedroom, her closet. She wasn't the typical teenager. And she did things because she wanted to, not for recognition." Definitely an endearing quality.

"One way to find out." Trent raised his eyebrows, challenging her.

"Okay, let's see." Amanda pulled out her phone. "I'll google her name and see what comes up."

"My guess is *a lot.*"

Amanda smiled at her partner and googled Chloe Somner's name. And she hated to give it to Trent, but he was right. She scrolled down the screen. There were a lot of results. Most of them linked back to some type of social media account, but there were also some articles issued from Geoffrey Michaels University that mentioned Chloe. She clicked on one of these and scanned the piece. From the looks of it, Chloe was quite involved in the community. She was a champion for the environment and vocal about climate change. This was also supported by the event flyers in her bedroom of the family home.

"Here you go." May set their sandwiches in front of them.

"Thank you," Amanda said.

"No problem, hon."

As much as Amanda wanted to just relax and enjoy her food, there was no time for that. They owed it to Chloe to find out who her killer was and bring her justice sooner than later. "Let's make this quick. We have lots to do."

They didn't say much else as they scarfed down their food and swigged back their coffee. During that time Mitch Somner had forwarded the numbers for Chloe's roommates and the address of the place they had rented with Chloe. He also included a phone number for Josh Ryder but no address for him. Amanda made a call to get a uniformed officer on Chloe's residence until she and Trent had a chance to get there.

Just twenty minutes after they'd entered the diner, Amanda and Trent were loading back into the department car. The clock on the dashboard read 1:10 PM.

"All right, get us over to my brother's shop," she began. "Do you remember where that is?"

"Remember? I was never actually told where he worked."

"Mack's Garage. You know where it is?"

"That I do." Trent put the car into gear.

The ball of anxiety in her chest knotted tighter the closer they got to the garage. She and her brother used to be very close before she'd pulled back from her family and before their mother had killed a man—the taboo subject. Her relationship with Kyle was on the mend, but it was still a work in progress. She just hoped he'd be cooperative and maybe even give them a lead on the vehicle seen on the park video.

TWELVE

Amanda held the door for Trent, and they entered Mack's Garage. Melvin Gray was behind the counter and grinned at the sight of her. He was twenty-three and still an apprentice, but he was given a lot of free rein. "My, my, Miss Amanda is in the house."

She laughed. Melvin had a way about him that could calm a person on death row. "Kyle wouldn't happen to be in, would he?" Rhetorical, really, as there was nowhere else her brother would be this time of day. Her brother could be a stickler during business hours and focused on his work to the extent that all else around him disappeared. He considered breaking for lunch a weakness. No one could say he didn't work hard.

"You don't need to ask. And just go back. You're family here." Melvin smiled at her and let the expression carry for Trent.

"In the shop or his office?"

"Not sure. Might as well try his office first since it's on the way."

"Thanks." Amanda lifted a section of counter, and she and Trent ducked to the other side. She knocked on a closed door with a nameplate that read *The Boss.* Definitely her brother's sense of humor. She hoped that he wasn't behind a desk; he was always in a more favorable mood covered head to toe in grease.

Air compressors started up in the garage bays, seeping into the retail front and making it hard to hear and be heard. She raised her voice when she called out, "Ky—" The door opened mid-name.

"Mandy? What are you— Nah. No. You get out of here." He thrust a pointed finger toward Trent, nostrils flaring.

"Kyle!" Amanda reached out to stop her brother from advancing on Trent. "He's my partner."

Kyle shrugged free of her hand. "I know exactly who he is."

Trent had been the one to officially arrest their mother, and he'd testified on the stand against her. "He was doing his job."

"That the excuse you're always going to hide behind?"

All the wind left her, and it took her a while to compose herself. They'd been down this road so many times it was worn and full of potholes. "Mom was exonerated."

"Yeah, lucky thing too." Kyle was seething and glaring at Trent.

"I'll wait in the car." Trent jacked a thumb over his shoulder. To his credit, he was calm and collected despite Kyle's hostility. He moved to leave.

"Good idea," Kyle called after him. The bell on the door jangled as Trent exited the shop.

"You've become quite an ass," Amanda snarled.

"Maybe that's what happens when my sis cuts me from her life."

"Is that the story *you're* going to hide behind?" she volleyed. She was heaving for breath. As much as they had conversed about their mother's actions and the trial, they still had to address the fact Amanda had cut him out of her life for a time. It was a conversation she really didn't look forward to, but maybe it was better to rip the Band-Aid off and deal with the gaping wound. Just not now. "I thought we were moving forward."

"Trying to. Just keep *him* out of my face and give things time."

"It will take a long time if you're going to be a bull-headed —" She stopped when a customer came through the front door.

"In here." Kyle ushered her into his office, and he sat behind the desk.

"I'm not here to talk about ancient history." She was panting, trying to get a solid breath. If she didn't need his help with solving a murder, she would have regretted being here. She somewhat did anyway.

"Ancient?" he scoffed. "Her trial just ended two months ago."

"Might as well be ancient. Mom knew I had a job to do. She doesn't blame me for anything. She's forgiven me, so why can't you?" Amanda could only imagine how much animosity her brother would hold if their mother had been convicted.

Kyle clenched his jaw and held it for a bit before letting out a rush of air. "What is it?"

She pulled out a data stick that Todd Hampton had given her with the video surveillance of the lot. "I need your expertise."

"Finally, some credit." A small, cocky smile. A flash of the brother she remembered and adored, even idolized when she was younger.

"Credit where credit's due." She could play nice.

He plucked the USB stick from her hands and put it into his computer. "What am I looking at?"

"I just need to know if you can recognize a vehicle from the spread and shape of the headlights. Which I'm sure you can." *Laying on the flattery now...*

He held eye contact with her. "You might be giving me more credit than I deserve."

"Am I?" She batted her eyelashes.

"All right, then." He pointed to the monitor, and she walked around to look at the screen. She told him the rough timestamp, and he brought up that section. She had him pause when the headlights of the mystery car came into view.

Kyle angled his head left, right, then left, right again. "It's obviously a sedan. I'd say import given the shape of the headlights."

"All right, this is great. Do you know make and model?"

He looked at her, smiled. "You must think I'm a genie in a bottle."

"Aren't you?"

"Oh, flattery, Mandy. It works on me."

"It always has." She was grinning at his profile, his gaze back on the screen. She hoped he wanted to heal things between them, but would he be able to let go of his hurt feelings long enough to do so? There were times she couldn't blame him for being bitter. They had been best friends before Kevin and Lindsey had died, or more accurately, before she had pulled away. She'd thought it would hurt less to be on her own instead of being around her family, a constant reminder of what she no longer had. The pity she sometimes witnessed in their eyes... she despised it. Like she was some fragile doll that needed handling with kid gloves.

Kyle tapped his fingers on his desk. "My guess is a Honda or Toyota."

"Model? Year?"

"Again, I'm not a genie, but within the last five years."

"Still, you're the best." She tapped a kiss on her brother's forehead and held out her open palm. "The USB stick?"

He pulled it from the computer and put it in her hand. "Glad I could assist the PWCPD."

"Remember that." The words slipped out, and she immediately wished she could retract them. The light disappeared from her brother's eyes, probably at the thought that he'd helped the same police department that had charged their mother with murder. "I didn't mean anything by that."

"I really need to get back to work. Parts don't order themselves, and I have an engine in the back that needs my expertise."

She should just leave. After all, she got the answer she'd come for. She reached the door and found herself turning around. "I'm sorry, Kyle. If I could turn the clock back, I would have done things differently." Her heart was aching so much it was hard to breathe. She'd let him down.

"Would you have? That's easy to say now."

She sniffled and tears welled in her eyes. "It just hurt so freaking much, Ky. You could never understand unless you lost Michelle or the kids. Trust me on that." He went to speak, but she held up a hand and continued. "I know you loved Lindsey and you liked Kevin." She gave him a partial smile. It was just a case of big brother not thinking anyone was good enough for his little sister, but in all honesty, her brother and husband were friends as much as family.

"They were amazing. Both of them."

"Yes, they were." She paused a few beats and added, "When I lost them, well, I lost my way. Guess that's the best way to describe it. I was utterly destroyed. Broken."

"Then you should have leaned on me and the rest of your family." Kyle's voice cracked, and his eyes became wet.

"I know." She swallowed a sob. "But I can't go back in time. I can only move forward. I'm hoping we can rebuild the trust between us."

"Me too."

"Do you think we can?" She could barely scrape that question from her throat. What if he sent her away?

"I'd like to."

She blinked and dipped her head. "I guess that's all I can

ask." She opened the door and added, "Thanks for your help today."

"That's what big brothers are for." He gave her a subtle smile, one that barely ticked up the corners of his mouth.

Though she left Mack's Garage with a lead for the case, she felt wrecked, like she'd faced an emotional hurricane. Family was never simple. A lesson she'd relearned in the last few months. Her parents' marriage wasn't as perfect as it had once appeared. Her father's affair and illegitimate child was a secret her parents had held for twenty-some years. The entire situation had shaken Amanda's foundation, making her question what and who could be trusted more than ever before. And she was sure before Chloe's investigation could be resolved, there would be lies and secrets to wade through. There always were.

THIRTEEN

Trent flicked the stereo off as Amanda climbed into the car. When she'd walked up, she'd heard the beat of modern country, and this wasn't the first time she'd caught him listening to the genre. She didn't mind but wasn't much of a music person. Kevin wore his earbuds any chance he got. He loved Bruce Springsteen and classic rock bands. All this danced through her mind—anything a welcome distraction from replaying the interaction she'd just had with her brother.

"He figures the vehicle in the video was either a Honda or Toyota sedan," she said. "From within the last five years."

"That's all? No model?"

"He's not a genie." The comment was meant to be amusing, but one look at Trent told her he wasn't in the mood to jest. "He shouldn't have kicked you out."

"No, he shouldn't have." Trent faced the windshield and twisted his hands on the steering wheel as if cooling his temper —and he rarely got angry. There was only once that she could recall, and that was when they had to deal with a woman-beating asshole. The situation hit home because his aunt was still a victim of domestic violence. Their efforts to save her had gone unrewarded.

"I don't know what to say."

He slowly faced her. "There's nothing for you to say." Dry. Clear. No subtle meanings to ferret out.

She met his gaze, silence budding between them, and she almost hated that she found herself empathizing with her brother's position. From his standpoint, he still needed someone to blame for things outside of his control—Amanda pulling back from her family and their mother facing a murder charge. Trent had become that face. "We should go see Josh Ryder," Amanda said.

"Yeah." Trent sat up straighter. "I pulled his background while you were in there. Twenty-one, no criminal record. His parents live in Dumfries, but Josh's address is in Fairfax."

"Okay. Great." Now, if Josh was guilty of killing Chloe, there would be some red tape to wade through. They'd have to coordinate their efforts with the Fairfax PD before making the arrest. Still, that was a small price to pay for justice. It brought to mind something else. Josh would need some way of getting to Woodbridge to see Chloe. "Does he have any vehicles registered to him?"

He checked the onboard system. "No vehicles."

"He could take public transportation, including taxis and car services." *Just like their killer could have done.* There was another possibility though... "What about Josh's parents? What vehicles do they have? Josh could drive one of theirs."

"Bruce and Molly Ryder." Trent clicked away on the keyboard. "Looks like they have three: a BMW X2, a Chevy Equinox, and a Toyota Prius. All are models from within the last five years."

"Why would one couple need three cars? Josh might drive one, and the Prius is a sedan. It could match the headlights in the video. Either way, we should take a drive up to Fairfax and talk to him."

"I'm not going to dispute that, but we're only assuming Josh even drives that car. And the video shows someone whom we assume to be the killer being dropped off. If we think Josh may be that person, and the vehicle was his parents', then who was driving? Are we looking for an accomplice?"

"Let's not go there until we have to."

"You still want to fit him in before the autopsy?"

The clock on the dash told her it was going on two o'clock. Fairfax was thirty minutes from Manassas where the autopsy would be held. "If he's Chloe's killer, that trumps the morgue."

"Suppose it does. Do you really think the boyfriend is behind this?"

"We need to rule him out." She thought back to how happy Chloe and Josh had looked in the photographs that lined the mirror over the vanity. But something could have drastically changed. Amanda's own life was a testament to how things flipped in an instant.

"All right." He put the car into drive, and they headed in the direction of Fairfax.

They were almost to Fairfax when Amanda's phone rang. Caller ID told her it was Malone, and she answered immediately. "Do you have news for me?"

"Well, hello to you too." Malone usually got to business just as fast as she did, but something had him taking a step back.

She put the call on speaker. "It's me and Trent, *and* hello," she said slowly. "We finished up notifying Chloe's parents."

"How did that go?"

"About as well as could be expected. They lost their only daughter."

"Definitely wouldn't have been an easy message to deliver."

"I'm assuming you have something for us?" She was surprised she needed to corral him.

"One of the K-9s found a running shoe in the woods. Right foot, correct size for Chloe. It's been bagged and tagged as evidence."

"Just a shoe?" She'd hoped they'd found her clothing, phone, or laptop, or even that the APB on Chloe's car had a hit.

"That's it. What are you guys following up on now?" he asked.

"We're almost to Fairfax. That's where Chloe's boyfriend, Josh Ryder, lives. He goes to the Geoffrey Michaels University campus in Fairfax."

"Any reason to suspect the boyfriend?"

"Just checking off the boxes, Sarge," she said with a smirk. The direct answer to his question would have been *no*, but it would be premature to assume the boyfriend was innocent. Stabbing was often a murder of passion, but the rest of the scene didn't complete that picture. The cleaning, posing, and the orchid. All of that was saying something else entirely. She had to figure out what.

"Let me know how it goes with him."

"Will do." She always kept him in the loop with investigations and wasn't quite sure why he'd felt the need to say that.

"And next... after the boyfriend?"

"We're headed to the autopsy."

"They're never fun when the victims are young. It doesn't matter how long I've been on this job, it never gets easier."

So much for Amanda's hopes that she'd eventually become callused and desensitized...

Trent pulled into the parking lot of a townhouse complex.

"We're at the boyfriend's now. I'll update you when I have anything," she assured him again and ended the call. Since when did the Sarge push to that extent? Was that new or had he been that way a while now? She wasn't entirely sure. Her own life was undergoing a transformation and had become quite chaotic ever since Zoe entered her life in September, leaving her mind preoccupied most of the time. Waiting for the adoption to finalize was painful, and she was only a couple of months in. She couldn't imagine being a number in the system waiting to hear when a child was available. At least she was already ahead of things and fostering Zoe full-time. The rest was just legal checkboxes to tick off. One of which was a detailed background check on Zoe's family to ensure there wasn't anyone with a legal right to claim her as theirs.

As far as Amanda knew no such person existed—the Parkers had no living family members. But there was one name she'd provided the state out of due diligence. During the Parker investigation, it had come to light that Angela Parker, Zoe's mother, had an affair with a Colin Brewster around the time Zoe was conceived. Colin had moved to California years ago for a job, and Amanda doubted he'd be concerned with whether Zoe was his or not. Even if he came forward to stake a claim on Zoe, it would just take a paternity test to send him on his way again.

Trent parked the car in front of unit 18, and they got out.

"Here goes nothing," Amanda said as she pocketed her phone and walked to the front door.

She knocked, rather heavy-handed, and strained to hear if anyone was inside. Silence. She was starting to second-guess her decision to come. They could head over to the campus, but that would take more time than they had right now.

She banged again. Footsteps headed toward the door. It swung open, and the young man captured in the many photos in Chloe's childhood bedroom was standing in front of them.

Amanda held up her badge, and Trent held up his. "I'm Detective Steele, and this is Detective Stenson, from the PWCPD. Are you Josh Ryder?" Pretty much a rhetorical question.

"Yeah, that's me." He angled his head. "You said PWCPD? As in Prince William County police?"

He was a good-looking kid and, according to Mitch Somner, was intelligent with a bright future, but so far he wasn't living up to the praise. "Yep. Can we come in for a minute?"

"Sure." Josh backed up to let them inside, and Amanda rushed to hide her initial reaction. Being with her brother earlier might have stirred up an emotional hurricane, but a physical one had passed through this place. Clothes, dirty dishes, empty bottles—you name it—were scattered all over the place. She'd guess, and maybe she was stereotyping, that only college boys lived here.

"Anyone else home with you?" Amanda asked.

"No." The way he said the single word was like he was confused why Amanda even cared.

Cute but not bright, she thought again. Though maybe she was rushing to judgment. She could have caught him at a bad time. On the flipside of a bender and hungover, or... well, there was a much worse possibility. If he had killed his girlfriend, his mind could be a mess from that. "Do you have roommates?"

"Nope. Just me."

It must have been party central last night, then. "Is there somewhere we could sit and talk?" She peered around him and eyed a battered couch. "That would do," she said as she pointed toward it. Though a part of her cringed at the thought of sitting on it.

Josh led the way to the couch. He turned around and said, "Oh, don't worry about taking off your shoes."

She didn't have the heart to tell him no worries existed as far as that went. First of all, as cops, they had to be ready to move. Second, she wouldn't be subjecting her socks to the floor. She could imagine the fabric sticking to the laminate like shoes in a movie theater.

"Please, have a seat." Amanda gestured to the couch, and

Josh sat. She'd prefer to remain standing given the looks of that couch, but it didn't feel right to stand over Josh while they informed him about Chloe. She took a seat, and Trent followed. "We're here to talk to you about your girlfriend, Chloe Somner," she said.

Josh opened his mouth like he was going to speak, but then snapped it shut. That made Amanda curious what he was going to say, but she wanted to get on with the notification portion of this visit.

"I'm sorry to tell you that Chloe was found murdered this morning in Leesylvania State Park." Amanda wanted to witness his reaction to the news firsthand. It could be telling as to whether he was guilty and hiding something, or innocent.

Josh's cheeks flushed red, and he wiped his brow. "What now?"

"We were hoping you could tell us." He could genuinely be in shock, but Amanda needed to shake him a bit more to make a better judgment.

"I... I... haven't seen Chloe in a few weeks." He cleared his throat and scratched the back of his head. "We broke up." His eyes scanned Amanda, then Trent, back to Amanda.

Amanda adjusted her posture, squared her shoulders. The pictures of them together were still in Chloe's bedroom, though her parents had said she hadn't been home since school started. Did she also not communicate with them about her relationship? Her parents had given the impression Chloe and Josh were still seeing each other. "Whose idea was it to break up?"

"Honestly? It was a mutual decision. We've known each other forever and were just the comfortable choice. Man, I can't believe she's..." Josh's face knotted in anguish, and his entire complexion reddened. "What happened to her... exactly?"

"She was stabbed numerous times."

Sorrow played over his facial features and demonstrated in his body language. Tears pooled in his eyes, and he sank farther into the couch and rubbed his forehead. Signs that he was genuinely upset—but was it because someone he'd cared for had been murdered or because she had been killed at his hand?

"Is there anyone who can substantiate it was a mutual breakup?" Trent asked.

"Do you really think I had something to do with what happened to her?" If agony had a voice, this was it.

"I don't know, Josh," Amanda said softly. "Did you?"

"You can talk to her parents. They will tell you I'd never hurt Chloe. Hurting her would be like hurting myself."

They *had* told them that, but that didn't make it gospel. She also didn't have names of anyone who could back up Josh's claim the breakup was mutual. She'd bench that for now but would come back to it later today or in the days ahead. "Where were you this morning between three and seven?" The mystery figure had been dropped off at three thirty, but she padded it with another thirty minutes.

Josh raked a hand through his hair. "I definitely would have been sleeping. Not feeling too good this morning. Flu or something."

Amanda was quite sure it wasn't a flu. A hangover, if the empty bottles were to be believed. "Can anyone confirm you were here, sleeping?"

He shook his head.

"Think carefully. It would help the investigation and get us out of your way sooner," she said.

"I didn't kill her. That's all I know." Tears beaded in his eyes. "And you said she was at Leesylvania State Park? Was she there for the snails? Who did this? Why?" Pain creased his face.

"We're trying to figure all that out," she said. "You brought up the snails. Did you know she went to the park?"

"Not this morning, but I know that she does." His voice cracked. "But you said three this morning? Why would she have been there then?"

"Another question that needs an answer. And did you ever go with her to the park?" She was testing what the ranger had told them.

"Sure, but not in a while. Certainly not after we broke up, and never before six in the morning. That was enough of a stretch for me. I prefer sleeping in. God, I loved her," he said between gulps for breath. "Sure, we broke up, but that didn't change how I felt about her. I did love her. I still do."

Trent said, "It must have hurt to go your separate ways, then."

"Yeah, but as I said, it was mutual. We were still good friends."

"And the reason you broke up was because you were the comfortable choice for each other?" Amanda was having a hard time accepting that. But people could make strange decisions, and she certainly wouldn't claim to understand all of them.

"We had to expand our horizons. Work out who we were as individuals." His tone was flat, like he was repeating someone else's words, not his own belief.

"We'll need some names of friends who could testify to the breakup being mutual." Trent handled the request like it had been made during the course of a casual conversation.

"I'll get you their names. They're from Dumfries, Wood-bridge area." He drew his sleepy gaze to Amanda. "Prince William County."

"Are they students at Geoffrey Michaels?" Trent asked, his pen paused over the page of his book.

"Yeah. Heck, her roommates, Jayne and Lauren, could tell you the breakup was mutual. You have their information?"

Amanda nodded. They had their home address and knew they went to the science center. "We'll reach out to them. What kind of car do you drive, Josh?"

"What kind of car— What does that have to do with anything?"

"Again, elimination purposes."

"I drive an Equinox sometimes. It belongs to my parents. Why?"

"Do you ever drive their Toyota Prius?"

"Nope."

"And that's what your parents would tell us if we asked?"

"You don't need to talk to my parents."

Now she wanted to. "And why's that?"

"They loved Chloe. Let me break the news to them." He ran a finger under his nose, but he easily met her gaze, which led her to believe his request was made from a place of integrity.

"Are you aware of anyone who had a beef with Chloe?"

"A beef?"

The tone, the enclosed mocking at her turn of phrase, made Amanda feel old. "Someone who didn't like her and might have had reason to kill her?"

Josh looked from Amanda to Trent, back to Amanda. He wasn't in any hurry to assure them Chloe was perfect and loved by everyone, like the girl's parents had been. He had someone in mind.

"Josh?" she prompted. "If you know of someone, tell us."

"Yeah, okay, she had her haters. She had a lot of friends, but she probably had an equal number of people who were envious of her and despised her. You know how beautiful she was, but she was smart too. The world doesn't seem to quite know how to handle both in one package."

Deep thought. Maybe she'd judged him too soon. "We're going to need some names."

Josh got up without a word and, a few minutes later, returned with a piece of paper that looked like it had been ripped out of a notebook. He gave it to Amanda. Two names were scrawled in messy handwriting.

"Just two?" she asked.

"You want more?"

"Are there more?" It had sure sounded like there were a second ago.

"Those two probably disliked her the most."

"Why?"

"Best you talk to them."

"Okay," she dragged out. "Do they both go to Geoffrey Michaels?"

"Uh-huh, at the science center with Chloe."

"Thank you." She moved to get up.

"They're not the only ones by far," he reiterated.

So much for Chloe's mother's claim that her daughter was liked by everyone. It was just the idyllic hopes of a parent.

Josh glanced at Trent. "Surprised that I have to tell you this, that you don't already know... Or at least I don't think you do, but Chloe was a brand ambassador on Snap VidPic."

Amanda had heard of the new social app, which had recently gone viral. She didn't know much about it other than it was a place for people to share pictures and videos. As for what a brand ambassador was, the generational divide was rearing its head again, and Amanda's thirty-six years might as well have made her an old lady for the breakdown in communication that was happening.

"What products did she endorse?" Trent said when Amanda hadn't opened her mouth to speak. He was roughly the same age as Amanda but obviously more knowledgeable with social media.

"Mostly workout wear, but she also did some jewelry. All of it environmentally friendly. No need to even say that, as everything she did was to help the planet. But it also attracted a lot of haters online."

"For one company or several?" Amanda's mind wasn't far from that logo on those flyers.

"Just the one. Planet Rebirth. They're out of Washington."

And they come up again... Did Chloe's murder have something to do with this environmental group or one of their enemies? She'd been found in nature, naked as the day she was born, cleansed, and left with a flower. Still, their involvement would be a great stretch at this point in the investigation, but she'd keep them in mind. "We'll need her Snap VidPic handle." At least she knew that much. But in her defense, it wasn't like she had a reason to be savvy with the new social media site. It probably didn't help there was a new one popping up every other day either.

Josh rattled off the handle like he'd said it a million times before. "There were some people who got really nasty on there. You'll notice it if you go to her profile and read the comments."

Amanda was grateful for the lead but also a touch over-whelmed. Depending on just how popular Chloe had been online, there could be a lot of information to wade through. A lot of false leads. A lot of wasted manpower.

But one step at a time. That was the only way any case ever got solved, and they had somewhere else they needed to be. "My partner and I are going to leave now, but we're very sorry for your loss." *We're* sorry...? Either that was the first time she'd phrased it that way or it felt different this time. Even Trent glanced over at her.

"I honestly don't know what I'm going to do without her." Josh's gaze fell to the floor briefly, and he sniffled.

"We're going to have to ask that you stay in the area. Just in case we have more questions. Do you understand?" she asked.

"I'll do whatever I can to help."

"Actually, one more question before we go. Does a black orchid mean anything to you?" She'd thought maybe the inquiry would catch him off guard; she never expected absolute confusion.

"No..." He shook his head. "Sounds like it could be a rock band."

"It's a flower."

"Never heard of it." She could see in his eyes that he didn't understand why she'd brought it up, but he never verbalized his curiosity.

"We'll see ourselves out," she said.

He'd put on a good performance, but it was hard to believe he had no concept of what a black orchid might be.

Back in the car, Trent got the vents blowing some heat, and faced her.

"Do you think he did it?"

"Too soon to say. Not sure he's as naive about black orchids as he'd like us to believe."

"That niggled at me too."

"At least we're walking away with something." She held up the paper Josh had given her. "Stephanie Piper and Luke Hogan. Right now, though, we better head over for the autopsy."

Trent got them on the road.

"How did you know what a Snap VidPic brand ambassador was?" The question spilled out.

Trent didn't look at her, but it was clear from his profile that he was grinning. At least he found her ignorance amusing.

"Come on, tell me."

"You know that younger sister I've told you about before?"

"The Jabba girl?"

"That's the one." He glanced over at her. "She's the only reason I know what it is. She was a brand ambassador on Instagram."

She fought the urge to laugh but lost the battle.

"Glad you find this so amusing," he said.

"You have any idea how old I was feeling in there?" Laughing felt great, like all the tension and stress was releasing from her body.

"Oh, I see what this is. It's misery loving company. Glad I could make you feel better about yourself." He winked at her.

In that instant, her stomach fluttered. What the heck? She continued to stare at his profile as he drove, completely confused by her reaction. Trent was handsome by anyone's standards, with his neatly trimmed blond hair and blue eyes. He had a nice jawline and kept himself in good shape.

But this was Trent! That flutter had to have meant nothing. Maybe indigestion, her last coffee not sitting well. After all, Trent was like a second brother she didn't have. To think of him as anything more was utterly ridiculous. Preposterous.

She shook aside all insane notions about Trent and buried her nose in the piece of paper.

Did one of these names belong to Chloe's killer?

FOURTEEN

There was always a sense of finality to seeing a body on a slab in the morgue, but Chloe Somner didn't look much different than she had next to the river. Just her skin was more translucent and held more of a bluish tinge under the harsh lighting.

Rideout was standing next to the autopsy table and appeared rather solemn considering his normal upbeat nature, even in the face of death. But there was something about seeing a young woman ripped from this world so unexpectedly—it went against the fiber of humanity. It stung. It enraged. It was unnatural and demanded a righting of a wrong.

"Glad to see you made it all right," Rideout said and waved a greeting.

"I wish I could say that we meet again under better circumstances." Amanda nudged her head toward the body. "Do you have anything for us so far?"

"Yep." Rideout snapped on some gloves and pulled the white sheet down to Chloe's waist. "Just to get this out of the way, I stand by what I'd surmised on scene. She wasn't sexually assaulted."

"One glimmer of good news despite all this..." Amanda waved a hand over Chloe.

"We take what we can, Detective. And there's no evidence that she was even sexually active recently."

More good news. It could support Josh Ryder's claim that they'd broken up. "Is there anything you can tell us that will get us closer to her killer? Possibly the type of weapon used or whether there were any defensive wounds? Maybe she scratched her assailant and attained epithelia." As she spoke, Rideout's face fell, and he frowned. She could read his expression like a book: he didn't have too much good news, if any, to share from this point forward.

"It doesn't look like she had a chance to defend herself," he said. "No evidence of that, anyway. I've scraped under her nails, but it's not promising. The killer did quite a thorough job of cleaning up trace."

"Missed the snail," Amanda said, inserting some humor into the moment.

"I heard about that. Yes, it might help the case. But there's also this." He snatched a vial off a metal table and handed it to her.

It was just a tiny piece of yellow fiber. "What am I looking at?"

"I believe it's a piece of a sponge."

"So he stripped her, laid her out, and sponge-bathed her. Probably using river water. It would also account for the blood on her back and on the soil." Her mind assembled the image. The killer put her body on the ground, and some of the blood dripped around and behind her torso. He hadn't been completely thorough, but damn close to it.

"I believe so." Rideout took back the vial and returned it to the table. "She was stabbed seven times, as you know from the scene. After being stabbed even once, instinctual reaction would have you reaching out to defend yourself."

"She might not have been able to reach him." Amanda was building a picture in her head—the killer lunging forward with the knife, keeping his distance, juking left, right, left. How could Chloe have reached him to defend herself? But then that raised another question. "Okay, I can follow what you're saying, but then why didn't Chloe run? There wasn't any indication at the scene that she had."

"Probably because of this." Rideout lifted Chloe's left arm and pointed to light bruising on her tricep. "These contusions indicate the killer grabbed her."

The impressions of fingers were plain to see. Amanda's stomach knotted into a ball. That poor girl must have been so terrified, held in place and stabbed repeatedly—and possibly by someone she trusted.

"Given the bruising is on the left arm and the angle of the wounds, I'd conclude she was attacked from the front, and that the killer used their left hand to inflict the blows. Her killer would have required a lot of physical strength to hold onto her while they stabbed her."

Trent glanced at Amanda. "Strong and left-handed."

She shook her head. "Not necessarily on the latter."

Rideout was smiling. "She's right, Trent. Just because the killer may have used their left hand in this situation that doesn't mean it's their dominant one. They could be ambidextrous and even be primarily considered right-handed. However, I will say this: given the clean edges to the cut, using their left hand to stab Chloe came naturally to them."

Naturally... That word was unsettling, given the context. "You think they've killed before?"

"I think it's quite possible, but I'll leave that for you to determine."

Tremors ran through her. He might as well have just come out and said he suspected a serial killer at work.

"Told you on scene, the wounds showed no hesitation. Well,

the weapon was a non-serrated blade approximately five to seven inches long." Rideout drew a circle with his finger around one of the stab wounds. "As you can see, the incision is very clean. The killer did attack her aggressively—she was consecutively stabbed seven times—but also showed restraint. There is no indication of the knife's hilt hitting the skin, so they drew the blade out before going that deep."

Amanda rubbed her arms. Another serial killer in Prince William County? Would there be more young women before this was over? *Not on my watch.* "What can you give us that lends a clue to the identity of the killer?"

"The angle of the wounds tells me her killer was taller than her. I'd approximate at least six feet. Probably no taller than six four."

Likely a man, then, as they'd already assumed. Luke Hogan, one of the names Josh had given them? There was also the possibility Chloe was attacked by a tall woman who may have bolstered her height by wearing heeled shoes or boots to impede the investigation. Could the other name on the list be the culprit—Stephanie Piper? Or was it wishful thinking that Chloe's murder was an isolated incident, executed at the hands of someone within her circle? After all, the alternative was terrifying—a psychopathic killer who might strike again.

Rideout went on. "Also, one thing with this sort of repetitive action is that the killer's hand could have slipped down the side of the blade, even if they were exercising restraint. You might be looking at someone who was cut."

"The least of what he deserves," Amanda spat. Chloe would have encountered her would-be killer in the dark. She must have been terrified upon realizing she was going to die. But did she know her killer's face? The question was haunting. The repercussions of her being the victim of a serial killer unthinkable. "In your professional opinion, this killer was controlled and experienced?"

"Absolutely."

Would a one-off killer be able to show such poise?

"You said it was a non-serrated blade, but do you have any knife types or brands in mind?" Trent asked.

"Unfortunately, no. But there is one more thing I can tell you. The width of the blade would be about one inch."

"A hunting knife?" Trent looked over at her, and she could surmise what he was thinking. They'd had a case before that involved a bowie knife. It was possible such a knife had been used on Chloe. But narrowing down a knife type and, from there, finding the specific one that had been used as the weapon would be like searching for a needle in a haystack. Things would work the other way around, instead. Find the suspect, see if he had such a knife.

"And what about time of death?" Amanda asked.

"I've run more tests here. Given the timestamp on the video from the park and approximating thirty minutes to walk to the point where she was found, she died not long after reaching the riverbank. Somewhere between four and five in the morning." Rideout moved around the body and added, "Something else you'll be interested to know. I pulled cotton fibers from some of the wounds. Could have come from her clothing."

"Sounds like proof her killer stabbed her while she was clothed," Amanda concluded.

"I'd say that's a fair assessment."

"The undressing came afterward," she said, ruminating on that. "Could also have been an effort to remove evidence that could implicate the killer."

"Could be. Maybe something would match up with another crime scene," Trent kicked out, and she really wished he hadn't. Her mind was running wildly enough on its own. "And there's something that's occurred to me now. We've been trying to figure out why Chloe was at the park so early, which we still don't know. *But* if she was meeting up with someone she knew, why didn't she wait for that person in the lot or even carpool there with them? Does that mean something? Did her killer follow her?"

"A stalker? *Two* stalkers? The person driving and the one who actually stabbed her?" she theorized. "It's sad when that sounds like the better option, but compared to a serial killer, it is."

"I didn't think we were supposed to go there—a partnership or a serial killer," he volleyed back. "Besides, I thought we were hoping the second car was a taxi or driving service?"

"You're right—not that I like the direction any of this takes us."

"Me neither," he said.

But they had to explore all the angles in an investigation. She hated that one of these raised the possibility of a serial killer, let alone maybe two working together. Was it a matter of time before they'd find more young girls stabbed and laid out, a black orchid on their torso? She took a deep breath and rested her gaze back on Chloe. "Were you able to figure out which stab was the fatal blow?"

Rideout pointed to the wound near her heart. "I still believe this was the one."

Was the killer sending a message by stabbing her in the heart, or was it just coincidental? Amanda wanted to ask whether Chloe would have suffered for long but hesitated. Some questions were better left unanswered—some even unconsidered.

Rideout wheeled over a table with his autopsy tools on it. "Shall I get started?"

Amanda crossed her arms, hugging herself lightly. "I'm as ready as I'm ever going to be."

She and Trent stood by as Rideout performed the autopsy on Chloe, dissecting her and weighing her organs, cataloging her as an inventory of parts. It was something Amanda had witnessed too many times to count. And while she could stomach the sights and smells, she always hated the thought that in the crassest of terms, humans were glorified machines. A cold, unfeeling viewpoint, to be sure, but it was an observation she had made over the years. It was also something she tried to put out of her head the moment she left the morgue. Easier said than done.

FIFTEEN

Amanda and Trent left the ME's office at eight thirty. During the time she'd been in the morgue and watching the autopsy, she received a few phone calls. Someone in Tech had left a message to say there was no luck in tracking Chloe's phone, and she shared that info with Trent. Her favorite caller had been Zoe.

Even standing at a distance watching Rideout take apart a beautiful young woman, Zoe's voice was able to lift Amanda's spirits. She'd certainly made the right decision to open her heart to the child.

She couldn't wait to get home to her. It was horrible enough that she had to get Becky to step in and babysit Zoe tonight. Hopefully Zoe understood why Amanda was away so often.

There was something else Amanda should take care of tonight—making sure Jacob Briggs got the video from the park. Then there was this niggling fear that the killer they were after might have struck before. The experience, the restraint, the organization. She and Trent should be scouring the internet for past cases or even looping in the FBI with their Violent Criminal Apprehension Program, which allowed them to search unsolved crimes.

In short, there was a lot keeping her from home, but one small, precious thing pulling her there. She'd forgotten how tough it could be to balance family with the job. But maybe she didn't need to carry everything on her shoulders. She did have Trent.

She looked over at him as he drove them back to Central. "I'm wondering if you'd be able to do something tonight before going home."

"Name it."

She had to admire his willingness to do whatever it took to solve a case. "I need to get home to Zoe. I *want* to," she corrected.

Trent smiled. "I'm sure you do."

It was like this unspoken conversation between them, but when Amanda had first met Zoe, she'd denied how much the girl meant to her. She had downplayed Zoe as merely an eyewitness in a case Amanda needed to solve, but Trent quickly saw through that false wall.

"Could you follow up with Briggs to make sure he got the video from the park?" Briggs worked nights and was always willing to help when he could.

"Of course. Guess we have our killer's approximate height from Rideout, but we're wanting to see if Briggs can gauge the height of the mystery figure?"

"That's right. Let's see if both Rideout and Briggs agree on height."

"I'll ask Briggs about that. Other than that, we're hoping he can discern the license plate on the car that dropped off our mystery person, correct?"

"Yep." Discussing what they needed from Briggs emphasized how long ago it was that they'd first had that conversation.

It had been just that morning, though it felt like a day or two ago. She yawned and slapped a hand over her mouth.

Trent laughed. "Not easy being a mom again?"

She hesitated, not sure how to respond. It was absolutely glorious, though it definitely did upend her life. It had caused her to face some cold, hard truths she'd done her best to avoid for years. Namely that her husband and her daughter were never coming back, and it was time to allow herself to open her heart to new people and experiences. "It's challenging, but one of the most rewarding jobs."

Trent smiled. "I knew you two would wind up together."

"Yeah, yeah, you told me so? Zoe *was* more than just an eyewitness."

"She's very lucky she has you."

Lucky was relative. The only reason Zoe had Amanda was because she'd lost her parents—that hadn't been lucky. "I'm going to do my best by her."

"I know it."

Her chest warmed at his expressed confidence, and her cheeks flushed. She didn't know when she'd started caring so much about Trent's opinion of her. "What about you?" The question slipped out, and she wanted to reel it back in.

"What about me, what?" He glanced over at her.

"Ah, do you ever want to be a dad?" She'd already started down this path, might as well keep going.

His mouth twitched, then he burst out a laugh that had her chuckling.

"Me...? A dad? Yeah, no thanks."

"What? Really? You've never thought of it?"

"Oh, I've thought of it. It's just not who I am."

"Maybe you just haven't met the right person."

He moaned and took the exit ramp off the highway that led them toward the station. "I don't know if that's all it is."

"What about Cassie, the CSI? You guys still hitting it off?"

They'd met at the Parkers' crime scene and gone out a few times.

"More off, but we're taking things slow." He looked over at her. "Why the sudden interest?"

She squirmed inside but concentrated on keeping herself perfectly still otherwise. "No interest really. Just making conversation." Her tone was convincing, and really that's all it was—making conversation. About kids. "I'm just going to call home, give them an ETA." She called Becky's cell phone. She answered in the middle of the first ring.

"I was just starting to wonder where you were."

"Sorry. Things ran a little long. Zoe still up?"

"Depends on your definition. She's not in bed, but she's in her pj's and zapped out on the couch."

Amanda smiled. Just the thought of Zoe resting—her blond hair spilled around her head, her soft breathing that bordered on outright snores—warmed her. "I'll be home in about twenty minutes, if that. I can put her to bed when I get there."

"Okay. Good thing you called because I was just going to have Brandon carry her there."

"Glad I called, then. See you soon." With that, Amanda ended the call.

Trent's mouth was set in a straight line, brows drawn downward. At the sight of him, her thoughts went dark. The lightness that had been there, infused merely by the thought of seeing Zoe, was squashed.

"Just a feeling you're thinking this right now, but we need to consider that a serial killer may have done this to Chloe," she said.

He looked over at her, his grip on the steering wheel tightening, his knuckles showing white as they drove under streetlights.

"The experience, the restraint, the organization," she said, sharing her earlier thought. "We should see if we can find any similar cases to Chloe's."

"Probably a good idea." Somber, reflective.

Trent parked at Central, and they went their separate ways.

They were going to meet at the station at eight in the morning and go from there. Time to shake the ugliness of the day, the nightmare of homicidal shadows lurking in the darkness. She was going home to the light of her existence, a reward at the end of a hellish hard day.

She let herself in and found Becky, Zoe, and Brandon all nestled on the couch. They'd make a good-looking family—not that she'd be saying anything of the sort. While Amanda didn't know how her friend felt about having children of her own, she couldn't really see it. Becky was such an independent spirit and loved her freedom. Though she had kept Brandon around longer than any other boyfriend, despite their rough patches.

"Hey, guys," Amanda said softly, noticing how Zoe was lying across the couch—her head on Becky's lap, her feet on Brandon's, and her favorite stuffed dog, Sir Lucky, gripped closely to her chest.

"Hey," Becky and Brandon chortled back. Zoe whimpered and twisted. She never opened her eyes.

"Sorry to keep you so long. I can't thank you enough."

Becky waved her off. "Don't mention it." She carefully peeled herself out from under Zoe and made it to a standing position without disturbing her.

Brandon did his best to imitate Becky's moves but wasn't as successful. Zoe bolted upright and blinked wildly, looking around the room like her eyes were trying to adjust into focus. Her gaze landed on Amanda and immediately her eyes lit up.

"Amanda." Zoe hopped off the couch and ran to her. She

threw her arms around her legs before Amanda was able to get down to her level.

"Well, we're going to head out," Becky said, nearing the front door and slipping into her shoes.

Brandon was grabbing their coats from the coatrack, already in his shoes. He held Becky's jacket out for her to slip into, then put on his own. Amanda hadn't taken to Brandon at first. He was arrogant and cocky, past the point of confidence. He also worked with an ex-girlfriend of his, which Amanda didn't like one bit, but he'd assured Becky the relationship was long over. Amanda didn't trust the situation—especially when Brandon and his team were often jetting across the United States. They were hunting serial killers, not exactly fodder for romance, but still...

Amanda would now admit, though, that she'd come to cautiously like the guy. He had helped her with a previous investigation, sharing his expertise on serial killers. And he couldn't be that bad of a person if he was willing to babysit on one of the rare occasions that he was home and not on the road.

"Bye, sweetie." Becky waved at Zoe from the front door, and Zoe waved back from where she was, clinging to Amanda's leg.

"Bye," Amanda said to Becky and Brandon.

They shut the door behind them, and Amanda went over and threw the deadbolt. She turned and faced Zoe. Now the girl's arms were hanging at her sides, and Lucky was dangling by an ear.

"I'm thinking it's time we got you into bed."

"Okay." It came out as a mumble.

Amanda held out her hand for Zoe to take, and they walked down the hall to her room. There were times when it arrested Amanda's heart to cross the threshold with Zoe, knowing that the space they were about to enter had once been Lindsey's. It still held memories of her daughter. The walls were the same soft pink, and the curtains remained the same. Some of her toys were around. The Barbie picnic that had been going on for years had ended. The dolls were now stacked in a small tote in the closet. Zoe sometimes played with them.

The coloring book Lindsey had been working on was tucked away in Amanda's bedroom closet. The pages would forever remain her daughter's alone. She couldn't bring herself to part with the book altogether. She let Zoe use the crayons in her own coloring books that had been brought over from her family home, along with other toys and books. The furniture had been swapped out—Lindsey's was piled in the garage and Zoe's brought in. The bedroom was a mishmash of Zoe and Lindsey—and that was the best Amanda could hope for. It hadn't been an easy process, though necessary to move forward. They say forgiveness is hard, but acceptance was equally so.

Amanda pulled back the comforter and sheets, and Zoe crawled into the bed, but she didn't lie down. She sat with her back against the headboard, her legs and stomach covered.

"Will you read to me?"

Amanda tucked some of Zoe's long, blond hair behind an ear and smiled. "I'd love to but it's getting late, and you're tired." She poked Zoe's nose playfully.

Zoe giggled and swiped her hand away. "I'm awake." She was looking at Amanda with those blue eyes of hers that were nearly electric.

Amanda scooted Zoe over and sat on the edge of the bed, grabbing the book they'd been reading from the nightstand.

"Yay!" Zoe clapped her hands, releasing her hold on Lucky. It catapulted Amanda back to a time when the girl never let it out of her hand. Then again, Zoe and Lucky had been through a lot together. Zoe had been with the doll in the storage ottoman at the time of her parents' murders, when she'd witnessed her father's shooting.

Amanda flipped open to where they'd left off the night

before. They were reading *Alice in Wonderland*, a special edition with stunning illustrations and lots of text.

"Down the rabbit hole we go," Amanda said and began to read.

She continued until Zoe's head started lolling forward, her little chin dipping to her chest. "All right, sweetheart. Time for your own adventures."

Zoe shuffled down the bed, the covers coming to her chin. Amanda positioned Lucky so the dog's head was also above the sheets, and pecked a kiss on the girl's forehead. She flicked off the main light, turned on one that cast stars onto the ceiling—another item that had been Lindsey's—and left the room, leaving the door open a crack.

She stepped into the hall and leaned against the wall, feeling incredibly blessed. It was as if the slate was wiped clean, and all the nasty things that she'd seen since leaving home that morning had disappeared. Sadly, Amanda knew this euphoria would be fleeting. The moment her head hit her pillow, the ugly would wash over her again. But until then, she'd savor this sweet moment.

SIXTEEN

Surprisingly, Amanda slept like the proverbial baby. She'd expected the investigation to seep in, but it had thankfully remained at bay. She couldn't remember if she'd even dreamed, but she felt rested. She usually didn't need much sleep but that had apparently changed with the added responsibilities of taking care of Zoe. There had also been a time when the only way she'd get any rest was with a sleeping pill, but that felt like another lifetime ago. She hadn't taken them in months, the last package untouched in the top drawer of her nightstand.

Libby had come over to collect Zoe and take her to school. It was convenient, as Libby worked at Dumfries Elementary, where Zoe attended, and lived nearby.

All that morning's activities were in the rearview now, though, as she walked toward her desk at Central. She and Trent, and the other detectives in Homicide, were set up in a warren of cubicles with low dividers. They were just high enough to afford some privacy but low enough to encourage ease of communication.

Trent was already at his desk. "Good morning."

"Good morning." She held up a tray with two large coffees

from Hannah's Diner as if it took all the credit for it being "good." But there was so much she had to be grateful for. She'd certainly woke up renewed and ready to tackle this investigation with a fresh mind. She was more determined than ever to get to the bottom of what had happened to Chloe. Both the girl and her parents deserved as much. And if they were looking at a serial killer, best they know sooner than later. The last thing she was wanted was more young women being murdered. "You follow up with Briggs?"

"You know it. He received the file, and he'll work on it."

She walked into his cubicle and held out the tray for him to pluck a cup.

"Wow. Really? Thanks."

"Hey. Don't say that like I never do anything nice for you."

"Never." He smirked, tore back the lip of the lid, and took a sip.

She tossed the tray into the garbage and perched on the edge of his desk. "We've got a busy day. Figured we could use the caffeine. I want to talk to Chloe's roommates and see if they can point us in anyone's direction. I also want to go to the townhouse Chloe rented and take a look in her room."

"We have those two names from Josh Ryder too. I pulled backgrounds on them, as well as the roommates. No arrest records of any kind. Then I looked at Chloe's Snap VidPic profile. She had a lot of haters on there like Josh told us. She's also got herself thirty thousand followers and followed all of twenty-five."

"Does she only follow close friends of hers? Are the roommates on there?"

"Yeah, they are." He lifted a sheet from his desk and handed it to her.

There was a list of names accompanied by photos. "What am I looking at?"

"The twenty-five who made the cut."

She pushed off his desk and scanned down. "All right, well, this could be helpful." One of the profile pictures was of Josh Ryder with the handle of high_ryder21.

"This could be too." He handed her another printout that was several pages and stapled.

She lifted it and raised her eyebrows as if to ask, *What's this?*

"I came in at six." He raised his cup from Hannah's Diner.

She touched hers to his. "To catching a killer." Then she looked down at the printout. It was a newspaper article: "College Girl Stabbed to Death." She almost dropped the papers. *Please don't tell me...* She read the article.

Trent summed it up when she was done. "Annie Frasier, murdered at twenty-two years of age, twenty years ago in Washington, DC. She was found with a flower."

"That's all? No flower type mentioned or where it was placed? Whether or not she was naked?" Amanda set her coffee on Trent's desk, no longer interested in drinking it given the turn in their conversation—it was churning to acid in her gut. "Could just be a coincidence."

"Sure, but it might not be. The case is still open. Now, I hope you don't mind, but I called the lead detective from the investigation and left a message for him."

"He's still on the job?"

"Wasn't told otherwise, and he had a voicemail greeting."

"It says it was a flower. Might not have been a black orchid. We don't know how many times she was stabbed, what the scene looked like..." She was grasping, not wanting to roll right over to a serial killer. She was desperately trying to cling to *isolated incident.*

"Might not have been a black orchid, but maybe the killer picks a flower that represents each victim."

"Thanks for putting that in my head."

"We seriously need to consider a serial killer. They have a

type, right?" He brought up an image on his computer. A young brunette was looking out at them. "That's Annie."

"Long hair, like Chloe."

"And brunette. Chloe's natural color."

"Could just be a coincidence, Trent." *Please!*

"And it might not be."

"Their ages are different. Chloe was nineteen and this Frasier woman was twenty-two." She jutted out her chin. "Before we get carried away, we'll rule out people in Chloe's life." She pushed off his desk and left the article on it. Was it too much to ask that the killing stop?

They hit the administrative offices for the Potomac Center for Science and Environmental Studies and followed a nice-looking, fifty-something man named Craig Perkins to his office. They'd been told to speak with Craig regarding Chloe Somner and any other students they may want access to.

Craig entered a modest office and sat at the desk. "Please sit wherever you'd like."

There were a few options available, but it seemed most appropriate to sit in the chairs across from him.

"You wanted to talk about Chloe Somner?" The senior associate dean leaned forward, clasping his hands on his desk.

The introductions had already been done, and he knew they were homicide detectives with the PWCPD. There was no apparent concern that Chloe was in trouble or had found herself the victim of a crime. If anything, he was completely unfazed by their presence.

"Chloe Somner was found murdered yesterday morning," Amanda laid out, doing so matter of factly.

Craig leaned back in his chair, gripped the arms of it with his hands, and swiveled ever so slightly. "Dear me."

"You're surprised or...?" It was hard to read his reaction.

"Shocked." He made eye contact with her. "Chloe's parents must be beside themselves with grief. I heard about the woman found murdered on the shore of the Potomac on the news last night. Was that...?"

Amanda nodded.

"Wow. Never in my wildest dreams would I have guessed it was someone I knew. A student, no less."

"Please accept our condolences," Amanda said.

"Yes, well..." He adjusted the lay of his jacket's lapel.

"We understand that Chloe had a bright future ahead of her," Trent interjected, paving a path for the associate dean to take.

"Absolutely. She was the star of her classes. It's such a shame."

Amanda imagined him *tsk*ing, though he didn't actually do such a thing. She was starting to see him as very dry and one of those people who rarely got excited or upset about anything. Even his office didn't have any personal touches. There was one framed photo in which Craig was standing next to a handsome woman, and while she was smiling, he appeared stiff, his smile bordering on a grimace.

"Was she a popular girl?" Trent asked.

"She seemed to be, yes. From what I saw anyway. Kids can be one thing in front of adults and another behind their backs, especially as they get older and assert their independence. And, really, by the time they get to us, they're adults—at least legally. True maturity takes more time, I believe."

Amanda smiled. "And some people never grow up."

"Very true." Not so much as a flicker of a smile.

"Do you know of anyone who Chloe didn't get along with?" she asked.

"Do I..." He tapped his chin with his index finger. After a few seconds, he shook his head. "Enough to kill her? I don't see anyone having that big of a grudge or vendetta against her."

"Let us decide that," Amanda said. "You're obviously thinking of someone."

He nodded. "Stephanie Piper. The two of them are awfully competitive."

Piper was on Josh's list. "Did you ever see the two girls get into a physical altercation?"

"No, I can't say I did. But Stephanie really didn't take kindly when Chloe scored higher than her on a recent exam. Word about that made it all the way back to me from Professor McMillan's class. Advanced biology."

Rideout had estimated the killer to be at least six feet tall, but Amanda wouldn't dismiss the possibility of heeled shoes. The video from the park had certainly been too dark to discern whether the person dropped off was male or female. "We'll want to speak with Stephanie Piper and Professor McMillan."

"Certainly. I can have them paged to come to the office." Craig looked at the clock on the wall. "The professor breaks from class at eleven. Can you wait until then to speak with him?"

Amanda glanced at the time. 8:25 AM. "Sure, but we'll need to speak to a few students in addition to Stephanie. We'd actually like to start with Jayne Russell and Lauren Bennett, and then we also want to talk to Luke Hogan." Considering Jayne and Lauren were Chloe's roommates, it was best to start with them. It wouldn't be nice if word got back to them about Chloe's death from a third party. And that was assuming they hadn't already heard. In the least, they must be curious about the police officer posted at the curb outside their townhouse.

Craig reached for the phone on his desk. "I'll request they come to the front office."

"Is there somewhere private we could speak with them?" Trent asked, beating Amanda to the same question.

"Certainly." Craig picked up the receiver and directed the person on the other end to have Jayne and Lauren removed from class. A few moments later, he hung up. "I wish there was more I could do to help."

Amanda was ready with her business card. "If you think of anyone who might have hurt Chloe or had anything against her after we leave, call me. Day or night."

"Will do." Craig tucked the card into the breast pocket of his shirt and stood. "Now, if you'd follow me."

He took Amanda and Trent through a few corridors to a large conference room that he'd told them was used for overflow or special lectures the university booked periodically.

As they waited for the students, Amanda couldn't help but think how they were about to upend more people's lives. It was only the good cases—the wins—that pushed her through. Otherwise, it would be far too easy to roll over and give up.

SEVENTEEN

The door swung open, and two young women walked into the room. The air between them seemed charged. Both frowned when their eyes fell on Amanda and Trent, and one girl nudged the other. Either they suspected bad news was coming or the associate dean had told them of Chloe's death, despite Amanda asking him not to.

Amanda gestured to chairs across the table from her and Trent. "Hi, girls. You want to take a seat?" It would be more effective presenting it as an invitation, rather than a request.

"Ah, sure." The one who spoke had bleach-blond hair swept back in a high ponytail. The other seemed timid and withdrawn. It was hard to know if it was because of the circumstances or if it was her normal nature. But there were a few strands of her brown hair that had been colored purple, suggesting to Amanda that she wasn't always quiet.

"I'm Detective Amanda Steele, and this is Detective Trent Stenson."

The girls dropped down into the chairs across the table. The one with the ponytail set her messenger bag on the table, and the other one hugged her textbooks to her chest—uncomfortable and closed off. Was it the reaction of a person with something to hide or was she naturally nervous around cops?

"You're Jayne?" Amanda took a guess and addressed the girl with the purple highlights when neither of them reciprocated Amanda's introduction by supplying their name.

The ponytail girl shook her head, her hair swaying with the movement. "She's Lauren. I'm Jayne."

Amanda nodded, curious why Lauren couldn't speak for herself. Jayne did have a way about her that sucked the air from the room, though. "We understand that Chloe Somner was your roommate?"

"Uh-huh. And a good friend." Jayne had this confident air about her, and Amanda hated that the news she had to deliver would probably tear it apart chunk by chunk.

Lauren nodded but said nothing.

"Unfortunately, we have bad news about Chloe. She was found murdered yester—"

"No! Shut the—" Jayne jumped to her feet. "You're shitting us. You have to be. She can't be..." She lowered back into a chair, opting for one a bit farther down the table, though still opposite Amanda and Trent.

Lauren's eyes filled with tears, and she stared blankly at the table.

"She was stabbed to death," Amanda said, laying Chloe's fate out more clearly.

"Who would—" Jayne rubbed her mouth and blinked rapidly. She shook her head. "No, I can't accept this."

"You were quite close, then?" Trent asked gently.

"Uh-huh." Jayne regarded him like the question had been a stupid one.

"And you, Lauren?" Amanda leaned forward, dipping her head low enough to meet the girl's gaze.

"She was my best friend." Her voice was gravelly.

"Jeez, thanks," Jayne groaned.

"Not everything is about you!" Lauren snapped, set her books on the table, and turned her body toward Jayne. "Don't make what happened to her about you. Don't even dare."

The quiet girl had a temper. Those who bottled up their feelings were the most volatile. She'd come into the room almost as if she were being led to the execution chamber. Had she known what happened to Chloe before coming here? "Lauren, did you hear Chloe had been killed before we told you?"

"No."

"She's just a bit of a witch," Jayne said.

"Would you shut up?" Lauren's face contorted into a mask of anger.

"No, I won't shut up, bitch!"

Amanda held out a hand like a referee official at a football game. "Hey, let's stop with the name calling and the outbursts. Do you know how lucky the two of you are? Your friend, not so much." Her redhead temper had enough of listening to these two bickering back and forth when a supposed friend of theirs was in a fridge at the morgue.

Both girls held each other's gazes and grimaced.

"You two are friends, as well as roommates, are you not?" Amanda suspected she might have made a false assumption before the girls had entered the room, but it was possible they were just in a tiff at the moment.

"No way," Jayne pushed out. "And she gets these woo-woo feelings." She wriggled her fingers. "Thinks she's psychic or something."

Lauren shuffled farther down in her chair and crossed her arms. "I get feelings," she mumbled. "Something you wouldn't understand."

"Lauren, you got a feeling that something had happened to Chloe?" Amanda would roll with this and see where it got them.

"Yeah. I mean she didn't come home last night, and she wasn't answering her phone all day."

"She could have hooked up with a guy, you know. You mother us and smother us." Jayne curled her upper lip in a repulsive expression that certainly wiped away any natural good looks she had.

"Enough," Amanda snapped, and Trent wheeled his chair back a few inches. She kept her gaze on the girls. "Your friend is dead. Murdered. We're here talking to you to see if we can figure out who did this and why. Do you want to see justice for her, or is it more important that you continue to argue? Honestly, we have all day, but the longer this takes, the longer her killer is out there free."

Deafening silence.

"Good. Now, let's continue." Amanda coached her breathing to slow and continued. "Jayne, you mentioned Chloe hooking up with someone. Her boyfriend or someone else?" There was no evidence Chloe had sex recently, but that didn't mean she wasn't seeing anyone, and they still hadn't confirmed her breakup with Josh.

"You know about Josh?" Jayne asked.

"Yes, and we'll get back to him. But was she seeing or sleeping with anyone else?"

"No, but she could have." Jayne crossed her arms and pushed her chin out.

Amanda took a deep breath, trying to cool her temper. "Did either of you think to report Chloe as missing?" The answer to that question would reveal just how tight the group of girls was.

"No. Because of this one." Lauren shot a glare at Jayne. "She thinks I make things up, but it's not true. I *sense* things."

Amanda wasn't there to delve into the spiritual universe and its inexplicable mysteries. She didn't even buy into them. It's said a person can sense when a loved one is hurt, but had the two girls been that close? Then there was the one aspect of the symbolism for the black orchid: black magic. She shook aside any suspicion in that regard. There was nothing at the scene to indicate Chloe was killed as part of a magical ritual. "Do either of you know why Chloe would have been at Leesylvania State Park at three thirty yesterday morning?"

The girls looked at each other. Both shook their heads.

"Did she go to the park regularly?" Trent interjected.

"Yeah," Lauren said. "She studied the mystery snails."

Not news. "Would you know why she was there so early? Or was that the time she normally went?" A little fishing expedition. Line cast.

Jayne chewed on a hangnail. "Well, she hasn't been there in weeks... not since she and Josh split."

Amanda would get back to the subject of the breakup, but she wanted to pursue the other part of what Jayne had said. Helen McCarthy made it sound like Chloe had been a regular visitor, right up to the previous week. Had she lied intentionally, or had she been speaking in generalities as to Chloe's schedule? "Did Chloe go to the park regularly before that?"

"Yeah," Jayne said.

"I think she and Josh would sometimes hook up in the woods," Lauren added softly. "I got the impression it was too hard on her emotionally to go back there after they split. I'm surprised to hear that she was there yesterday."

"What? You don't have any *feelings* about it?" Jayne gave Lauren a smug grin.

"Tell me about Josh," Amanda started, not even about to let herself get worked up this time. She'd save her breath. After all, what would be the point? No matter what she said, they continued to bicker. "He and Chloe used to date. Tell us about their breakup."

Jayne dropped her hand. "It was about time they called it quits. She was with him way too long if you ask me. We're young, and we should be having fun." Jayne winked at Trent.

"My God!" Lauren threw her arms in the air. "She's like a walking hormone."

Well, this is proving to be fun...

"You probably slept with him behind her back," Lauren accused.

"Hold up. I'm going to pretend you never said that, or I'd come over there and—" Jayne made a move like she was going to spring from her chair and lunge at Lauren.

Lauren didn't even twitch.

All right... Amanda's temper was sizzling beneath the surface of her skin. These two were best to remain miles from each other, yet they were roommates. "When did Chloe and Josh break up?"

Jayne shrugged. "Say, three weeks ago."

The timing lined up with what Josh had told them. "Whose idea was it?"

"They both decided it would be best. But Chloe was starting to become quite a... how would you say it, a nerd?" The way Jayne put that felt like she'd searched for terminology Amanda's generation would understand. Maybe Amanda was more sensitive about her age after not knowing what a brand ambassador on Snap VidPic was.

"She was more interested in her studies than dating?" Amanda asked. "Is that what you mean? If so, that's admirable."

"That's what I think." Lauren knotted her arms tighter and shot off another glare dagger at Jayne.

Amanda didn't want to know what it was like at home in the townhouse with these two. And now with Chloe gone, who had possibly been a mediator between them, it wouldn't be surprising if Jayne and Lauren went their separate ways. It would probably be healthier for both of them if they did. "You two obviously don't... see eye to eye." Amanda took the time to put it delicately. "But you were both close with Chloe, so we need to know if either of you were aware of someone who had an issue with her. Someone who might have a reason to kill her."

The girls looked at each other, and for one moment in time, all nails were retracted.

"That guy," Lauren said.

"Stephanie," Jayne chimed in at the same time.

Amanda looked between them. "Stephanie..."

Jayne nodded. "Piper is her last name. She was like Chloe's nemesis."

There was that name again. "And this guy you mentioned, Lauren, who is that?"

Jayne turned on Lauren. "Yeah, who are you thinking about?"

"Luke Hogan," Lauren answered Jayne, and Jayne's eyes widened.

That name...

Jayne faced Amanda. "She's right. He is a bit... off."

"What's *off* about him?" Amanda needed a lot more clarity on the matter.

"He's in love with her, follows her around like a puppy dog."

The skin tightened on the back of Amanda's neck. *Follows her around...* They'd theorized that Chloe's killer might have stalked her. "Did Chloe give him the time of day or...?"

"You're kidding, right?" Jayne said. "He's a real dork, nerd, whatever you want to call him. But he had it bad for her and never took the hint that she didn't even want to be his friend. She was constantly brushing him off. Smart, but dumb, because he couldn't take a hint."

Lauren rolled her eyes.

"You don't agree?" Trent asked her.

"It's not that. I just don't know why she has to be quite so judgmental."

"I just call it how I see it. Like you *sense* things." Jayne used finger quotes.

"All right. Thanks, girls," Amanda said, stepping in. She pretty much reached her limit with these two. "One more thing, though. Do black orchids mean anything to either of you?"

Jayne made this stumped face like she hadn't a clue, but Lauren picked at the spine of a textbook.

"Lauren?" Amanda prompted.

"Don't they mean death? But they can also carry a positive meaning such as success and strength."

"How do you know that?"

"She's weird like that too!" Jayne jumped in. "All into astrology and horoscopes. Don't bug her when Mercury is in retrograde. Whooo." She shook her hands in the air.

"Enough," Amanda barked, pinched the bridge of her nose and shut her eyes for a second. She should have more control than that, but these two were really irritating. She regrouped and continued calmly. "Thank you, Lauren." Amanda pulled out two business cards and handed one to each of them.

Jayne stood and eyed Trent. She held out her hand. "I'll take yours too."

"You can reach me through Detective Steele." All business.

The smirk on Jayne's face dissolved, and her eyes became ice before she turned on her heel and left.

"Sorry for your loss." Amanda called that out after Jayne's retreating form and let it carry for Lauren, who was a little slower collecting her books. "Let me know if you'd like someone to speak with you about what happened to your friend... To help you process it all."

"Thanks." Lauren dipped her head and left.

"Let's hope the two of them don't kill each other," she mumbled to Trent.

"Right? A valid concern."

EIGHTEEN

Amanda asked for Luke Hogan to be paged next. While they waited for him to come to the room, she turned to Trent. "Lauren knew exactly what a black orchid stands for."

"Could be the one we least expect."

Amanda's phone rang, and she checked the caller ID. *Deb Hibbert.* She was her contact at the adoption agency. "I've got to get this," she said.

"No problem."

Amanda stood, answered, and stepped into the hall.

"Amanda..."

Her stomach clenched at the way Deb said her name, at the woman's pause. She had bad news. Amanda had already experienced enough of that for a lifetime, but with all that misfortune, it had emboldened her to face it head-on. It also made it so Amanda could sense bad news coming. "What is it? I sense something is wrong." As she said the words, she recalled Lauren and her *feelings* about things. It could just be evidence of strong intuition—nothing sinister.

"Guess I should have known better than to think you might not pick up on it. You are a detective." Deb took a deep breath that traveled the line. "I reached out to Colin Brewster in California."

Amanda tensed and started pacing. She watched students and faculty move in the hallways around her, hoping the distraction would aid in calming her nerves. It wasn't working.

"He wants to contest the adoption."

"He can do that?" She started to whirl into a cyclone of deniability. She knew when she'd handed over his name that it was a possibility he'd come forward and try to claim that Zoe was his daughter, but there was an easy way to fight his attempt. "So, we just get a paternity test." Rational, level-headed, even if she wasn't feeling either of those things.

"Yes, but if the DNA comes back and says that he's Zoe's father, I think you know what that means."

Apparently, it was too much to hope that the man wanted nothing to do with Zoe—not even enough to bother with a paternity test. She doubted he'd even met the girl, and he probably hadn't known of her existence before Deb had reached out. But now Amanda was faced with the real possibility that he might want to swoop in and take Zoe with him to California. The girl had only been with her a couple of months, but Amanda already couldn't bear the thought of life without her. Amanda wanted to see Zoe grow up, find out what kind of person she was going to become, what she was going to do with her life, who she was going to fall in love with, be at her wedding and the birth of her children. Whatever stops on the journey, Amanda wanted to be there for all of them, or at least as many as possible.

"I know this wasn't what you wanted to hear, and it might not end up affecting the adoption. Let's keep positive, and I'll be in touch."

"Thank you for letting me know." Amanda ended the call realizing the irony of being told to keep positive. Usually that was a line she fed herself, even when she didn't believe it.

Honestly, the whole "keep positive" adage only surfaced when the opposite was the more natural response. Amanda laid a hand over her stomach and tried to coach herself into thinking this was for the best. Let it come up now and be done with it. Then Zoe would legally become her daughter, and there would be nothing but the future to look forward to.

Amanda turned to go back inside the room and came face-to-face with a young man just outside the door. He towered above her several inches. He had brown hair and a solid build, and he wore glasses. Genetically he was an attractive kid, but his slumped posture suggested a lack of confidence.

"You must be Luke Hogan," she said, holding out a hand.

He looked at her extended hand as if it were a foreign entity, but eventually he took it. His palms were clammy, and his grip weak. "I am, ma'am."

"I'm Detective Amanda Steele." Holding the door open, she motioned for him to go first. She gave him a gentle smile as he walked into the room, hoping it would set him at ease.

Trent stood and walked around the table to greet Luke and introduce himself. The two of them were about the same height. That would make Luke six foot one—within the estimated range for Chloe's killer.

"Please, take a seat." She gestured toward the numerous chairs that surrounded the table. "Wherever you'd like."

Luke dropped into the chair that Lauren had vacated, and Amanda and Trent went back to where they had been sitting. Luke's eyes were scanning the room. It was clear he was uncomfortable. Had he killed Chloe and was nervous he might have gotten caught? Or was it simply being asked to come here to talk to two police detectives?

"Do you know why we're here, Luke?" Amanda figured it might be best to go the more indirect route with him.

He met her gaze and slowly shook his head.

"We're here because one of your classmates, Chloe Somner, was murdered." She let it root as she watched for a reaction.

Luke's chin quivered, and his eyes pooled with tears.

"Were you close?" she asked.

He slid his bottom lip through his teeth and shook his head. "I wanted to be. She was one of the prettiest, brightest girls in this college."

Now Luke was demonstrating some confidence. He wasn't shy about his affection toward Chloe, even in the light of being told she'd been murdered. "How did she feel about you?" Amanda leaned forward ever so slightly.

"Sometimes I wondered if she even knew I existed. It was like I was invisible to her, and regardless of what I did, it didn't matter."

"And how did that make you feel?" Trent asked. "I mean, as a guy myself, it stings when a girl doesn't reciprocate my interest."

"Should I get a lawyer?"

Amanda sat back in her chair, surprised by his defensiveness. "I guess that depends, Luke. Did you kill Chloe?" She hadn't intended to go down this direct path, but it was the one on which she'd landed.

"No," he spat. "But it's obvious you guys are wanting to pin her murder on me. I watch those crime shows. I know how important it is for the police to close cases—even if the wrong guy goes to prison."

"I can assure you, Luke, my partner and I are only interested in finding the killer, not some scapegoat to settle the case. So just answer my question: did you kill Chloe?"

"I told you no!"

She recoiled at his brash reaction but did her best to hide the fact. She'd try another tack. "How did it make you feel knowing Chloe would never be interested in you romantically?"

A rogue tear fell down a cheek. He swiped it away and said nothing.

"Did it make you angry?" She realized she was getting aggressive, but sometimes it was called for. She wanted to see if she could provoke a telling reaction.

"Sure, yeah, it made me angry sometimes. I would have made her happy, and I would have treated her right. Not like that Josh guy. I don't know what she ever saw in him. It was like he had her blinded somehow."

Amanda glanced sideways at Trent.

"Josh didn't treat her right?" Trent asked.

"I doubt it. The guy was more jock than academic. Chloe has a future. *Had*." He looked down at the table and wiped his eyes.

"Did you ever see him hurt her or mistreat her?" Trent inched forward on his seat, his energy buzzing beside her. It would just take Trent hearing that Josh had hit Chloe to send him on a tangent.

"Not directly. But I'm pretty sure he was seeing other girls behind Chloe's back."

Josh Ryder was at the Fairfax campus, a half hour away. "And how would you know this, Luke? I'm not saying you're lying, but I'm guessing you must have a good reason to make this claim."

"All you have to do is look at the guy. All the girls like him."

Amanda studied Luke. It was obvious that just as much as he cared for Chloe, he hated Josh. Could her murder have been a case of Luke not being able to have Chloe, so no one could? Jealousy was an age-old motive for murder. She relaxed her body language before she proceeded. "Where were you yesterday morning between three and seven?"

"Sleeping."

"Can anyone attest to that?" she asked.

"My parents were home."

"You live at home." It was a statement, not a question *and* not a judgment, but Luke glared at her like he'd taken it as such.

"Yes, I live with Mom and Dad. It's not a crime, you know."

"No one is saying that it is. We'll need their information," she said firmly.

"No way. You can't go asking them where I was at the time of the murder. They would never understand that."

"Have you been in trouble before?" She recalled Trent saying he didn't have a record so Luke's reaction was surprising.

"No."

"Then what wouldn't they understand?"

"The police coming around, asking questions."

They didn't need Luke to track down his parents. All it would take was searching their names in the system. "It's just procedure. Nothing to worry about. Unless, that is, you did kill Chloe. But"—she held up her hand to stay him from talking—"you said you didn't."

"That's right." Luke clenched his jaw.

"Guessing since you don't live on campus, you need to catch a bus or take a taxi?" Trent put the question out in a casual, conversational manner.

"I drive myself."

"What do you drive?" Trent countered.

"A Honda Insight. Why?"

Trent gave him a pressed-lip smile. "Just asking some questions here. Another one. Do black orchids mean anything to you?"

"The flower?"

"Yeah," Trent said.

"It doesn't mean anything to me, but I think it represents death and evil."

"And how would you know that, Luke?" Amanda asked, feeling a small shiver run down her back. He'd stuck to the one side of the symbolism, leaving out the positive aspects. Not reassuring. His unrequited love could have turned dark.

"I don't know. My mom is into things like that. I probably just heard her say something about it."

Amanda would take his word for now, but they would verify his alibi with his parents. They could also obtain a subpoena for the GPS in his Honda Insight to see if it ever went to the park, specifically the morning in question. They'd need more to get that authorized, though. And if they could place his car there, was he the one behind the wheel or had someone dropped him off?

"Have you ever been to Leesylvania State Park?" Depending on how he answered and what they may find out from the GPS, they could catch him in a lie. And there was still the real hope that Briggs would be able to get a license plate for them.

"Ah, yeah. I've taken part in some studies on the mystery snails."

"Did you ever go with Chloe?"

"Alone?" He smirked and gave a small chuckle. "You're kidding, right? I just told you I was invisible to her. She wasn't hanging around with me for any reason. Not even snails. But she'd take that boyfriend of hers there."

Amanda leaned forward. "And how would you know *that*?" She remembered what Chloe's roommates had said about Luke, how he followed her around like a puppy dog. Did he stalk her and kill her? This wasn't the first time suspicion ran through her about Luke Hogan, and she doubted it would go away unless she was given good reason. He was shaping up to be her prime suspect.

"I just know. Okay?"

"It's not okay if you were stalking her, Luke."

He frowned. "I wasn't stalking her. Is that what her friends told you?"

Amanda wasn't going to respond to that question. "We need you to stay around town. We'll be speaking with your parents and verifying your alibi."

His cheeks flushed, and he licked his lips, looking like he might vomit. "I didn't kill her; I swear to you."

"From our perspective, that's not certain," Amanda said. "You loved Chloe and never had those feelings returned. You hated her boyfriend, and you knew about her comings and goings."

"That's a stretch. I just know she went to that park sometimes, often with Josh."

"Again, I'm going to ask how you know that," she pressed.

"I'd hear her talking to her friends about it."

She let a few beats pass in silence. She'd never say as much to a suspect, but it might be a good time for Luke to secure that lawyer. "That's all. For now." She gave him her card and told him he could go.

Luke didn't waste any time leaving and slammed the door behind him.

"Do you think we did the right thing, letting him go?" Trent asked her.

"I sure hope so." But the truth was they didn't have enough to justify holding him—yet. And while they *could* hold him for twenty-four hours without pressing charges, it was best to do so only when charges were imminent.

"Do you want to go talk with his parents now or speak with Stephanie while we're here?" Trent asked.

She considered. Luke Hogan was looking good for the murder of Chloe Somner, but she didn't want to have tunnel vision and fixate on one person too soon. The truth was they needed more evidence before they could avidly go after him. The cold case of Annie Frasier in Washington also wasn't far from her mind. If Chloe was a victim of that same killer, that eliminated Luke. He wouldn't have been born yet. "We'll talk with Stephanie and Professor McMillan, then we'll head over to see the Hogans."

"Sounds like a plan. I don't know about you, but Luke comes across guilty as hell."

The fact he agreed with her made her second-guess herself about letting Luke leave, but ultimately she knew it was the right thing. And by speaking with Stephanie and the professor, they might be able to find out more about Luke and how he was with regard to Chloe Somner. At least for now Amanda could release some fear that a serial killer was out there, lurking in the shadows, ready to strike again. After all, they had a viable suspect from right within Chloe's circle.

NINETEEN

Stephanie Piper had barely got herself positioned in the chair across from Amanda and Trent when she started to cry.

"Did someone tell you what we wanted to speak with you about?" Amanda asked, curious if the news about Chloe's murder had reached across campus by now. After all, there were already four people who knew, including the senior associate dean.

"No." Stephanie sniffled.

"Then why are you crying?"

The girl pulled a tissue from her backpack and blew her nose. "You're cops, right? Just makes me a little nervous."

More like Stephanie was falling apart. Amanda and Trent hadn't yet said a word to her. "No need to be." Unless she had killed Chloe, of course. Then Amanda would come at her with the full force of the law. "I'm Detective Amanda Steele, and this is Detective Trent Stenson. If it makes it easier on you, you can call us by our first names."

"Okay." The word was barely coherent.

"We're here today because a student from this campus was found murdered in a local state park," Amanda said, as delicately as possible. She waited until Stephanie met her gaze before continuing. "Chloe Somner. Did you know her?"

Stephanie nodded, completely devoid of emotion at the mention of Chloe's murder. Very strange considering how upset she was at the start of the meeting.

"What was your relationship like with her?" Amanda knew what they'd been told by the associate dean, Chloe's roommates, and even Josh, but she wanted to hear what Stephanie herself would say.

"We never saw eye to eye." Calm, collected, as if Chloe's murder had no real impact on her. The transition raised the hairs on Amanda's arms. If Chloe had always excelled at the top of the class, her death would leave the position open for Stephanie. Had Stephanie killed her, or was she simply dazed due to shock?

"How is that? On a social level or...?"

"On any level." Stephanie worried her lip. "You might hear or have heard, but we had a bit of a rivalry between us, but it's not what people think. Sure, as I said we didn't gel or see eye to eye, but things became exaggerated. We actually—I believe, anyway—had a mutual respect for each other. My mom had someone like that when she was in school too. She told me it only pushed her to work harder."

A glimmer of pain flashed across Stephanie's eyes. Amanda believed her when she said the animosity was hyperbole. She was also starting to see the lack of emotion Stephanie showed about Chloe's murder as being shock. "Where were you yesterday morning between three and seven?"

"I was at home, sleeping."

Amanda nodded, leaving that uncontested for now. Stephanie was a tall girl, and with heels, she could reach the height of the estimated killer. It also looked like she had a strong upper body. While Stephanie might be physically capable, Amanda was still determining motive, means, and opportunity.

She wasn't seeing all three yet, but that didn't mean they weren't there to find. "What kind of car do you drive?" Again, the question born of due diligence. The girl could have had someone she knew drop her off in her car, someone she was even working with.

Stephanie blinked and sat back. "Kind of a strange question, isn't it?"

"If you could answer it." Amanda gave her a kind smile.

"I don't have a car. I take public transportation or ride with friends if I need to go somewhere. My parents would never let me drive their vehicles."

"Why's that?" Trent interjected.

Stephanie looked at him. "They have a BMW and a Mercedes and don't trust me behind the wheel of either one. Can't really blame them. I tend to be a nervous driver."

Amanda wasn't doubting that claim for one minute. The girl had cried at simply being brought in to speak with the police. Expanding on that thought, did she possess the spite to carry out a murder and one that was so organized? "Do black orchids mean anything to you?"

"The flowers?" Stephanie shook her head. "Not really. Why?"

"We can't answer why." She and Trent really needed to hit up florists in the area and see who may have purchased the plant. As for Stephanie, it didn't seem the girl was behind Chloe's murder. There was other ground they needed to cover with her, though. "Do you know of anyone who might have wanted to harm Chloe, or who may have stalked her?"

"We weren't close."

Trent leaned forward, putting his elbows on the table. "So, no boys hanging around... say, ones she didn't care for?"

Stephanie pressed her lips together and started to shake her head but stopped. "Luke, I guess, but I can't see him killing her."

Amanda angled her head, curious. "And why's that?"

"He's a gentle person. I've seen him capture a fly and take it outside and release it. I kid you not."

Amanda glanced subtly at Trent and found he was looking at her as well. That was an interesting viewpoint on their current prime suspect—and an observation Amanda would disagree with. Luke had gotten rather loud when accused of killing Chloe, and he had an age-old motive. In the least, Luke Hogan had a temper. But how far had he taken that temper? There could be a divide between how he treated insects and other living creatures, such as someone who had rejected him. And it actually could explain the scene—Chloe cleaned, laid out, a black orchid on her chest. Remorse through and through. Maybe. "All right, that's all our questions for now." She gave Stephanie her business card and ran through the spiel about calling if she thought of anything else.

Stephanie left, and there was an older man in his fifties standing in the doorway.

Amanda checked the time on her phone. *11:15 AM*.

"Professor McMillan?" she asked, though she was quite certain she had it right.

"You can call me William," he said pleasantly, but his tone and presence were formal.

Amanda gave the introductions for herself and Trent. William got seated, and they informed him about Chloe.

"Wow. I don't know what to say." He puffed his cheeks and blew out a breath. "Such a tragedy. She was an incredibly bright student."

"We've been hearing that," Amanda said. "Do you know of anyone who might have had an issue with her? Anyone who might have been stalking her? Whether she had any of those concerns herself?"

"From what I could see, she was quite a popular kid." His brow was perspiring, and he wiped it away.

"We've heard that, but we've also heard that some of the kids who go here didn't quite get along with her."

"Ah, sure. But you can't expect all the kids to get along with each other. It doesn't work that way."

Amanda didn't need him telling her how it worked, but she smiled. "Never does. The world would be a much better place if people could overlook their differences."

"That it would." He dipped his head and clasped his hands on the table as he did so.

"What was your impression of the relationship between Stephanie Piper and Chloe Somner?" Trent asked.

"Those two had a competitive spirit, and it really came to life when they were up against each other."

"You're talking about scoring better on certain tests?" Amanda asked, recalling that the associate dean had told them Chloe had beat Stephanie's score on a recent exam.

"Yes, and sometimes opportunities come up to assist professors in the field for studies."

"And Chloe often received that privilege?"

"She did."

"And the most recent time this happened?"

"Just a few weeks ago."

Stephanie hadn't mentioned a thing about this when she was in the room just moments ago, but maybe she'd thought it irrelevant. Or she'd intentionally kept it from them so they wouldn't suspect her of wrongdoing. "And how did Stephanie react?"

"She wasn't happy, sulked a bit, but she got over it. She put herself into her studies more than ever."

Amanda nodded. "And what about Luke Hogan? Did he hang around Chloe?"

"Ah, I felt sorry for that kid. She was never going to see him." He rubbed his jaw. "But he didn't seem to want to accept that he wasn't her type. He kept trying."

"Do know how her rejection made him feel or react? I'll get right to the point. Did you see him respond aggressively toward her or watch her in a silent, brooding sort of way?" Amanda asked.

William's forehead wrinkled in concentration. "Nah, I don't think so. But I saw that Stephanie was just leaving." He jacked a thumb over his shoulder. "She would have been a good person to ask. She and Luke are friends outside of school hours, from what I gather."

Huh. One more thing that must have slipped Stephanie's mind. "Okay, thank you for your time, Professor." Amanda stood and reached across the table to shake his hand. He had a strong, firm grip.

He moved to leave.

"Could you please close the door behind you?" she called out.

He waved a hand over his head, and Amanda turned to Trent once the professor had left.

"Stephanie omitted two things. One, she's friends with Luke Hogan, and two, she recently lost out on an opportunity because Chloe got it."

"In addition to the test Chloe scored higher on."

"That's right."

"Do you think she planned all this out—followed Chloe to the park and stripped her naked? I may be wrong, but would a woman do that to another woman?"

"I wouldn't think so, but there's always exceptions to the rules."

Trent bobbed his head side to side. "And in murder, are there any rules?"

"Don't think so."

"If it was Stephanie or a woman who killed Chloe, it would explain the lack of sexual assault."

"True." The facts in the case kept spinning in her head, as

did all the conversations they'd already had with people this morning. And while it could have been a woman who had killed Chloe, Luke Hogan, with his underlying temper, was still at the top of her suspect list. But what if Stephanie and Luke had teamed up to kill Chloe? Luke drove his car, and Stephanie did the stabbing, or vice versa? She'd bench her theories for now, but there was something that had to be checked off the list. "Let's go talk to the Hogans." She led the way out of the room, eager to get some forward momentum with this case. If they didn't find something that pinned Chloe's murder on someone in her social circle, the alternative could very well be that a serial killer was stalking college students in Prince William County.

TWENTY

Amanda and Trent grabbed a coffee and a muffin from a place in Woodbridge on the way to the Hogan residence. They'd also pulled the backgrounds on Ron and Judy Hogan. They found nothing interesting but did get an advanced look at their faces from their driver's licenses. The door was opened by Judy on the second knock.

"Yes?" Judy raised her eyebrows in perfectly matching arches. There was a hint of irritation in her tone, but also marked curiosity.

They held up their badges, and Amanda did the introductions and confirmed the woman was Judy Hogan, for the record. Then she said, "We'd like to speak with you about your son, Luke. If we could come in for a minute..."

Judy studied them. "Ah, sure." She backed up to allow them room to enter.

The house was spacious inside, just as the exterior had suggested. It was a brick, two-story home in an affluent neighborhood. Obviously the Hogans were doing all right for themselves given their zip code and the decked-out, current model Audi A6 in the driveway.

Judy led them to a well-appointed living room with furniture that appeared almost too proper and elegant to sit on. The space was flooded with natural light due to floor-to-ceiling windows that took up an entire wall. She lowered herself into a wingback chair, and Amanda and Trent sat on the couch. Judy crossed her legs. "What is this concerning my son?"

Two cops at her door, and Judy hadn't immediately jumped to a horrible conclusion that most mothers would. Like Melissa Somner, it didn't seem to occur to her that something may have happened to her child. Or was it denial, self-protection's armor? "A student from Geoffrey Michaels, the Potomac Center for Science and Environmental Studies, was found murdered yesterday morning." Amanda paused there, watching for any tells of recognition. There were none. Instead, Judy's mouth gaped slightly open, and her eyes watered.

"How horribly sad."

"Her name was Chloe Somner, and she was in some of your son's classes."

"Oh." Judy toyed with the buttons on her cardigan. "He must be upset. I know what it's like to lose a fellow student. I did when I was in college."

"It can be devastating, for sure. It often doesn't even matter if you were close to the person who died." Amanda could testify to that from experience too. High school. Wesley Ferguson. He'd hung himself.

"Yes, you're right about that. I wasn't close with Karen, but it still affected me. I should really call my son." Judy made a move to get up, but Amanda raised a hand.

"We'd ask that you refrain for the moment."

"Do you... do you suspect my son had something to do with this girl's death?"

"We just need to ask some questions, Ms. Hogan." Amanda would skirt around Judy's direct assumption for the time being. "Has your son ever mentioned Chloe to you?"

"Chloe, Chloe," she repeated as she tapped her fingers on the arm of the chair. Eventually, she shook her head. "I can't say that he has."

Amanda nodded. "Where was your son yesterday morning between three and seven?"

"Do you seriously suspect he killed her?" Her complexion paled, and her voice cracked.

"Just procedure, ma'am," Trent said. "Please answer Detective Steele's question."

Judy gripped her sweater, bunching the material and twisting slightly. "He was here—in bed."

"You're sure?" Her body language and articulation said otherwise.

"Of course. Where else would he be at that time of day?"

Amanda gave Judy a tight smile. "That is the timeframe in which Chloe Somner was tracked and murdered in Leesylvania State Park."

"My boy, even if he wasn't home—and I'm not saying he wasn't—wouldn't hurt anyone."

"But your son does have a temper, doesn't he, Ms. Hogan?" Amanda countered.

"What young man doesn't?" Judy flailed her hands in the air. "I'll get him a lawyer if you're going to come after him."

Amanda appreciated that parents wanted to believe the best of their children, and she also understood defending them—to an extent. But the parents who coddled their kids and refused to acknowledge they could do wrong only damaged their offspring. Those kids became adults who acted as they wished because there were no consequences. "We're just asking some questions at this time."

"Sure, but you suspect my son."

Amanda bit her tongue to avoid saying Luke looked like a prime suspect. "We've spoken with Luke, and he knew Chloe. She was in some of his classes, as I said, and more than that, he had a crush on her. His feelings were not returned. Not saying that he did something about that," she rushed to add as she watched Judy shift in her chair and the woman's cheeks grow a bright shade of red. "But he never mentioned her?"

"No." Curt, and she tilted out her chin with the reply.

"Okay." Amanda stood, pulled her card, and gave it to Judy. "If you have any reason to reach me, please don't hesitate."

Judy took the card tentatively, as if it could bite or burn her. She got up to see them out. Amanda stopped in the entry next to a table with a floral bouquet in a vase. The smells emanating from the variety was intoxicating. No sign of black orchids, however. And none anywhere in the parts of the house that they'd seen.

Amanda gestured to the flowers. "Beautiful arrangement."

"Thank you." Judy stiffened and crossed her arms.

Amanda lightly brushed her fingers beneath the petals of an orange Gerbera daisy. "I'm horrible with remembering the symbolism of different things. What do these mean? Do you know?" Luke had told them he was aware of the black orchid's meaning due to his mother's interest in symbolism. Amanda wanted to test that claim.

Judy's posture relaxed, and she stepped next to Amanda. "The very base meaning is happiness. But also beauty, purity, and innocence." She wasn't looking at Amanda when she spoke but rather had her gaze on the flower.

"How lovely," Amanda said. "What about black orchids?"

The woman pulled her attention from the bouquet. "That flower holds dual meaning—good and bad, light and dark. Why the interest?"

"No reason." Amanda then turned for the door, leaving behind a confused Judy Hogan.

Once in the car, Amanda turned to Trent. "We've got nothing solid to go after Luke at this point, but I'm not ruling him out. There isn't even a verifiable alibi."

"He wasn't lying about his mother knowing the meaning of things. I noticed the pop quiz in there." Trent smirked.

Amanda chuckled. "Stellar detective work." Sarcasm. Thinly veiled. "I do have a question for my brother, though." She dialed his number. "Ky, do you remember the video I showed you?"

"It was just yesterday, so yeah."

She smiled at her brother's attitude. "Remember the head-lights? Could they have belonged to a Honda Insight?"

There were a few seconds of silence on his end.

"Kyle?" she prompted.

"Just thinking."

"Hence the smell of smoke."

"Funny, sis. A Honda Insight? No, it wouldn't have the right headlights."

"You're sure?"

"I am."

"Okay. Thanks for nothing." She smiled and ended the call, shook her head. "If Luke did kill Chloe, he didn't have someone take him in his car. The Honda Insight doesn't have the right headlights." There went her passing thought that Luke and Stephanie had paired up and used his car.

"Would be too easy if everything just lined up."

She could hope for once that it would, but hope really meant nothing—something she knew firsthand. She'd hoped for a long life with Kevin and Lindsey, and that hadn't happened. She felt a ribbon of heartbreak lace through her as her thoughts bent toward Zoe and the latest possible kink in the adoption process.

"So, next steps? Want to question more students and see if we can determine if Chloe had any other enemies on campus?" Trent was looking over at her from behind the wheel, just waiting for direction.

"I think we've spoken to enough students for now. What I'd

really like is Chloe's phone history, but we know that may take a while to come through. We haven't heard from Briggs to see how he made out on the video yet." She could call him. He normally worked evenings, but she had his cell phone number and knew where he lived. He'd always been eager to help out after hours before. She gave Briggs's number a try but had to leave a message. "Okay, we'll need to wait to hear from Briggs. That leaves us with one thing. Florists. Let's see if we can hunt down where Chloe's killer got the black orchid from."

"We can start with the florists in the area."

"Didn't I just say that?"

"Just wanted to say it for myself." He smiled at her.

Orchids, florists, flowers... "Did you hear from that Metro PD detective?"

"You've been with me all day."

Was it too much to hope that the cold case from twenty years ago and Chloe's weren't connected at all? That Chloe's killer had been someone she'd known and not a serial killer targeting female college students? "I'm thinking we might have been getting caught up in seeing a serial killer where there isn't one. We both see motive with Luke. He's our most likely suspect right now." Hearing her words made it feel like she was trying to convince herself. Maybe she was.

"Sure, but we need means and opportunity."

"We'll find it if it's there." She'd do her best to stubbornly cling to Chloe's murder being an isolated incident.

He held her gaze, and her words echoed back in her mind. *If it's there.*

"All we can do is follow the evidence," she said. "And that's taking us to local flower shops at this point. Agree?"

"I do." He pulled out of the Hogans' driveway.

Her mind was still chewing on what she'd said. *Local* flower shops. So someone from the area, presumably in Chloe's life. But who could have hated her so much as to stab her seven times and leave her the way they had? How had Chloe wronged her killer? From what they'd discovered, she was a down-to-earth person who did things because she was moved from her heart—not motivated by praise or glory. She was interested in healing the planet and caring for the environment.

Chloe hadn't deserved what happened to her. Amanda would make sure that Chloe's killer would pay for robbing the world of the young woman's light.

TWENTY-ONE

Just an isolated incident, Amanda repeated in her head, trying to convince herself. Skilled at handling a blade. No hesitation marks. Organized. But there had only been one victim. She'd latch on to that. Sure, there was the case of Annie Frasier from twenty years ago, but what were the chances it had any connection to Chloe Somner's murder? Probably small.

Malone surely wouldn't support her pursuing a serial killer who may not even exist. He'd tell her to treat it as an isolated incident and continue to look at the people in Chloe's world. In fairness, she and Trent hadn't even tapped into Chloe's haters on Snap VidPic, and they could still explore Luke Hogan more.

Regardless of how they viewed the murder, it would have taken meticulous planning. How long had the person been scheming Chloe's death? Was the black orchid picked with intention? Had the killer been stalking Chloe to know her routine? Even if that was the case, it didn't answer how they'd know she'd be at the park so early Monday morning.

So many questions that frustrating doesn't begin to cover it!

Trent pulled into the lot of Lee's Flowers, located in Woodbridge, a short distance from where the Hogans lived.

"Luke was certainly close enough to a flower shop," she said, getting out of the car with Trent.

A bell chimed when they opened the door, and a smiling woman behind the counter welcomed them and introduced herself as Lee, the owner.

The fragrance of all the flowers bombarded Amanda's senses and propelled her back to the funeral home where the service had been held for Lindsey and Kevin. How much time had to pass for that to stop happening? Would it ever? She'd just like to be a normal woman who could enjoy a bouquet for the sheer pleasure of its colors and smells rather than any attribution of meaning. *Meaning...* They'd been focused on what the black orchid represented, but flowers in general stood for good and bad. They were present for death, but they also marked happy occasions and celebrations—graduations, the birth of a child, marriage, anniversaries. The mile markers of life.

Amanda looked around the store, passing refrigerated units and displays of flowers in pails with water. No black orchids.

"Can I help you with anything?" the woman asked.

They gave the formal introductions, and Amanda asked, "Do you sell black orchids?"

"Ah, no, sorry." Lee winced. "Though we do have some white and pink ones." She came out from behind the counter and led them to a table with a few potted orchids climbing up a slender bamboo stem.

"They're beautiful, but we're interested in black ones. Can you order them in?"

"Yes, of course."

The black orchid that had been left on Chloe's body appeared to have been rather fresh, but also like it came from a mature plant. "And do the orchids arrive fully matured?"

"They do."

"Just out of curiosity, how long does it take the black orchid to get to that point?"

"Full maturity would take, say, eight to ten months."

Amanda nodded. "Is there any way for you to see if anyone has ordered this plant from you—recently or ever?"

Lee smiled. "I can check the book." She returned to the counter, and the bell over the door rang as a woman entered. She smiled and waved at Lee, who said, "I'll be with you shortly, Carol."

"No problem." Carol extended her smile to Amanda and Trent, but her eyes narrowed slightly, human curiosity at work. She shuffled around the store, putting her nose to most flowers as she went along.

Lee pulled a large book out from behind the counter and thumbed through its pages. After a minute or so, she shook her head. "I didn't think so—no one has ordered any black orchids from me in some time."

"But someone has before?" Trent asked.

Lee pressed a manicured fingernail to the page. "Uh-huh. Three years ago. Does that help?"

Amanda leaned over the counter and caught a glimpse of the name on the page. *Leah Turnbull.* "Probably not, but thank you for your help."

"Which I'm afraid I didn't really provide." Lee closed the book, and it gave a soft thud as she did so.

Amanda and Trent left the store and went on to mark off the other florists in Prince William County. None got them any closer to the killer they were after.

It was going on four PM by the time they'd finished.

"If we spread out even further, we'd need to consider floral shops in and around Fairfax as well, but this avenue could be never-ending." She was so frustrated with all the dead ends in the case thus far. "There's also the possibility the orchid was ordered online, and without a suspect, there's no place to even begin with that."

"Yeah, and it's possible the killer had their own greenhouse they pulled from."

She massaged her temples. "Sometimes it feels like we're bashing our heads against a wall."

"You can say that again."

She looked over at her partner. Normally he was the positive one; this case must have been getting to him too. "I just want to close this case. Chloe deserves that much, and so do her family and friends."

"We will. It just might take more time." He paused, his blue eyes taking on a deep intensity. "We need to go easier on ourselves. It's only day two of the investigation."

Two days since a young woman was killed. Two days behind her killer. Two days closer to another victim? She closed her eyes.

"Hey, we'll get this bastard."

She leaned back into the neck rest and rolled her head to face him. "You know what?"

"What?"

"You're right."

"I tend to be sometimes." He smiled.

"Let's hit Chloe's townhouse. I think we might also need to make the haters on Chloe's Snap VidPic account more of a priority, ferret out their real identities."

"Good idea."

"I just don't want to give in to thinking it's a serial killer. Not yet." That was despite the circumstances surrounding Chloe's murder being unique and rather troublesome—namely the cleansing and posing of her body with the black orchid. Both things could send a chill through her with little thought.

"But I'll still follow up with that Metro PD detective?"

She nodded. "To be thorough."

Trent took them to the girls' townhouse, and Amanda called home on the drive.

Libby Dewinter, "Aunt Libby," was with Zoe today. Libby had adopted the Parkers as her own family, and the more Amanda got to know Libby, the more Libby was becoming family to her too. There was a part of Amanda that warned her to pull back and protect her heart in case Zoe's adoption fell through. But despite life teaching her that the ground could fall out at any time, she was choosing to put her faith in a happy outcome when it came to Zoe.

Libby answered.

"How's everything over there?" Amanda asked, smiling—all it took was the thought of talking to Zoe.

"Going good. She's just eating some apple fries."

An apple sliced into thin strips. Presenting them to a kid as fries made them more desirable.

"Mandy?" Zoe's small voice carried across the phone line from the background.

She had no desire to have Zoe call her anything other than Amanda, or Mandy for short. Even if Amanda wanted the role as Zoe's mother, she'd never replace the actual woman and had no intention of trying. That would make her not only cruel but a hypocrite. She'd never been able to address her mother-in-law as Mom. Amanda had one mom—Julie (Jules) Steele. But thinking of Maria James, Amanda should reach out. "Can I talk to Zoe for a second?"

"She wouldn't have it any other—"

"Hey, Mandy." It was Zoe. She must have snatched the phone from Libby's hand. "I had fun at school today. There was a toad..." She went on, chuckling as she did, to tell Amanda about a boy in her class who had brought one into the classroom.

"A toad?" Amanda glanced over at Trent, sensing him looking at her.

"It was sooooosooooo ugly."

She listened to Zoe for a little longer and hated to end the call, but they were getting close to the townhouse. Just a couple more hours at the most, and she'd be home.

"Sounds like someone had a good day," Trent said as he pulled into the townhouse driveway.

"You heard all that?"

He was smiling. "Most of it."

Amanda laughed. "Yeah, she can be quite loud when she gets excited." It was one quality that Amanda loved about the girl. Honestly, it reminded Amanda of her own mother. But the livewire energy that Zoe brought into Amanda's life was invigorating and restorative. For the first time in years, Amanda could actually see herself clear of the grief that weighed her down. Before Zoe, that was something she hadn't imagined was even possible.

TWENTY-TWO

Amanda and Trent hadn't told Jayne Russell and Lauren Bennett that they'd be coming around to look at Chloe's bedroom. It was best these things be done impromptu, in case the girls had something to hide. The downside to that was no one was home. They checked in with the uniformed officer sitting vigil in his cruiser, and he told them he hadn't seen anyone go in or out of the townhouse but Lauren and Jayne. Officers on previous shifts had passed on the same to him.

"We'll wait for a bit." Amanda was back in the department car with Trent and watched the minute change on the dash clock. She desperately wanted to be home on time to be with Zoe tonight. It was Pizza Tuesday—a weekly ritual they'd initiated. Mondays were hard for everyone, whether it was returning to school or going to work. But by Tuesday evening, you'd survived two days of the week. Doing something "fun" made it easier to face the three that remained.

There was a rap on the driver's window, and Amanda jumped. It was Jayne, and Amanda had been so deep in thought that she hadn't even seen her approach.

"All right there?" Trent smirked at Amanda and then lowered the window.

"Detectives? What are you doing here?"

"We're here to take a look in Chloe's room," Trent told her.

"You're fine with that?" Amanda said. Such authorization wouldn't have been necessary if Chloe had lived alone, but to get to her room, they would need to go through other areas in the home that were inhabited by her roommates.

"I'm fine with it."

They got out of the car.

"Do you know when Lauren will be home?" Amanda asked.

"Nope. Don't really care either."

Apparently, the homefront is bliss... "I'll need to get permission from her as well. Do you have a phone number for her?"

Jayne rattled it off from memory as Amanda tapped the digits into her phone.

Lauren answered on the second ring and gave Amanda the approval she needed. She pocketed the phone and said to Jayne, "Ready when you are."

"All right." Jayne led the way into the townhouse. Immaculate. It had Amanda thinking about Chloe's crime scene and how clean it had been.

"Someone's good at cleaning house," Amanda tossed out casually.

"That's Lauren." Jayne rolled her eyes. "She's a freaking neat *freak*."

Jayne took Amanda and Trent to the second story and cracked open the second door on the left. "This was Chloe's."

"Thanks."

"Don't mention it. If you need me, I'll be downstairs."

The two of them stepped into Chloe's room and snapped on gloves. The space was about fifteen feet square with one decent-sized window that let in sunlight, but it was on the north-facing side of the building, so the room was dim. Amanda flicked the switch next to the door, and the ceiling light came on, deepening the shadows.

The room was tidy, but not immaculate like the rest of the house. The bed was made but in a rushed fashion, the act of simply pulling up the sheets and comforter. Though the last time Chloe had left here, it had been in the early hours. She probably hadn't even been that awake yet.

There was a simple student desk with no drawers, a wheeled chair, a small bookcase, and a nightstand by the bed.

Amanda opened the closet's bifold doors. Clothes on hangers were crammed together with no apparent thought as to organization. On the floor, there was a rack for shoes, and Chloe had plenty.

"More clothes here than at her parents' house." Amanda looked at some articles of clothing. No fancy labels or anything flashy. *Down-to-earth.*

She returned to the desk. No laptop or desktop computer. Strange for a student not to have one. But there was that backpack she'd had with her when she arrived at the park. It hadn't been found. It may have had her phone and other electronics in it.

She went over to the nightstand and opened the drawer. Foiled condoms and a tissue box. Nothing else.

"Look at this." Trent was pointing to a frame on the wall.

Amanda walked over. A certificate noting Chloe Somner as a top financial contributor. "Planet Rebirth."

Trent said, "She didn't just participate in their events, she donated money to the cause."

"An angel," she said softly.

"What was that?"

She blinked Trent into focus. She hadn't realized she'd said that out loud. "It's just such a shame she was killed. Like her parents said, the girl would have changed the world for the better."

"She certainly had the passion."

Amanda snapped her gloves off, tucked them into her coat pocket, and headed downstairs. Trent followed.

Jayne was at the kitchen counter leaning over a laptop; a binder was next to it along with a couple of textbooks. She was bobbing her head, and Amanda imagined she had earbuds in, listening to music. Amanda treaded slowly so as not to startle her.

"Oh." Jayne yanked a bud from an ear.

"We're finished up there, but we have some questions. Has anyone been in her room since Monday?"

"Nope."

"Not even her parents?" Amanda was just verifying what the officer had told them.

"Not that I'm aware of."

"Is it possible they came when you weren't home?"

"Don't think so, and Lauren hasn't mentioned it."

"Where is Lauren now, by the way?" Amanda asked.

"Probably out with some of her hippy, tree-hugging friends."

"You're not into the environment?" Trent raised an eyebrow. "I'd think you would be, given where you go to school."

"Oh, I am. I'm just not risking a bulldozer running me over to save a tree." She tapped a finger to her head as if to imply she was a genius for that.

"What do you know about Planet Rebirth?" The name kept coming up. Had it just been a part of Chloe's life, with nothing to do with her murder—or was something there? Maybe they should pay the place a visit, but unless something significant led them there, they already had more than enough to keep them busy.

"They're an environmental group, dedicated to fighting

climate change. Chloe loved them. She was a brand ambassador for them on Snap VidPic."

"Yeah, we found that out," Amanda admitted. "Were you or Lauren a part of the group, or supportive?"

"Lauren more than me. I tagged along to a couple of their events."

"Why only a couple? Something rub you wrong?" Trent asked.

"I just have enough on my plate with school. I need to study harder than some people just to get a passing grade."

Amanda nodded, closing the subject on Planet Rebirth for now. "Did Chloe have a computer, a laptop, tablet?"

"Uh-huh, a laptop. It's not in her room?"

"No," Amanda said.

"Well, she was inseparable from it, and her phone."

"Okay, thank you for your time and cooperation."

Jayne hopped off the stool she'd been on and put both earbuds on the counter. "Are you getting any closer to knowing who did this to her?"

Jayne was one multi-faceted girl. It wasn't *what you see is what you get* with her. Amanda would guess Jayne was much deeper and far more sensitive than she let on. While it might seem she took the murder of her friend in stride, Amanda didn't think that was the case. Jayne was struggling. And hurting. "We're doing all we can to find out who killed Chloe."

Jayne let out a deep breath and briefly shut her eyes. "Did you talk to Luke?"

"We have," Amanda said.

"He really was obsessed with her, and don't forget Stephanie. She was a loser next to Chloe."

"You really think one of them killed her?" Amanda asked outright.

"Not sure about Stephanie. Probably not. But Luke? Maybe, even though I think Stephanie has a thing for him."

First time hearing that. "You mentioned he stalked Chloe when we spoke before. Did he ever show up here at her home?"

Jayne shook her head. "Not like that bad, but he was just always around, or so it seemed. Lurking in the shadows type of thing."

"I see. How long have you known Chloe?"

"Since elementary school."

"And how long had Lauren and she been friends?"

"Just since Chloe started at Geoffrey Michaels."

"Okay. Thank you for your cooperation." Amanda bit back the urge to say, *Hang in there.* She just wanted to offer some encouragement, but the best thing she and Trent could do for the girl was find Chloe's killer.

TWENTY-THREE

Amanda drove home, her foot heavy on the gas. Tomorrow she and Trent would start looking into Chloe's haters on Snap VidPic. Tonight, she was all Zoe's. And this Saturday, she planned to take her to the aquarium in Washington.

The sky was dark as she reached Dumfries. Thunder rumbled in the distance and lightning streaked across the sky. Zoe was terrified of storms, and for good reason. The night her parents were murdered, she'd been in their bed due to a thunderstorm.

Amanda hit the pedal a little harder and was pulling into her driveway at five forty-five. The front light was on, thanks to Libby's foresight. Amanda rushed from the car to the door as the sky opened. The rain pounded the pavement and bounced, splashing up to her knees.

By the time she burst through the door, she was soaking wet. For a moment, she envied dogs and how they could simply shake the extra moisture away.

"Oh my, look at you." Libby came hustling over with a towel extended.

"Thank you." Amanda wiped herself down and slipped out

of her shoes. A puddle spilled out around them on the tile floor. She hung her jacket on the coat rack and looked into the living room that was off to the left of the entry. The couch cushions were askew, like they'd been tossed, and the throw pillows were on the floor. "Where's Zoe?"

"In her room."

Amanda raced down the hallway. Zoe's bedroom door was shut, and Amanda knocked. "Zoe, sweetie, I'm home." She waited, trying to afford the girl opportunity to respond and invite her in, but there was nothing but silence. "Zoe, I'm coming in, okay?"

Quiet except for some rumbling thunder that was getting closer.

Amanda slowly turned the handle and entered the room. The comforter had been yanked from the bed and sat in a pile on the floor. Even the bedsheets had been tugged off. Her pillow was across the room. The stuffed doll collection she'd brought from her family home had been knocked off the bookshelf.

All signs of a tantrum.

"Zoe?" She could barely get her name out. Just seeing the room in this state, imagining what the poor child was going through, wrenched her heart. "You're safe, honey."

The sound of sniffling.

It got louder as Amanda approached the closet. The bifold doors were shut. She slowly opened them and announced what she was doing so as not to startle her. Zoe was huddled against the wall with Lucky hugged tight to her chest.

A clap of loud thunder shook the house.

Zoe screamed out, and tears snaked down her cheeks. Amanda dropped to her knees next to Zoe and scooped her into her arms. Zoe slapped at her.

"No. Go away! You're not my mom!"

The reaction might as well have been a knife to Amanda's

heart. The burning sensation coursed through her, setting her on fire. "Sweetheart," she cooed softly.

"No. Go!" Zoe yelled at the top of her lungs.

All Amanda wanted to do was pull the girl to her, protect her, and heal her hurts, but Zoe needed to process these emotions for herself. Amanda would have to settle for being next to her for support. Amanda moved back from the closet, giving Zoe some space, and the girl looked at her. Zoe's blue eyes were even more piercing when wet, like they were electric and carried a current.

"I'm not going anywhere. I'm right here." Amanda settled with her legs crossed, sitting with her back against the edge of the bed frame.

Zoe shot daggers at her but remained silent.

More cracks of thunder had Zoe jumping. It took all of Amanda's willpower and respect for Zoe's wishes not to reach out to her.

"Do you know what causes thunder?" Amanda tossed the question out like she was making casual conversation—a feat, considering her heart was thumping.

Zoe didn't respond, though Amanda hadn't expected she would.

"It's caused by lightning, when the sky lights up. That's basically an electric charge. A lot of energy. The lightning heats the air, and it explodes, which creates the sound we hear as thunder."

"An explosion?" Zoe shuffled farther into the corner.

Amanda tried to think of another way to put it and then remembered how she'd framed it for Lindsey. "You ever rub a balloon on your head?"

"No."

All right, there's something we need to add to the to-do list. "Well, if you do that, the contact between your hair and the balloon creates static energy. It makes your hair stand on end, but it's nothing that can hurt you. Just like thunder."

"Thunder can't hurt me?"

"No, sweetie." Zoe would have lots of time to learn that a person could get struck by lightning, however.

"But it hurt Mommy and Daddy." Tears spilled down her cheeks.

Amanda considered her words and, when she spoke, did so gently. "It wasn't the thunder, honey. It was a bad man. But you don't need to worry about him anymore."

"Why?" She pulled the stuffed dog closer to herself, inching it up and tucking it under her chin.

Amanda had told Zoe many times about the fate of the man who'd killed her parents, but she told her once more and repeated, "You don't need to worry about him anymore."

Zoe didn't respond.

"Do you trust me, Zoe?" Amanda eventually asked.

A small nod and eye contact.

"Then believe me. You're safe." Amanda almost added the girl was safe as long as she was with her, but that wouldn't be the right thing to say. Zoe could become dependent on her, and what if Colin Brewster was Zoe's biological father and took her away? The possibility jabbed her with pain.

The thunder continued to shake the house, but Zoe began inching her way out of the closet toward Amanda. There was a loud *boom*, and she closed the space between them in one lunge forward.

Amanda caught Zoe in her arms and held her tight. She swept her blond hair from her forehead and tapped a kiss there.

The two of them stayed in the embrace until Zoe had enough. And while the storm still circled, Zoe claimed her independent space.

"I'll clean up my mess," she said, standing up and heading toward the bed.

Amanda got to her feet. "I'll help you, but first... do you want pizza?"

Zoe's face lit then shadowed. "Before I clean up?"

Amanda hesitated, deciding how to respond. Zoe's parents had run a meticulous household where all the beds were made in the morning. Amanda could imagine if Zoe had caused this same mess when her parents were alive, they'd have requested she clean it up before dinner. But Amanda didn't run that tight of a ship. She appreciated that life could be messy. In fact, it was a little more fun that way. "After dinner," she affirmed and held out her hand to Zoe.

TWENTY-FOUR

While the evening seemed iffy at first due to the unexpected situation with Zoe, it had turned around. Amanda was still smiling for how well things had gone as she parked in the lot at Central the next morning. Libby had stayed for pizza and her girlfriend, Penny Anderson, had come over and joined them. Zoe's spirits had lifted, and she'd started making a game of the storm that circled the area for hours. Every time the thunder cracked, she'd point up and giggle. "Can't hurt me," she'd say.

It warmed Amanda's heart, but she was also aware that not far off in the distance was the grief, the hurt, the anger that circled Zoe—much like that thunderstorm. While they'd weathered the storm last night, there would be more in the future. Amanda was prepared to face it all by Zoe's side.

As Amanda had tucked her into bed, Zoe had said, "The balloon thing sounds like fun."

"Yeah, it does," Amanda had agreed. Maybe she'd change up their plans for the weekend—the aquarium *and* the science center. In the least, Amanda would pick up balloons for some hair-raising fun.

"Good morning," Trent said from his desk, eyeing her over the divider, then getting up to join her in her cubicle.

"Hey. Considering you're on my heels already, I'm guessing you have something?" She sipped her Hannah's Diner coffee, longing for it to wake her up. As good as the evening had gone, her sleep had been choppy, causing her to toss and turn, doing the typical worrywart thing about Zoe and the challenges they faced. Not just with Zoe processing her parents' murders but with Colin Brewster popping up.

"I do." Trent leaned against the partition, perching his elbow on the top of it.

"Hit me." She dropped into her chair and swiveled to face him.

"Good news? Bad news? Any preference?"

"Always bad. It's only up from there."

"Thought you'd say that. All right, I heard from Detective Briggs last night."

Interesting that he'd called Trent and not returned her call, but all right. It was probably a good thing, considering. But she was cringing inside to think this was supposed to be the bad news. "He didn't have any success with the video?"

"Ah, yes and no." Trent rolled his hand like a teeter-totter.

Another draw on her coffee to help with her patience, which was wearing a little thin. "Trent," she said.

"He wasn't able to gauge the mystery man's height, but he got a partial plate." He rattled off three digits. "These are from the middle of the plate."

"Okay, it could be worse. That's the bad news?"

"Yeah," he dragged out.

"We can take those digits and do a search by also cross-referencing the type of vehicles that have the right type of head-light. Which you've done?" *Call it a hunch.*

"Which I've done." He grinned.

"And?"

"Last year's Toyota Camry, registered to Ashton Chambers, nineteen years of age. Now, he's also got a juvie record from when he was fifteen. I've googled him and read his social media posts. He's extremely unhappy and angry at the world. And..."

"Drum roll?" She snickered.

"He followed Chloe on Snap VidPic and spewed hate at her."

"So this may not have been some random car service dropping off that mystery person."

"Nope. He could have been the killer's partner."

"Shit. Well, it sounds like we have our next stop. Grab your coat. We just got our best lead yet."

"Ashton Chambers, Prince William County PD!" Amanda called out and banged on the door again, hard enough it could be assumed the place was on fire and she was trying to rouse the resident.

"Hold up!" A man's voice volleyed back from inside, and footsteps plodded toward the door. A security chain was slid across, and several deadbolts unlatched. The door swung open. "What do you want?"

Ashton Chambers certainly wasn't Mr. Congeniality. He was wearing stained jogging pants and a plain gray T-shirt. His short hair was mussed and sticking up in spots, like he'd just crawled out of bed. His eyes were also bloodshot, either from exhaustion or tipping a bottle the night before. She held up her badge. "Ashton Chambers, we need to bring you in for questioning in regards to a current investigation."

"What the— Why?"

"We'll be happy to fill you in down at the station. Come on." She wriggled her fingers, motioning for him to get him moving.

"Fine. Give me a minute." He huffed and grabbed keys

from a bowl on a hall table. He put on a coat and pushed his feet into running shoes that were already laced.

They didn't cuff him, but Trent frisked him, as per procedure, to make sure that he didn't have anything on his person to inflict harm. He was loaded in the back of the department car, and they took him to an interrogation room at Central. They'd just escorted him inside when Malone showed up behind Amanda and Trent. He jabbed his gaze in Ashton's direction and raised his eyebrows.

Amanda and Trent stepped back into the hallway and shut the door. They brought Malone up to speed.

"Huh. So we can connect him to Chloe Somner, but we don't know if he was aware the person he had dropped off at the park intended to kill her? Or even whether they were friends? Is that right?" Malone was looking at her for an answer.

"We're going to find out," Amanda said.

"Well, good luck." Malone dipped his head and set off in the direction of his office.

Good luck had very little to do with investigations, but it was always welcome. She turned to Trent. "You want to take the lead with the questioning?"

"Sure."

She smiled and gestured for him to proceed into the room. She followed and shut the door.

Trent sat and placed a folder on the table. It held Ashton's background, some crime scene photos, and the one of Chloe Somner that her mother had provided. "Mr. Chambers, do you know why we brought you in today?"

Ashton slumped in his chair. "Can't say I do, and I really need to catch up on my sleep, man."

"It's Detective Stenson." Trent pushed out the correction in a measured tone, establishing the pecking order.

Ashton rolled his eyes, and Trent smacked the table. Ashton twitched.

For some reason, a tiny whirl of excitement rushed through Amanda every time Trent showed his temper. Maybe it was because when they were first paired, he'd been rather quiet and timid.

Trent withdrew the photo of Chloe and pushed it across the table in front of Ashton. "Do you know this woman?"

Ashton paled and rubbed his stomach.

"Give it some thought if you have to," Trent said.

"I didn't kill her." Ashton was trembling.

Trent angled his head. "I never said she was dead or murdered."

"That's got to be why you're interested in me. I heard that some woman was murdered. Chloe? You're probably thinking I had something to do with it just because she ruined my life!"

Amanda was quite sure it took more than news of a murdered woman for him to make that leap.

"She, ah, ruined your life?" Trent looked at Amanda, as if to say, *This just became more interesting.*

"Don't pretend like you don't know. She's why I live on my friend's couch and have a dead-end job at a pizza shop."

Amanda was thinking there were worse fates for a nineteen-year-old who was still figuring out his path in life. He spoke as if he were middle-aged and his life had been crap for decades.

"How is she responsible for that?" Trent asked.

Ashton certainly wasn't making the case against him any weaker.

"Never mind." Ashton snapped his mouth shut and glanced up at the ceiling. If Trent didn't back off the intensity just a little bit, Ashton might clam up and request a lawyer.

Amanda approached the table. "We're just covering some bases here, Mr. Chambers. No one's claiming or saying you did anything to Chloe. Not yet anyway."

"No?" he shoved out. "You come to my place and drag me here."

She wanted to correct him with *your friend's place.* "No one dragged you anywhere. We asked you to come with us. You did so willingly. No cuffs were used."

"Willingly? You patted me down," he scoffed. "If I didn't go with you, I'd have been cuffed. I know how the system works."

"Of course you do. After all, you have a record from when you were young. But we're not concerned with that." She caught Trent's side-glance and subtle smirk. *Oh well, someone in the room needs to be Good Cop.*

"You're not?" He sounded like he wanted to believe her but was wavering.

"We're concerned with the here and now."

"Well, *here and now*, I didn't kill her."

"All right, let's say you're telling the truth. How did she ruin your life?" Trent pressed.

Ashton narrowed his eyes. "She's how I ended up with a juvie record. In high school, she bullied me relentlessly until one day I just couldn't take it anymore."

"And you hit her?" Trent asked, tossing out a hypothetical.

"No way. She's a girl."

Amanda crossed her arms, not convinced his claim absolved him of all guilt. He could have just been working in partnership with the person who had killed Chloe. And liars excelled at saying whatever necessary when it benefited them.

"You did something bad enough to land you in juvie," Trent said.

"I keyed her car."

"Oh." The word escaped Amanda's lips on a breath. She'd built up his juvie record to be indicative of something far worse than keying a car, though in the eyes of the law it was considered vandalism and an act of criminal mischief.

"But I served my time for that and did some community service."

Amanda was processing what he'd told them. While the

criminal charges surely hadn't helped Ashton get off to a good start in life, the matter had happened when he was younger. He could have made the best of things and still gone on to have a bright future. There had to be more. "Did Chloe do something else that supposedly ruined your life?"

Ashton met her gaze and shook his head. "Pushing me until I snapped was enough. That got me a juvie record, which on its own ruined my future. I couldn't get into any good colleges, just community ones."

"They can still offer a decent education," Amanda said.

"Not interested."

"What did she do to make you key her car?" Amanda asked.

"No, I'm not saying. It's far too embarrassing."

"You realize you're being questioned in regard to her murder," Trent pointed out.

"It's history."

"Though it doesn't sound like it is to you. You're still embarrassed by whatever she did," Amanda interjected. "And you blame her for the direction of your life."

"I was overreacting."

"Huh. So you had aspirations to pursue a career making pizza?" Not that there was a problem with that if it was his ambition. Given his bitter attitude, though, she doubted it was his chosen life path.

"I don't make the pizza. I deliver them."

She had a spark catch fire in her belly. There was the possibility that the person who had dropped Chloe's killer off was either unaware or an accomplice. It was crucial she find out which. And if the only work that Ashton did was deliver pizza, how did he afford last year's Toyota Camry? He'd admitted he was sleeping on his friend's couch, didn't have a place of his own.

"You have a nice car," she said. "A Toyota Camry, last year's model."

"So what?"

"How can you afford it?"

"Credit."

She eyeballed him until he sighed loudly.

"Not that it's any of your business, but my dad co-signed on the loan."

"So, delivering pizza brings in enough cash for you to afford the payments?" She was leading him, curious where they'd end up.

"That and my side gig."

Trent leaned forward. "Which is?"

"I use the Camry like a taxi. You know the app, Pick Me Up? I'm with them."

Amanda had heard of the car service, and she finally had something to show for all her leading questions. Though it didn't yet excuse Ashton from all culpability. It could just be a nasty coincidence that he'd given a ride to Chloe's killer *and* had a connection to her himself. If that was the case, the killer was even more thorough and organized than she'd originally thought. But there wasn't a lit sign on his dash announcing him as being with the driving service—not a good indication. She'd get to that. "Where were you Monday at three, three thirty in the morning? Taking any fares at that time?"

"Anytime between eleven at night and six in the morning."

His quip wasn't working in his favor. "And in direct answer to my question?"

He turned away from her.

She went on. "I think you know exactly where you were and why you were there."

He swallowed roughly, his Adam's apple bobbing.

"So I'll ask again, where were you Monday morning at three thirty?"

"Fine, I was at Leesylvania State Park, but it's not what you think." He straightened up in his chair.

"No? Chloe Somner was murdered there that very morning," she pushed back.

"Well, I didn't kill her! I just dropped off my fare there. Thought it was odd as hell because it was so early, but who am I to question a paying customer?"

"Was your fare a man or woman?" Trent asked.

"I'm not entirely sure. They didn't say one word and wore a hoodie. I couldn't see their face."

"Okay, what about a dashboard camera. Do you have one of those?" Amanda was ready to pounce. So close to a break in the case, her insides were jumping.

"I don't."

No sign on the dash *and* no camera. "Isn't it the law for those offering public transport to have cameras? For safety reasons?"

"I dunno."

"Well, you might want to look into it," Trent seethed.

"Also, why wasn't your sign on?" It might not sound like a big deal, but a light told customers that the car was accepting fares. Without it on, one could assume the driver was off the clock.

"What do you mean?"

She sat next to Trent. "We have your car on video dropping someone off at Leesylvania State Park, and it was your headlights and a partial of your plate that led us to you."

Ashton flailed a hand. "Then why ask where I was if you already knew?"

Amanda shrugged. "I wanted to hear it from you. Now, why didn't you have the dash sign turned on? Surely the car service provides you with one of those."

"I often forget to turn it on."

"Huh. Convenient."

"I swear. I'm telling you the truth."

"You're going to have to do a lot better than that. We need

the name of your fare, an origin point where you picked them up. For starters." Amanda's entire body was quaking with excitement like the case was finally getting somewhere. Up, down, up, down. Just like the elevator business.

"I can tell you all of that." Ashton held up a hand. "Just going to get my phone." He pulled it from a pocket. "No real name but the account's profile nickname is right here." He showed them the screen.

High_ryder21.

Amanda looked at Trent. That was Josh Ryder's handle on Snap VidPic. Was that telling or just a coincidence?

TWENTY-FIVE

Minutes later, Amanda and Trent were standing outside of the interrogation room. She was pacing.

"We've got to bring Josh in immediately," she said and stormed down the hall to Malone's office. Trent kept stride with her.

They found Malone's door shut, but she could see through the glass that he was on the phone. He looked up and saw her, but when she cracked the door open, he stopped her by holding up his hand. A couple of words from his conversation filtered to her ears. *"Not sure where that would leave things... I know. It could be a good thing."*

The discussion could have been about anything, but whatever it was, it was clearly none of her business. In all the years she'd reported to Malone, she never recalled him having her wait in the hall for him to finish up on a phone call. He was usually very much about transparency.

After a few minutes, Malone waved her and Trent in.

She didn't bother to sit, even when he gestured for her to do so. "We have an incredible lead. The boyfriend." She went on to inform him a pickup had been requested at Tipsy Moose Ale

House in Woodbridge by the same name as Josh Ryder's Snap VidPic handle. "This was the morning of the murder," she added.

"Huh." Malone twisted his lips, dropped his hand. "Could just be a coincidence? Someone else could be using that handle on the car service app. It doesn't mean it was Josh Ryder."

Amanda found it curious that Malone was knocking down their suspects one by one. She squinted at him, and he looked at Trent and raised his eyebrows.

"What else is this Chambers kid saying?"

"We asked him what he knows about black orchids, and he was clueless," Trent told him.

"But he is still bitter toward Chloe for the path his life took." Amanda filled him in on the past.

"The kid's—what?—nineteen? He has his life ahead of him. Or did, if he conspired to kill Chloe Somner. Do you think Chambers and Ryder collaborated on her murder?"

"Not entirely certain yet. I'd like to hold Chambers for a while longer, though," she said.

Malone tapped his chin, tugged on his short beard. "Given what you've told me, I'm not sure how we can justify that."

"He has a history with the victim, and he dropped off the person who was likely her killer at the park. His car is on video, and he admits to being there. That's not enough justification?" She was getting worked up, but she wanted to talk more with Josh Ryder and maybe even play him and Ashton off each other to see what shook loose.

"I'll give you until the end of the day." Malone shifted some papers and folders around on his desk. "If that's all...?"

"Not exactly." Now she sat down. "Josh Ryder is a resident of Fairfax. We'll need to at least notify the local PD that we're interested in one of their residents for the murder of Chloe Somner."

"I'll call the commander of their Criminal Investigations Division."

"You know the commander?" Trent asked.

"I'm about to." Malone laid his hands on top of the paperwork that awaited him and looked at them with the question *That all?* running on a ticker tape in his eyes.

Amanda stood and turned to Trent. "Let's go."

Her partner led the way out of the room, and she looked over a shoulder at Malone. He sure was acting strange lately.

They hit a drive-thru for a burger on the way to Fairfax and were in the administration office of Geoffrey Michaels University by twelve thirty. Malone had called Amanda during the drive to let her know the commander of the Criminal Investigations Division of the Fairfax PD was aware they were going to bring in one of their residents for questioning on a murder case. In addition, they had no interest in getting involved with the process. *Perfection!*

"We need to speak with one of your students, Josh Ryder," Amanda said while holding her badge for the woman at the front desk.

She squinted as she read the engraving. "Prince William County PD? Aren't you out of your jurisdiction?"

"We'd like to retrieve Josh Ryder from whatever class he may be in at the moment." Amanda could have had him paged to the office but didn't want to take the chance of spooking him and having him run. That's assuming their visit the other day hadn't already had him taking off.

The woman regarded her and Trent for a few seconds, and Amanda wasn't sure she was going to cooperate, but she started typing on her keyboard. She proceeded to let them know he was currently on lunch break and where he'd be afterward.

They made their way through the numerous corridors and

were outside the classroom with five minutes to spare before class would start. Still no sign of Josh Ryder, but other students were inside the room. Amanda flashed her badge to the teacher who was in there, a middle-aged man with a paunch. He agreed to let her and Trent wait in the room, out of sight of the door and the window in it. This way, they should see Josh before he saw them and it would prevent him from taking off with she and Trent none the wiser.

Each time the door opened and a student walked in, Amanda found herself holding her breath. Each time it wasn't Josh was another twist to her gut. When it was time for class to begin and there was still no sign of Josh, she was certain he wasn't coming. Still, they waited it out for ten minutes before quietly slipping from the room.

"He's made a run for it," Amanda said once they hit the hallway.

"Possibly. It's certainly not looking good for him. We should visit our friend at the front desk again and see if he's showed up for any of his classes this week."

"Good idea."

A few minutes later, they were standing across from the woman again.

"Detectives? Did you find him?"

Amanda shook her head. "Why we're back. Are you able to see if Josh Ryder attended any of his classes this week?"

"I can, but I'm not sure if I should divulge that information."

Amanda didn't want to come out with the fact that Josh Ryder was a suspect in a murder investigation—just in case they were wrong. The repercussions of such an allegation on the innocent could be long-lasting and devastating. "I'm sure you're aware one of the college's students was murdered Monday morning. Josh Ryder knew her, and he may have important information for our investigation. That's all I can say at this time, but if you could help us out here..."

The woman locked her gaze with Amanda's. Eventually, she broke eye contact and clicked on her keyboard. "Attendance is taken at the beginning of each class and recorded by the professors electronically and in live-time. One minute..." More tapping away. "Ah, yeah, from the looks of it, Josh Ryder hasn't been to class since last week."

"Not one class this week? You're sure?" They'd talked to him on Monday afternoon and had found him home. He'd said he had the flu, but he could have lied and been preparing to run then.

"Yes, I'm sure."

"Thank you," Amanda said over a shoulder, already on the move. "Trent, get us to his place faster than lightning."

"I'll do my best, but lightning... that's pretty fast." He smirked, and she appreciated the dose of joviality at a time when the entire case was blowing up. If Josh Ryder was the killer and in the wind, then what?

TWENTY-SIX

Trent parked across the mouth of Josh Ryder's driveway and looked over at Amanda. "How do you want to handle this?"

"Head-on. You good with that?"

He nodded, and they got out of the car and trudged to the door.

She knocked and called out, "Josh Ryder, police. Open up!"

The door opened. "Why are you yelling? Jeez." Josh wrinkled his forehead.

She stepped forward, and he backed into the house. "Do you have a minute to talk with us?" She didn't have the legal right to enter his residence without his approval, but depending how he wanted to play this, they could drag him straight to Central. Probably just should.

"Okay." He let them in, and Trent shut the door behind them.

"Why aren't you in school, Josh?" she asked.

"Why?" The question ripped from his throat almost as a garbled cry. "My girlfriend was murdered two days ago."

"I didn't think she was your girlfriend anymore," Amanda

countered. "Was that hard to get used to? Hard to accept? Maybe you never did accept it?"

"What are you getting at?"

Amanda played the power of silence, and Trent followed her lead.

"Oh my God, you think I killed her?" Josh ran a hand over his mouth. His eyes beaded with tears. "There's no way I ever could have hurt, let alone kill her. Talk to her parents. They loved me."

She was fooled by his tears the first time; she wouldn't be again. "Can you explain why you ordered a car from the Pick Me Up app on Monday morning?"

"What? I never did that."

"Someone using the profile name of High Ryder twenty-one did."

"Well, it wasn't me! Why would I kill her?" He turned to walk away, spun, and raked a hand through his hair. "Is some sicko pretending to be me?"

"Come on, Josh. You can do better than that." But what if someone did use Josh's Snap VidPic name to cast suspicion in his direction, as Malone had suggested? But who and why? Did the killer hold something against Josh and Chloe? Luke Hogan came to mind. She shook the thought aside for now.

"I don't care if you believe it, because it has to be the case."

"You're trying to sell us on someone using that handle to set you up?" Trent asked.

"Exactly."

She shook her head. "Nah. I don't know, Josh. Who would want to do that?"

"I don't know." His voice held desperation. "Ah, this... this driver, can't he tell you that it wasn't me? He must have seen this person's face."

"Apparently he didn't, and the person didn't say anything."

She'd withhold the fact the driver didn't even know if his fare had been male or female.

"Well, track the payment."

"Oh, we will. I assure you." Her phone rang in her pocket, and she pulled it out. ID told her it was Malone. She gave Trent a look, a silent message to manage Josh while she took the call.

As Malone shared his news, Trent's and Josh's voices blended in the background as white noise.

"You're sure?" she said to Malone.

"One hundred percent."

She eyed Josh, took in his defensive body language. "We're with him now." With that, she ended the call and moved toward the student. She pulled her handcuffs. "Josh Ryder, you're under arrest for the murder of Chloe Somner."

"No! I didn't kill her! I swear!" He tugged and yanked, trying to free himself of her grip, but she held strong, and Trent helped steady him.

She snapped on the cuffs and fed Josh into the back of the department car. Once he was situated, she updated Trent on the situation. "That phone call was Malone. Chloe's car was recovered from the university's Fairfax campus." They were just there and hadn't seen it or any police activity, but it was a big area. It was also possible the car had been brought in for processing earlier and they were just hearing about it now.

"Where this guy goes to school? I'm not so sure that's a coincidence."

"That's why he's coming with us." But there was this little niggling in the back of her brain. Josh had told them someone was setting him up, and if he had killed Chloe, would he have been stupid enough to park her car on the Fairfax campus? Surely, he'd have to know it would lead police straight to him. And she supposed the same could be said about ordering a car to the murder scene using the same profile name he used on social media.

They drove Josh to Central and shut him in an interview room before bringing Malone up to speed in the neighboring observation room. From there, they could look in at Josh through a one-way mirror while they spoke.

"He's been off school since Monday," Amanda began. "Claims he had the flu on Monday. Then on Tuesday and today, he was sick from heartbreak." He'd told them this on the way from Fairfax to Central.

"Huh. Hearing some tiny violins," Malone responded.

She was surprised by his complete lack of empathy but shook it off and shared Josh's claim with Malone, so he had the full story. "Josh told us someone was setting him up."

"He can pretty much say anything he wants to at this stage. And he's going to." Malone shoved his hands in his pockets, moved closer to the one-way mirror, and gazed in at Josh. "So, this kid dated the vic for years?"

"They recently broke up," Trent interjected. "He says it was mutual, which was verified by Chloe's roommates."

"Seems to me this guy is saying a lot. See if you can get him to say something that either hangs him or sets him loose." Malone jutted his chin toward Josh, and it felt like she and Trent had just been dismissed.

Again, Malone was acting strangely. It was as if he was in a hurry to wrap up the case—either lay charges or move on. Not typical Malone, who was more methodical and not in a rush.

Amanda led the way into the room, Trent following her.

They both sat across from Josh, who was fidgeting. "I told you I didn't kill her, and I mean that. What am I doing here?"

He'd protested his innocence all the way from Fairfax, and they had to remind him several times of his right to remain silent.

"You know why you're here, Josh," she said slowly. "We suspect you killed Chloe Somner. Maybe it was out of jealousy, or being upset over the breakup?"

"I swear the breakup was mutual."

"Doesn't mean it was easy to take." Her mind circled back to the jealousy motive. They were still waiting on Chloe's phone records, but her friends hadn't known of anyone she was seeing after she and Josh had split.

Josh crossed his arms. "I'm not sure I should respond to that." He snapped his mouth shut for five seconds—if that. "Yeah, I was upset. But I didn't kill her over it. And I understand why we went our separate ways." His gaze slipped to the table for the briefest instant before raising to meet her eyes.

"So it wasn't mutual?" Trent asked, pouncing on the discrepancy.

"No, it was."

"But you weren't happy about it. I mean, I get it, man. You cared about her." Trent was well on his way to earning the Good Cop badge this time around.

"I can't just turn those feelings off. It's also why I could never hurt her." He hurled the words out with such fierceness that drool bubbled at the edges of his mouth.

"Explain the car service and being taken to Leesylvania State Park on Monday at three thirty in the morning," Amanda said, pulling a printed screenshot from Ashton's phone of the request.

"I told you, someone must be setting me up. Here"—Josh pulled his cell phone from his pocket—"search it. I don't even have the app you mentioned."

"Pick Me Up," Amanda provided.

"That's right. Look." He tossed his phone across the table and proceeded to give her the password to unlock it.

She picked up his phone, got into it, and searched the apps. No sign of the car service. She set the phone on the table. "All it proves is you uninstalled the app to cover your tracks."

Josh's face paled, and he shook his head. A single tear fell.

"You regret what you did," Amanda began. "It's understandable. Sometimes those we care about let us down."

"She never let me down," he hissed. "I'm telling you someone is setting me up."

She leaned forward, placing her arms on the table. "But who? Give us a name."

He remained silent as tears pooled in his eyes. "I'm not saying another word until I get a lawyer."

"Suit yourself." She got up, stopped at the door, and looked back at him. She'd started having doubts, little tiny fractures that chipped away at her seeing him as guilty, but his defensive nature and request for an attorney were certainly not helping his cause. And for all his claims of being set up, he wasn't pointing them in anyone's direction. That didn't make sense. What did was that Josh Ryder had motive to kill Chloe Somner.

TWENTY-SEVEN

"We need to subpoena for the payment records on this transaction from Pick Me Up," Amanda said to Trent as they headed to their desks. "See if it can lead us back to Josh Ryder, and if not, the killer—whoever they are."

"Got it." Trent went to his cubicle to take care of that, and she dropped in her chair. Swiveled side to side. Deep in thought.

Two people in holding—Ashton Chambers and Josh Ryder. Both had a motive to kill Chloe Somner. Both were supposedly at the state park Monday morning. Only one was denying that.

Josh repeatedly claimed someone was setting him up but still hadn't provided them with a name. Not even a theoretical one. Was it just a shallow defense that he was trying on in hopes it would remove him from suspicion? Or was he genuinely innocent and grasping to understand how the evidence was leading back to him?

She listened to Trent tapping away on his keyboard, working on the subpoena request, and felt stumped. Though *stalled* was probably a better word. They were in a holding pattern, waiting on Josh's lawyer to arrive, and who knew when that would happen. Sometimes it took attorneys a long time to show up. Josh could be spending the night in a holding cell. But if he killed Chloe, that was the least of what he deserved.

She turned on her monitor and brought up some pictures from the crime scene. She stopped on the one of Chloe with the black orchid. Such care had been taken to stage her the way the killer had intended. In a way, the scene itself represented duality, just like the symbolism for the flower. The girl pale, white. The flower dark, black.

Chloe had embodied the positive aspects of the flower. The strength, virility, and success. She was certainly popular. Intelligent, pretty. That combination could be intimidating to some people, as Josh had pointed out—and it was true. She had contributed to society and wanted to better the world.

Had the killer stripped her and cleansed her to signify Chloe's innocence? Or to emphasize they hadn't viewed her that way in life? Was the black orchid simply picked for its macabre symbolisms of evil and death? Maybe even to imply that Chloe had brought her fate upon herself?

While they waited on Josh's lawyer, she and Trent needed to figure out the clues and burrow through the riddles. What could they find out that would implicate him so they could build a case against him? Did more telling evidence exist?

Chloe's car. They needed answers from it. Now. When Malone had told her about the car being found, he'd also shared that Chloe's clothing, backpack, laptop, and phone had *not* been recovered. So where were they? If the killer was smart, they would have disposed of these items.

She got up and went to Malone's office. Just as she was stepping away from her cubicle, Trent's phone rang, and he answered. She kept moving.

Malone was at his desk, and she filled him in on their interrogation results.

"A lawyer," he mumbled.

"Well, it is his constitutional right," she kicked back with a subtle smirk as she dropped into the chair across from him.

"Suppose it is. What can I do for ya?" Ruffled and irritated, like she'd interrupted something important.

"I just want to make sure Chloe's car is being processed as a priority."

"It is."

"Good to hear."

"Is there something else, Detective?" He raised his brows, and she was tempted to ask what was going on with him these days, but she had an inkling he wouldn't be receptive to the probing.

She'd bench her personal inquiry for now. "I think we should hold Ashton Chambers at least until we've had a chance to question Josh Ryder about him... That being whenever his lawyer gets here."

"All right. Fine."

Amanda dipped her head and left his office. She grabbed a coffee from the lunchroom. Her plan was to return to her desk and dig into Josh's online presence some more, see what he posted about, not just on Snap VidPic but on other popular social media sites he might have been on.

Her phone rang, and caller ID told her it was CSI Blair. "Detective Steele."

"There's something you might be interested in knowing."

No one could accuse the investigator of not getting to the point. "Which is?" Amanda headed to her desk, talking as she walked.

"The blood on that snail at the crime scene came back with two blood types."

"Two contributors. Chloe's and her killer's?"

"One is a match for Chloe based on blood type. It still needs to be run for DNA and comparisons made, but as you know that takes much longer. As for whether the other blood type belongs to the killer, I believe that would be most likely."

"What blood type?" Amanda chose to ignore Blair's snide tone.

"A-positive."

Amanda was going to respond with a thank-you or follow-up on Chloe's car, but Blair had already hung up. She probably didn't want to have a conversation about Amanda's father and their affair any more than Amanda did. Not that now would have been a good time—if one even existed.

"There you are." Trent stood in his cubicle, walked around and followed her into hers.

"Was I missing?" she joked. "I just went to see Malone for a minute. I wanted to make sure Chloe's car is being rushed with Forensics. And speaking of, the blood from that snail had two donors. One was Chloe. The other is presumably the killer, whoever that may be."

"I assume based on type only? It's too early for DNA."

"That's right. We'll need to find out what blood type Josh Ryder is."

"And the jackpot winner is...?"

"A-positive."

He nodded. "As soon as his lawyer gets here, which I've heard isn't going to be until tomorrow morning, we'll ask."

"Tomorrow?" she parroted, then snapped her mouth shut, frustrated. She just wanted to move on with questioning him and getting some answers. "The subpoena for the car service app?"

"Submitted for approval. Now we wait."

"Name of the game lately."

"Oh, I did hear from Metro PD."

"And...?" With the recent developments, she'd let the idea of a serial killer go, and she feared Trent might now resurrect it.

"Apparently, the detective I'd left the message for is out of town with a family emergency, but he has asked that a colleague call me."

"You got their name and number, I hope." She was more for proactive than *reactive*.

"Uh-huh."

"All right, well, we need to see if we can find anything to build a stronger case against Josh Ryder." Her mind went to the closet at Chloe's family home. "Maybe it's time to read some of her journals, see what she had to say about her relationship with Josh. I assume you have those in your cubicle?"

"Yep. And that works. We should also, at some point, visit the Tipsy Moose Ale House."

"Craving a beer?" she teased.

"That's where the car request came from. We could go over there and see if anyone recognizes Josh. Request came in at precisely three twenty in the morning, though, and last call at the pub is probably at two."

She nodded, knowing the place quite well. "It is, but they don't close the doors until the customers are finished. He could have been there drinking right up until the point he was picked up. But I'm not sure our killer—Josh, if that's the case—would have been drinking alcohol. Just thinking about the clean and organized crime scene. It's not fitting with a drunk person. The bar could have been nothing more than a pickup point."

"Yeah, I suppose," he said, deflated.

"It doesn't mean people at the bar didn't see him hanging around, but let's start with the journals." She got comfortable and waited while Trent returned to his desk. He handed her two journals over the divider between their desks. She flipped both open and looked at the dates of the entries. The ones she had were from a couple of years ago. "What about the two most recent ones?"

"Just a minute..." Trent put his head down and went through the books. "These two. I'll take one and give you one?"

"Works for me." She gave back the others, exchanging them for the more recent one. And speaking of, there hadn't been a single journal at the townhouse where Chloe lived. Maybe it had been in her backpack that was still missing. Either that, or she'd stopped writing in them. The last entry from the one in her hand was two months old. Flipping to the front, it looked like it covered August and the start of the school year. She shared this with Trent. "The dates in yours?"

"Uh...one second. Looks like May until July of this year."

"We could be missing her most recent one. Also the one that would have covered her breakup with Josh."

"Still want us to read what we have?"

"Yeah. In the least, it will help us understand Chloe more, and might give us a solid lead."

"You got it." He started reading.

Amanda got to work too. She wasn't a slow reader, but couldn't claim to be that fast either. The entries in August were brief and sporadic, often only a line or two, and it didn't take her any time to reach the first entry in September.

It's the first day of school. God, I'm more nervous than I want to be. Mom and Dad keep going on and on, telling me how this is my year. The year I'll really make a mark. But they say that all the time. They have no idea how much I work at being outgoing, how inside I'm so scared. But I do it anyway. Fear is only a state of mind. Maybe if I repeat that enough...

Amanda skimmed some pages and stopped at Luke's name.

Luke is buzzing around again. Always. When will he take the hint that I love Josh, that I'm with him? He's smart, he has to be to get the grades he does, but he doesn't seem to get that I'll never be with him. And he makes Josh soooo angry. I hate that!

I think back to the way I used to be when I was younger. It doesn't feel good.

Was she referring to the bullying she'd taken part in? So far they only had Ashton's word on that. And who knew if it could be trusted?

She read more.

I'll never even call someone a mean name again. Not after seeing what words can do.

She skimmed some more pages and stopped again at an entry dated September 28.

Ashton delivered pizza to the townhouse last week. I hadn't seen him since forever. He wouldn't look me in the eye. I know he's been hating me on Snap, but I can't blame him, I suppose. But he did key my car!

Maybe I pushed him to it.

Amanda marked the page with a sticky note. "Trent."

"Yeah?"

"Anything about Josh in your journal?"

"Oh, yeah. It's like I'm reading a steamy romance novel."

"I didn't realize that was a genre you're drawn to."

"Leave comedy for the comedians. What's up?"

"I've pulled out a couple things so far. Josh had a temper and low tolerance when it came to Luke Hogan."

"Gives Luke more reason to want to kill Chloe. Not sure this implicates Josh."

"Except for Josh got angry with Luke hanging around. What if Chloe stood up for Luke?"

"Josh wouldn't have liked that."

"I can't imagine he would have, and then the breakup could have been salt on an open wound."

"Okay, but why wait three weeks after they split?"

"Something must have triggered him." She paused, unsure what that was exactly. "Here's another thing about Chloe, though. She regretted being a bully when she was younger. She even mentions Ashton Chambers. And having run into him at the end of September. Ashton wouldn't even look at her."

"That's nearly two months ago. If running into Chloe triggered Ashton, why the delay?"

The second time she'd been presented with this question. First, in regards to Josh, and now Ashton. "We've already concluded planning the murder would have taken time."

Trent eventually nodded. "Could be that simple."

"Yep." She glanced at the clock. Three thirty. She wanted to get home at a decent hour for Zoe—especially after last night. Amanda had been shaken by the girl's reaction to the storm and the memories of her parents' murders. The police psychiatrist, Colleen Frost, had told Amanda how fragile Zoe's psyche was, given what she'd witnessed. Amanda recalled being happy at the time that it wasn't her job to worry about the child's long-term mental health. Now that responsibility had landed squarely on her shoulders.

"We should hit the bar and see if we can place Josh Ryder as having been there at the right time," Amanda said. "I'd also like to talk to Jayne Russell again. This time about Ashton. From the sounds of it, Chloe did something horrible to him. She even blames herself for the fact that he'd keyed her car."

"I'm ready to go. Reading's not my favorite pastime, and this"—he held up the journal—"should be X-rated. They say guys are bad."

She laughed, but the mirth was shallow. Hitting both places could take too long. *Divide and conquer* went through her mind, and that would get her home faster too. "You know what? I'll speak with Jayne. You go to the bar. That work for you?"

"Ah, sure?" He narrowed his eyes like he wasn't understanding why they were going separate ways.

She didn't want to come across like she was shirking her responsibilities to be with Zoe. She'd already mentioned getting to her at a decent hour enough in recent days. She stood and grabbed her jacket. "Keep me posted."

"You too."

She simply nodded and left.

TWENTY-EIGHT

Amanda parked outside the townhouse and stared at the building. On the way over, she'd had time to think in silence. She was failing as a parent, and she hadn't even assumed the legal role yet. After last night's events, she should have booked Zoe with the shrink first thing this morning. But Amanda had let the severity of what had transpired fade into the background. Probably because she wanted to—for her own comfort. At times, it was hard to swallow how much healing the little girl still had ahead of her. Amanda was well aware, too, of survivor's guilt and how it chewed away like acid. Zoe's parents had been killed two months ago. Amanda's life had been flipped for the better part of six *years*. She was, in a way, signing up for a version of that again. Would she survive it a second time? All these musings were likely brought on by reading Chloe's journal. Some actions had long-lasting repercussions. Chloe had felt bad for her treatment of Ashton, even though she hadn't seen him "in forever." Crap had a way of clinging.

Amanda knocked on the door. Jayne answered and stepped back for her to come in, no questions asked.

"How are you doing?" Stupid, *stupid*, question, but at least Jayne would know Amanda cared.

"Dunno." She shrugged her shoulders.

"Is Lauren home?"

"Nope. Just me."

That would probably work out even better, as Jayne was really the one Amanda wanted to talk with anyway. She had a longer history with Chloe.

"Want to sit down?" Jayne gestured toward the living room.

"Sure."

The two of them sat on the couch and turned to face each other.

"Have you ever heard of a guy named Ashton Chambers?"

"Ashton, Ashton," she repeated. "Oh, yeah." Her eyes went wide. "Haven't heard the name in a long time. Knew him in high school. Talk about a loser."

The girl's wall was instantly up, trying to appear tough and impenetrable. "Why's that?"

"He was just weird."

"So, because someone's different, they deserve to be mistreated?"

Jayne rubbed her cheek to her shoulder and didn't respond.

So she feels justified... Wow. "We know Chloe bullied him back in high school." She'd treat that as fact after seeing Jayne's reaction to his name.

"So? Why do you care about Ashton?"

She couldn't tell her they'd pulled him in for questioning. She went another route. "We have our hands on some of Chloe's journals."

Jayne pulled her legs up and folded them under her. "Okay...?" She chewed on that hangnail again like she had when she and Trent had first talked to her.

"What did you guys do to push him to key Chloe's car?

From the sounds of it, she felt pretty bad that she'd made him so upset."

"We might have taken things a little far..."

"What did you do?"

"It wasn't just Chloe and me. Josh was in on it too."

Amanda didn't have all night, but she'd sit there quietly until she heard the entire story.

"One day in the locker room, when Ashton was in the shower, Josh took all his clothes and his towel."

"Stranded him there naked? Real nice."

Jayne shrugged it off. "We were kids."

Then it hit. Naked. Just like Chloe had been. Could it be that Ashton was repaying the favor after all these years? But she had a feeling things had progressed beyond limited humiliation for high-school Ashton. "What happened next?"

"Josh took video of him and shared it online."

"Okay, and what was Chloe's role in this?"

"She was more tech savvy. She modified the video to have overlaid text..." Now Jayne squirmed.

Amanda hesitated to ask. "What did it say?"

"'Little pecker,' with an animated arrow jabbing toward it." Jayne mimed the motion with a pointed finger.

No wonder Ashton didn't want to tell them about it. "Too embarrassing," he had said. Anger heated her veins. She was biting her tongue because she had a lot she could say. How evil the group of them had been to do that to Ashton, how it honestly could have affected the trajectory of his life, how all of them should have been punished for their actions. But it was Ashton who ended up with a juvie record, even though criminal charges could have been laid against Chloe, Josh, Jayne, and any others for their role in bullying Ashton. Then again, did Chloe just get off with a keyed car or did this past act come back to kill her? And could good deeds make up for previous wrongs? Amanda had built up this saint-like image of Chloe, but finding out about the extent of her bullying past had tainted it. Then again, Chloe had sounded deeply sorry in her journal entries, and her life had been dedicated to noble pursuits in more recent days. There should be some forgiveness extended.

Amanda got up to see herself out.

"Wait, where are you going?"

"You answered my questions."

"Did Ashton kill Chloe?"

Amanda stopped, turned, and went cold as she met the girl's gaze. "It's an open investigation, and I can't say."

She left and got into the car, her entire body quaking. Why did some kids think it was okay to pick on someone who was different than them? Even to go so far as humiliating that person? The world had little hope if such thinking was a part of the future, but sadly it would probably still exist.

Her phone rang. It was Trent.

She let it go for a bit, trying to calm herself down. "Hey," she eventually answered.

"Oh, I got you. I'm done at the bar, and no one recognized Josh Ryder or Ashton Chambers, for that matter, for the time or day in question. How did you make out with Jayne?"

"Ashton would have had a good reason to hate both Josh and Chloe." She shared the prank they'd pulled. Not that *prank* was strong enough a word. "All because he was *weird*. Jayne's word."

"As long as people are threatened by differences, they'll justify bullying. But, wow. That's brutal. Maybe Ashton's recent bump-in with Chloe had him planning this."

"Though given the video, one person drove while another killed. Did Ashton and Josh pair up? I'd find that hard to believe, but we'll press him tomorrow when his lawyer is present."

"You bet we will. Also, if Josh really thinks someone is framing him, he's going to need to hand over some names."

"Only if he wants us to believe him." She realized it was on her and Trent, the side of the law, to prove guilt. She still wasn't quite sure where she stood with Josh. Even if he was one of the best suspects they had so far. "I'm going to head home, Trent. You should do the same. Tomorrow's going to be a long one."

"Sounds good. You have that right. By the way, the lawyer will be in at eight."

She groaned internally. That was earlier than she'd have liked, but he'd need time to confer with his client. "I'll be at Central at eight thirty."

"Okay."

They wished each other a good night and hung up. Now she just needed to return to the station and pick up her car. Then it would be a nice, relaxing evening with Zoe.

TWENTY-NINE

Amanda's phone rang as soon as she'd dropped off the keys for the department car at Central. "Hello." She didn't consult the caller ID, figuring it was probably Zoe, *hoping* it was Zoe.

"I know you said we'd call it a night, but..." It was Trent.

"What is it?" She had this strong feeling she wouldn't want to hear his answer.

"Chloe's phone records are in, and with Ryder's lawyer coming in tomorrow, I thought—"

"Son of a bitch." How could she go home and ignore this? Something in Chloe's records could give them what they needed to close the case. "You thought right," she said with a sigh.

"I didn't even say what I thought yet."

"You thought I'd want to look at them and see if there's anything we'd want to take up with Ryder and his lawyer tomorrow. And since they're going to be there first thing, we should look now. So we'll be armed and ready."

Silence.

"Trent?" It was okay for him to read her thoughts but not the other way around?

"Where are you?"

She was marching her way toward the warren of cubicles for the Homicide Unit. "Fifty feet from our desks, if that."

"I'll see you soon."

He was standing at his desk when she rounded the corner. The printer on his desk was doing full-time duty as it spat out page after page.

Shit. The realization that they could be looking at this for hours hit home. Chloe Somner had been a young woman with an active social life and a busy online persona. Amanda couldn't leave all this with Trent, or could she? There was a part of her that wished she could justify doing so, but there was a lot to review. If they were to have any hope of uncovering something useful to the investigation, specifically that might apply to their meeting with Josh and his lawyer tomorrow, they'd better dive in as a team.

"I need to make a call," she told him and walked back outside for privacy. The air was chilly, and a breeze gusted around her, causing her to burrow deeper into her coat. She pressed the number for home and stared at the digits on the screen. This was the last call she wanted to make. Yet another time that she'd be home late from work. She hit the Call button, and Libby answered on the second ring. "Libby, it's Amanda."

"Hi." One tiny word, and it was sucked dry of all energy and enthusiasm. She must have guessed what was coming.

"I'm not sure when I'll be home. Are you able to feed Zoe? Maybe even take her on a sleepover?" Amanda massaged her forehead with her free hand. A headache was setting in with a vengeance. Tonight was probably the worst time for this to happen, coming on the tail of last night.

"Yeah, sure."

"I really appreciate it. Thank you."

"You know how much I love Zoe."

Libby was technically the girl's godmother, though circumstances had changed in her life that made adopting Zoe not feasible. At moments like this when she had to stay late for an investigation, Amanda had to wonder if Zoe wouldn't be better off with the schoolteacher, who held predictable office hours. "I do. Can I talk to her for a minute?"

"Ah, sure. Let me get her."

A few seconds later, Zoe's voice pinged across the line. "When are you coming home?"

"As soon as I can, sweetie, but Aunt Libby and I were thinking that maybe you could have a sleepover at her place tonight." The thought of parting with Zoe stabbed her in the heart.

"On a school night?"

"Just for tonight." Amanda trembled, unsure if it was from the recent gust of cold air, or her insides freezing from the thought of disappointing this child.

"Okay."

"Hey, it will be fun, right? You love your Aunt Libby." Amanda did her best to infuse lightness and joviality into her tone.

"I love you too."

Amanda's chest paused on an exhale, which she slowly released. "And I love you."

"Bye."

"Zoe—" The line was dead. How had she really expected this conversation would go? Amanda felt like she was letting everyone down. Dramatic possibly, but it was how she felt nonetheless. She'd make things up to Libby and Zoe, but right now she wanted to make sure that she didn't fail Chloe Somner.

THIRTY

Waking up the next morning, the house had felt incredibly empty, like even the walls called out for life and energy. Amanda had none of the latter to give, and she missed Zoe like crazy. Making the call for her to stay with Libby last night had been the wise decision, though, as she'd been at the station with Trent until two in the morning.

She'd called Libby's to speak with Zoe at seven, but Zoe didn't want to talk to her, and that hurt like hell. Libby tried to soothe Amanda's conscience, but it felt like a half-hearted effort. She'd said it was only because Zoe was concerned about getting ready for school on time. Amanda could believe that to an extent—the girl certainly wanted to make sure she looked perfect every morning before heading out the door. She was six going on sixteen that way.

Amanda had stopped at Hannah's Diner on the way to work for a coffee and a muffin. That was about all her queasy stomach could handle this morning. While she'd let Zoe and Libby down, her efforts, and Trent's, had paid off. They had something that looked quite damning for Josh Ryder, and it answered one of their earliest questions about what had Chloe at the park so early in the morning.

She dropped off her coat at her desk at a quarter after eight. Trent wasn't in yet, but they'd discussed strategy last night—technically, this morning—about how they'd approach things with Josh and his lawyer. She drained her coffee and tossed the cup in her trash.

"Morning." Trent came in looking flushed from lack of sleep.

She managed little rest much better than her partner did. "Good morning. You ready for this?"

"Sure am."

"Let's go, then."

They went down the hall to the interrogation room and found Josh Ryder with a balding man in his late fifties, possibly sixties. Amanda recognized him from some previous cases. His name was Peter Wilson. He worked with a defense firm in Woodbridge and had created quite a formidable reputation for himself as a powerful attorney.

She knocked and entered the room. "Mr. Wilson."

"Detective Steele."

Josh's eyes darted between the two of them. "You two know each other?"

"Hang around this town long enough and run in similar circles, it's bound to happen," Peter said.

Amanda and Trent sat down across from them. Josh's eyes were underscored by dark shadows. A holding cell wasn't conducive to getting a good night's sleep. It was referred to as the drunk tank for good reason. All night, street cops would be pulling people in, many of them high or drunk. Most of them amped up and hostile. A fair number of them puking.

Josh had shared a cell with Ashton Chambers. She and Trent had requested the officer on duty watch them and report how they interacted, if they even did. When she'd popped by the cells before hitting her desk, she was told Josh and Ashton had stuck to different sides of the space. An act? Time would tell.

"Can I get you a water, coffee...?" Amanda asked Josh.

"I just want to get out of here."

"I don't think that's happening any time soon."

"What do you mean? I didn't—"

Peter laid a hand on Josh's arm. "From what I hear, Detectives"—he let his gaze swoop to take in Trent—"you don't have anything concrete against my client."

"That changed overnight," she said, then confirmed Josh's phone number with him. She didn't say a word as she pulled a printout of Chloe's phone records from a folder. She pushed the sheet across the table to Peter. "It's a text message from Josh to Chloe Somner sent this past Sunday night, requesting a meetup at Leesylvania State Park on Monday at four in the morning." She read the words again, upside down, even though she had them memorized. *Just want to talk. The park at 4 AM tomorrow. Meet by the water. Your favorite spot.*

Josh's face paled, and his mouth opened and closed like a fish. "I didn't send that!"

"Mr. Ryder, please." Peter leveled a look at Josh like a parent scolding a child.

"But, no! I didn't do that! Check my phone. You took it from me on lockup." Josh's cheeks were flaming bright red now.

"We'll look at it, I assure you," Amanda said. "But if we don't find the message, it doesn't mean you didn't send this. It just means you deleted it." She pointed to the page. "This came from your phone number."

"One that you just confirmed was yours," Trent stressed.

"No. This can't be happening." Josh shook his head wildly. "This has something to do with that Ashton guy. Has to."

"Ashton...?" She played dumb.

"I saw him in holding. No idea what he was doing there,

and he wasn't talking to me. But he had every reason to hate Chloe."

Reason to hate you too, she thought, but wasn't going to say that out loud in so many words, making it too easy for Josh's lawyer to shoot down accusations about his client and Ashton teaming up. And that was a road they had to go down. The fact remained that while they had Ashton and his car at the park, he couldn't have driven *and* been the mystery figure who'd emerged from the vehicle. "I heard about the prank you helped pull on Ashton Chambers."

Josh's brows bunched together. "The one in high school?"

"Some experiences never leave us."

"Then don't you see? He had more motive than me."

That took him all of five seconds... "I think you were far more upset about your breakup with Chloe than you're admitting. Maybe you and Ashton even teamed up and decided on a way to take out Chloe together? Two slighted guys against the girl who hurt them?" A baseless accusation and possibly a long stretch that Josh and Ashton would collaborate. And if Ashton had found it in his heart to forgive Josh's role in the prank, why not Chloe too?

"He's setting me up for this." Josh was heaving for breath, bent forward, gasping.

"We have Ashton's vehicle dropping someone off at Leesylvania State Park at three thirty in the morning. The request for this service was made using the same name you have for your Snap VidPic handle. We've been over this," she added.

"Detective, anyone could have used that handle. You can't prove it was my client behind it."

He had her there. They were still waiting on an approved subpoena to request the payment information from the car service. "We will."

"Awful arrogant to assume that's the case." Peter sat back,

tugged down on his suit jacket. "Did this Ashton character ID my client as being his fare?"

Amanda gave her response some thought and went with the truth. "No. But... he didn't see his fare's face."

"Ah, see?" Peter smiled at Josh. "They can't place you at the scene."

"We still have the circumstantial evidence. The lack of a verifiable alibi and a text message that took Chloe to the place where she was murdered. We have motive—your client's broken heart. We have also recovered Chloe's car."

"It was missing?" Josh screeched.

"It was found at the Fairfax campus. Where you left it?"

The lawyer frowned but didn't say anything.

Amanda went on. "It is being examined thoroughly. Will we find trace from you—fingerprints, DNA?"

"I'd suspect you'd find something from my client," Peter said firmly. "Josh had been dating the girl, something he's freely admitted."

That was the only problem with trace evidence—it was impossible to date. "Did you ever drive her car, Josh?"

"No. You kidding? She'd never let me."

Peter shook his head.

"What?" Josh said to his lawyer.

"We'll talk later."

Amanda refrained from basking too much in Josh's admission. If CSIs found Josh's prints on the wheel, he would have some explaining to do. "The next step will be a search of your client's home—"

There was a knock on the door, and Trent rose to answer it.

Amanda continued. "A search will be conducted of your client's home for the murder weapon and anything that may have belonged to Chloe Somner."

Trent stepped into the hall.

"I didn't do this," Josh said, repeating his claim.

"We'll figure this out," Peter assured him.

The door opened again, and Trent poked his head in. "Detective Steele? A minute?"

"Ah, sure. Excuse me." She got up and joined Trent in the hall, closing the door behind her.

Malone was out there, and both he and Trent were wearing grave expressions. Her stomach swirled, and dread squeezed her shoulders. They didn't say a word. They didn't need to. "There's been another victim."

Malone pinched his eyes shut briefly.

Trent nodded. "And since our prime suspects are in custody, that means—"

"We're back to square one," she finished. Just when she thought this case was coming to a close, there was another body. Maybe she should have taken that cold case from Washington more seriously. Maybe it was connected with Chloe's murder. Maybe there was a serial killer hunting in Prince William County. A lot of maybes with one result: due to her failure another girl had been murdered. "Has the victim been identified?" She could barely push out the question, her chest heavy and throat tight.

"Not yet," Malone said. "Just like with Chloe Somner, no clothes, no ID."

She laid a hand on her stomach. "And a black orchid?"

"Yes."

"Time of death?"

"You'd have to ask an ME about that, but she was found about seven this morning."

She wasn't even going to ask why they were just hearing about this now—after eight thirty. Sometimes it took time for the message to hit the right person. "Where?"

"On the edge of the Occoquan River on the campus for the Geoffrey Michaels science center."

"You've got to be kidding me." Vomit started up the back of her throat. She swallowed roughly, peaked.

"I wish I was. You guys need to go," Malone said, hurried. "I'll take care of what's going on in there." He waved a hand toward the room where Peter and Josh still waited.

But she was stuck on the text message from Josh to Chloe. How did that reconcile? And Chloe's car at the Fairfax campus? How could Josh have killed someone while he was behind bars at PWCPD Central? The answer was as simple as it was complicated: he couldn't have. And there was no way that Ashton Chambers could be behind this new murder either.

While she and Trent would be at another crime scene, their prime suspects would be released from custody.

As she and Trent rushed from the station, he said, "Are we looking at a serial killer, then? Do you think we can expect another college student in a few more days?"

"God, don't even say it."

THIRTY-ONE

Amanda hustled through the campus with Trent keeping up next to her. It wasn't hard to determine where the discovery had been made with the bulging crowd.

"Get these students to move back, but don't let them leave until everyone's been questioned and their names and numbers collected." She gave these directions to the first PWCPD officer she saw and shook her head. Part of a uniformed officer's job was crowd control, and the area was swarming with people who shouldn't be there. Contamination of the crime scene was at risk.

One officer had established a perimeter and held up a hand as they came toward him. "I'll need your names and badge numbers before you go any farther."

Amanda and Trent flashed their badges and gave their names.

"Go on ahead." He waved them through.

Amanda hurried across the grass toward the edge of the river. Crime Scene wasn't there yet, and neither was anyone from the medical examiner's office. But the closer she got to the victim, the more her heart raced. Another young woman killed on her watch, and she'd been powerless to stop it. That implication burrowed deep, but this job could eat you alive if you let it. It was why the importance of detachment was beaten into them at the academy. Career cops learned to preserve themselves emotionally because the alternative was landing in a psychiatric hospital or developing an alcohol or drug dependency. Amanda liked to believe she could balance the emotional aspects of the job, but there were still times when they caught her unaware. Like Zoe.

As much as Amanda had tried to convince herself that Zoe was just an eyewitness and nothing more, Amanda ultimately lost the battle. Detachment hadn't worked. She wanted to protect Zoe, heal her.

And now another young woman was dead. There would be no healing for her.

Was this all on Amanda's shoulders? Maybe if she'd put in more hours, sent Zoe to stay with Libby as soon as she'd picked up Chloe's case on Monday, it would have been solved already and this girl saved.

But she had to shake those thoughts. Could have, would have, should have. None of that mattered now—only the present moment.

The young woman had been stripped and cleaned, and as with Chloe, a black orchid had been placed on her chest. Its petals appeared crisp and fresh, like it had just been plucked. Amanda counted seven stab wounds, and if memory served her correctly, they appeared to be positioned in the same locations as with Chloe.

But it was the girl's face that had Amanda drawing back. "Jayne Russell," she muttered, unable to take her eyes off her. Amanda's penance for acting too slowly. Just yesterday she'd been in the girl's home and spoken to her. Jayne had been a living and breathing individual. Today, she was a body, a cadaver, a casualty at the hands of a killer. And she'd spent so much of her life putting on a tough front, like nothing could penetrate it, but Amanda had glimpsed some softer aspects to the girl.

Trent blew out a mouthful of air. "What the hell? Is someone out there targeting Chloe and her group of friends?"

Lauren! Amanda rushed to the closest officer. "I need you to find a Lauren Bennett and bring her to me. If she's not on campus, try her house." She gave him the address.

"Will do." He hurried off.

Amanda looked over her shoulder, doing so as casually and covertly as possible. Chloe and Jayne's killer could be among the crowd. But at first glance no one stood out—unless she counted Luke Hogan and Stephanie Piper, who were on the outskirts of a throng of people. She turned to Trent. "We need to start focusing on people who disliked both girls."

"That could be Ashton Chambers."

"Jayne was involved with that high school prank, but Ashton was locked up last night."

"What about Luke Hogan? He probably knew Jayne's opinion of him, maybe even suspected she had pointed us in his direction for Chloe's murder."

"Which could also mean that Lauren is in danger." She glanced at Luke again, but he was talking with Stephanie and not looking their way.

Trent put a hand on her shoulder. "That officer will get Lauren."

She met Trent's eyes and nodded. He had a way of calming and grounding her. She took a few deep breaths, and he removed his hand. "And Luke is right here. If he's the killer, he's within sight," she said. "But have you heard from that Metro PD detective? Maybe we should give that cold case more attention." She just hoped she hadn't dropped the ball there—and more importantly, that Lauren Bennett was safe. Two out of three roommates murdered. Horrid odds.

"I can call him and follow up."

"Thanks." Just when she'd started to relax, easing back from suspecting a serial killer at work, this happened. Another student dead. "Be sure to get all the details, crime scene photos, a list of suspects. See if there's any connection to Geoffrey Michaels University. We're going to want to talk to Luke and Stephanie again. Also, we need to find out who discovered the body and have a talk with that person too."

"Yep. Cover all the bases." He smiled, patient. He didn't need her to give him the blow-by-blow of their next steps but talking them out made her feel in control—far more than she was.

Trent got on the phone, and Amanda saw CSIs Blair and Donnelly coming toward them, holding evidence collection kits. Donnelly had a camera around her neck. The investigators offered Amanda and Trent a brief greeting and got to work.

"This can't be happening!" It was a man's voice, and it had Amanda turning around. It was Craig Perkins, senior associate dean. Gone was the initial image of a man who was calm and unshakable. She was curious why he was so upset this time—was it the victim or the fact another of his students had been murdered? Both? Or the fact this body had been found on his campus?

She trudged across the grass toward him. Trent held back, now talking on the phone. Hopefully to the actual detective and not his voicemail.

"Dean Perkins," she said, "I appreciate this is quite a shock, but I'm going to need to ask that you please calm down for the sake of the students."

"Do you know who it is? I mean rumors are going around, but I'm not sure if it's true."

"At this point, I can't confirm," she responded. "But if you'll go back to your office, we'll catch up with you shortly. We will have questions for you."

He hesitated, his eyes peering over Amanda's shoulders to the body. Eventually, he consented with a nod and walked off without a word.

Sergeant Malone came to the perimeter and was let through quickly. He beelined straight for her. Trent was still on the phone, so she'd take that as a good sign he'd gotten through to the detective.

"We were in such a hurry to get here. Do you know who found the girl?" Amanda asked him.

He nodded, slipped a hand into his jacket, and pulled out a small notebook from his shirt pocket. He opened it and said, "Lauren Bennett."

Trent joined them just then. He shot a knowing look in Amanda's direction.

"I take it this means something to you two?" Malone asked, eyebrows raised.

"You could say that. She's the roommate of both victims. Where is she now?"

"I suspect somewhere around here with an officer. But, wait a minute, you're telling me both of this girl's roommates have now been murdered? Do you peg her as a suspect?"

"Uncertain." There was the possibility Lauren had killed Jayne—the two of them didn't get along, to put it mildly. But Amanda couldn't see her killing Chloe. Trent's eyes kept darting at her. He'd found something out from that Metro PD detective worth sharing, but she wanted to filter what it was before Malone heard. She subtly shook her head at Trent. "Do you know why Lauren was out here at seven this morning?" she asked. Malone had said that was the time the body had been found.

"You're probably best to speak with the girl. But I believe she was just out here walking and getting some fresh air."

"Sounds like a rather convenient explanation," Trent began. "Is there anyone who could even verify that?"

"That's something for you two to figure out. And them"—Malone nudged his head in the direction of the arriving news media—"I'll deal with." He walked off.

With Malone out of earshot, Amanda faced Trent. "What did you find out?"

"The detective's going to send over some crime scene photos and the list of suspects, which he emphasized were tapped dry."

"But...?" She could sense one coming. It was going to be news she didn't want to hear.

"There are similarities and differences between Annie Frasier's murder and Chloe Somner's. Both were stabbed, though Annie three times not seven. Annie was clothed but Chloe was naked. The flower left with Frasier was a red rose, not an orchid, but it was left on her chest." He said the last part slowly. "Maybe the killer felt romantic love for Annie Frasier? I don't have to look up what a red rose means. But *if* this is a serial killer, he could pick different flowers for each victim, or he's decided to use only black orchids now."

"None of this is making me feel any better," she groaned.

"None of this means we're looking at the same killer either. Just a possibility," he said.

Again, he knew the right thing to say, but the truth still came down to the fact that there were two dead college students. "The murders do seem personal, more so than one would expect with a serial killer," she reasoned. "With our investigation, it's hard to ignore that both girls were from Geoffrey Michaels University *and* roommates. That makes me think the killer is from here." She took out her phone and snapped some pictures of the students standing around, and she turned toward the water and Jayne. It was always hard to reconcile death when you'd spoken with the person recently.

Trent stepped up close to her. "It's so exposed here. The killer really took a risk of being caught red-handed. Anybody could have stumbled on the scene."

"Which is kind of terrifying. Are they growing more brazen? Or are they escalating, trying to knock people off their hit list before we stop them?"

"Both scary thoughts."

"Uh-huh. And did no one hear anything? She would have screamed." She shook her head, trying to wrap her mind around how the killer had managed to execute their plan without getting caught.

"Her attacker had to prevent that somehow," Trent reasoned.

"It would seem. The aid of drugs or something more basic— say, a hand over her mouth to suppress the noise? Also, what brought Jayne down to the water this morning? There's no time of death yet, but it was obviously before seven. We need to consider it would have taken time for the killer to present her the way he did and then make his getaway."

Trent spun and jabbed the tip of his pen toward one of the buildings on campus. "It's quite a distance away from the water, but anyone looking out could have seen something."

"We'll need to find out who was in that building during the time of the attack."

"Yeah. There might even be surveillance cameras on the grounds that face the crime scene area."

"We'll need to find that out too." Her words tapered off.

Lauren Bennett was walking toward them with the officer Amanda had asked to look for her. She and Trent helped close the distance.

"Thank you," she told the officer.

"You're very welcome."

Amanda found herself almost wanting to hug the girl. She was alive at least. But Amanda had to remain detached. For now. Until they figured out what was going on.

Lauren's face was all blotchy. Tears were seeping down her

cheeks, and her chin was quivering. She reached for Amanda and hugged her. Amanda allowed it.

This was one of those lines that technically shouldn't be crossed between law enforcement and civilians. Touch only made things personal and more emotional. Amanda retreated from the embrace rather quickly and stepped back, putting a couple of feet between them.

"I'm so sorry for your loss," she said.

Lauren palmed her cheeks. "I never really liked her. Not a secret?" A small chuckle that fell flat. "But Chloe loved her, so I tolerated her."

"Not sure if Jayne told you that I spoke with her. You know I was at your house?" Twice, technically.

Lauren nodded.

Amanda continued. "She told me she'd known Chloe since elementary school, but that you two only met here at Geoffrey Michaels. Is that correct?"

"That's right, but I loved her like a sister. Chloe was the glue that held all of us together. After Chloe..." She sniffled and palmed her cheeks. "Jayne and I were already talking about going our separate ways. It just seemed like too much, you know?" Lauren sobbed softly for a few seconds, then added, "And now Jayne? Who's doing this?"

"We will find out," Amanda stamped out. "You can trust me on that." *Somehow, some way.*

"I just have no idea who would've done this to them or why. I mean, Jayne was a pain in the ass, but Chloe? She was a kind person."

Not that she'd always been that way, but maybe the fact she had changed was enough. Shouldn't people be forgiven for their wrongdoings? As for Jayne, Amanda felt certain the girl was mostly misunderstood.

"Do you know when she left home this morning?" Trent asked.

Lauren looked at him. "I'm not a hundred percent sure, but it was early."

"Just an approximate time?" Trent pushed.

"All I can say is it was before six, because that's when I woke up and she was already gone."

"Do you know why she would have come here that early in the morning?" Amanda asked, feeling a sense of déjà vu. She'd asked the same question regarding Chloe.

"Well, she's been a bit of a mess since Chloe's murder. I think she just came down here to have some time to herself before class."

They knew now that Chloe had received a text message to meet at the park at four in the morning on Monday. Had Jayne received a similar message? There was obviously no sign of her phone thus far, so they'd likely have to go about requesting the call history from the phone provider. A pain in the butt that would cause yet another delay to closing what was now two murder cases.

"Why were you down here this morning?" Trent asked, seeking a full answer directly from the source.

"Just wanted to see if I could catch up with Jayne." She sniffled. "It's been so hard... after Chloe. Either of you ever lose anyone you were close to?"

Amanda wasn't getting sucked into that emotional vortex. "It takes a long time for life to return to a new normal. So it wasn't just for fresh air?"

Lauren shook her head. "I know that's what I told the officer but... Now I realize this might look bad, but the truth? I had a feeling I'd find Jayne here—not dead obviously. But when I saw her phone on the counter, I was going to use bringing it to her as an excuse to talk to her."

"What were you going to talk to her about?" Trent asked, but Amanda's mind was on Jayne's phone and getting her hands on it.

Lauren glanced at him. "I wanted to come to a truce and stay living together."

"But you didn't care for her," Trent pointed out, wedging in again before Amanda could ask about the phone.

"No, but Chloe did, so there had to be some good qualities in her. Plus, you know how hard it is to find a roommate? At least I knew what I was dealing with when it came to Jayne."

"I can see that." Trent smiled. "But you said you had a feeling Jayne would be here this morning?"

"Uh-huh."

Amanda would let asking about Jayne's phone go for now, following the path Trent had laid out. "You also had a feeling something was wrong with Chloe, and she'd been murdered."

Lauren met Amanda's eyes in a relaxed manner. "I know how this could look, but I didn't hurt either of them. I just have what you might call a strong intuition."

As a cop, Amanda could appreciate strong intuition. But did she trust Lauren's claim? Amanda wasn't seeing any real reason to suspect her of murdering her two roommates. There was no obvious motive. If anything, Amanda would wager Lauren may be at risk. "You have Jayne's phone?"

"Oh, yeah." Lauren reached into her coat pocket and pulled out a phone. She put it in Amanda's hand.

Amanda hit the button to wake up the screen. "Do you know Jayne's password or how to unlock it?"

Lauren nodded. "It's a trace pattern."

Amanda handed her the phone and asked that she unlock it. She watched as Lauren swiped across the screen.

"There you go." Lauren gave the phone back to Amanda.

"Thanks." Amanda went straight to the texting app. She went cold at the sight of a message from last night.

Must talk to you. Meet me by the water on campus... next to the river at 4 AM. Your favorite spot.

Similar request and terminology that was sent to Chloe. *Your favorite spot...* But even more chilling was the name and phone number of the sender.

She excused herself and Trent, and they stepped a few feet away from Lauren. She held the phone so Trent could see the screen.

He leaned in. "Is that—"

"Yep. Josh Ryder."

"How is that even possible? His phone was in lockup last night."

"I don't know what's going on, but I don't like it, and I'm going to get to the bottom of it."

"*We're* going to get to the bottom of it."

It was strange, after all these months of having a partner, that sometimes she still failed to remember she wasn't in this alone. And knowing someone had her back felt good.

THIRTY-TWO

Amanda wasn't one to put faith in the "sunshine and lollipops" philosophy of life, like everything was chipper and rosy. Blame it on her job and seeing the ugliness of mankind on a regular basis. People kept secrets and told lies, and she was starting to wonder about some of Jayne's and Josh's. The message that had hit Jayne's phone wasn't just identified by Josh's number. He was in her contact list. The reason for that might be innocent— friends by mutual acquaintance—but it might not be. Jayne was obviously close enough to Josh to respond *"OK"* and to show up. She'd trusted him. Even in the light of her friend's recent murder, and the fact she'd been killed in the early morning, Jayne had left her phone at home. He also seemed to know her favorite spot—or at least the sender of this text had.

Amanda walked back to Lauren. "Do you know why Josh Ryder would have texted Jayne to meet up here?"

"Josh? No idea. That's what happened? He asked to meet her here?"

She held the screen for Lauren to see.

"Huh."

"Were they seeing each other behind Chloe's back? Or after

the breakup?" Jayne had defended the split, saying Chloe and Josh were too young to make a commitment. Did she have a thing for him? And him, her? Even Lauren had accused Jayne of sleeping with Josh, back when they'd first interviewed the girls.

"I don't think so. Not really. I know what I said the other day, but I can't see Jayne doing that to Chloe."

Her words seemed sincere, but maybe she was good at acting. "He mentioned her 'favorite spot,' do you know where that was?"

Lauren nodded, her eyes brimming with tears. "Right around where she was... uh..." She swiped a finger under her nose. "Where she was found."

That would explain Lauren's *feeling* about where to find her friend. It told Amanda, though, that whoever had sent Jayne the text to meet knew she'd respond to a message from Josh *and* the best place to set the meeting. That would suggest, though, that Josh had at some point been at the river's edge with Jayne for the killer to see. It also made everyone on this campus suspect. "Was Jayne prone to going to the river in the early morning?"

Lauren shook her head. "No, but she'd hang out here at lunch, between classes, whenever she could."

So the killer had been banking on Jayne's relationship with Josh to get her out for four in the morning. Still, Josh had told her and Trent that time of day was far too early for him. Surely, if Jayne knew Josh well enough, she'd be aware the guy liked to sleep in. But then maybe given the circumstances of Chloe's murder and his "must talk," Jayne thought nothing of the hour. "We're going to need to take her phone with us."

"I understand." They'd need to notify Jayne's parents and go through the proper channels to legally use whatever they found on the phone, but just having it and seeing the text had them miles ahead of the game already. "Lauren, we're going to need you to stay in town in case we have more questions."

"Okay. I understand."

"Also, is there somewhere you could go for a while? Maybe to your parents'?" Amanda didn't want to scare the girl, but if someone was knocking off the roommates, Lauren was in danger.

"I can go there."

"Great. We'll need their information."

Lauren proceeded to give them their names, address, and cell phone numbers.

Amanda gestured for the officer to come for Lauren. "Please see her home and then to her parents'."

He dipped his head, and the two of them walked off.

Please stay alive! Amanda took a deep breath, straightened her back, and faced Trent. "Maybe Josh wasn't so wrong when he claimed someone wants to frame him."

"We just have to figure out who."

"Not Ashton Chambers, because he'd have no way to do this. Even if it's possible that he scheduled a text message before we pulled him in, he was still at Central early this morning. He couldn't have been here killing Jayne."

"So Ashton being at the park the morning of Chloe's murder may have been a coincidence."

"Could have been." She still wasn't fully convinced. Her phone rang, and she glanced at it. Deb Hibbert was calling. "I need to get this," she said to Trent and handed him Jayne's phone. He walked over to the CSIs as she answered the call. "Amanda Steele."

Trent glanced over a shoulder at her, seeming to have pieced together that it was a personal call based on how she'd answered.

"Amanda, I'm just calling to give you some updates," Deb said. "Colin Brewster had a paternity test done."

Deb paused there, and every second that passed was excruciating. Amanda braced herself for bad news but tried to remain positive. What were the chances that he was Zoe's biological father? She supposed that would be about fifty percent, given the timing of the mother's affair, but she wanted to believe none of that mattered.

"I wish I had better news, but he is a ninety-eight percent match to Zoe."

"He's... That was fast." Her legs became weak and buckled beneath her as her entire world spun. Just when life had become worth living again. Zoe had given her a sense of belonging and purpose, and their relationship was so natural. Amanda blinked back tears, failing miserably as some snaked down her cheeks. She was quick to wipe them, not wanting to appear emotional at a crime scene. "What happens now?"

It felt like an eternity before Deb spoke, but in reality, it was probably only seconds. "He wants to contest guardianship."

Everything became a blur around her—colors and people blending into one another. She felt lightheaded, like she could pass out at any moment. *Breathe. Calm. Focus.* From Zoe's perspective, she had a chance of meeting and being with her biological father. Wouldn't that be in her best interest? Amanda couldn't accept that. After all, Colin Brewster lived in California. If Zoe went there, she'd be taken from everything and everyone she'd ever known. How could that be a good thing, especially in light of the great loss she'd recently suffered? And on that note, how would she even be able to process that the father she'd known wasn't really her father? At least not by blood.

Deb went on. "Now, just because he's her biological father doesn't mean the court will side in his favor. So, please, don't believe this is the end of the road for you and Zoe. Okay?"

"Okay." The small word barely escaped from her mouth.

Her tongue felt so dry. Her throat stitched together. "What are the next steps?"

"He is flying in and has requested to meet Zoe. We do have to grant him this meeting. Then a judge will consider his claim and rule whether he should be granted guardianship. But, as I said, all is not lost yet. He is brand new to her life, and he lives in California. He has no desire to relocate to Prince William County. The girl's roots are here, and with her parents' recent murders, I can't imagine a judge ruling in his favor. But he is her biological father. There is the possibility that—"

"A judge will think it's best for Zoe to be with him."

"Yes."

Amanda hugged herself with one of her arms, the other one holding her phone to her ear. She didn't know if she had it in her to remain positive. She'd seen heaven transformed to hell firsthand. Life didn't play favorites or extend any guarantees. That was the cold, stark truth, and there was the very real possibility that Zoe would be leaving her life. She cleared her throat. "I've got to go."

"Please just stay strong. Hang in there, all right? I'll keep you posted."

Amanda nodded, as if the woman could see her, and ended the call. She didn't have the energy to say goodbye. Would more heartbreak be her reward for setting her sights high, for thinking she could actually have something good in her life again?

"Amanda." Trent was waving her over.

In the time she'd been on the phone, Rideout had arrived with his assistant. She'd been so caught up in the call she hadn't noticed until now. She went over to the small group next to Jayne's body. "Yeah, what is it?"

Trent gestured to Rideout, who had his gloved hands on Jayne's jaw. When the ME seemed to realize that Trent was staring at him to provide the update, he spoke. "I could be wrong, but I'm quite sure that our girl here bit her attacker."

"Epithelia?" A solid lead, even if it would take time to process the DNA in the lab.

"Appears so."

"Let's hope it gets us somewhere." She put her attention on Jayne, contemplated how the killer had suppressed her screams, paired it with this new information. *Something as simple as a hand over her mouth?* "Does it appear she was also stabbed by someone using their left hand?"

Rideout dipped a gloved fingertip lightly into one of the incisions and angled his head this way and that. "I'll know for sure once back at the morgue, but I'd say that's right. That left is right." He snickered.

She was still trying to form the image. "Is there any indication on her left arm that she was held like Chloe had been?"

Rideout took a closer look and shook his head. "Not seeing that, but I am noticing that it's possible these stabs weren't made while her attacker faced her."

She glanced at Trent. "So the killer came up on her from behind, unlike with Chloe, who was attacked from the front?"

Rideout squinted. "Seems likely from what I'm seeing."

Amanda painted the picture in her mind, and she realized how terrifying those final moments would have been for Jayne. The girl would have been standing next to the river in relative darkness with nothing but moonlight to illuminate the area—assuming she hadn't brought a flashlight. A quick look around confirmed for Amanda there wasn't any lighting down here. "He wrapped an arm around her, covered her mouth with his hand. That's when she bit him."

"And maybe she got a scream out when he reacted to being bitten? It probably caused him to drop his arm," Trent suggested.

"I'm just thinking, though, was anyone around to hear?" It was probably too much to hope that someone had seen or heard something.

Trent bobbed his head at the building they'd talked about earlier.

"Time of death?" she asked.

"Covered that with him." Rideout flicked a finger toward Trent.

Rideout's normally chipper mood was gone. Maybe that's what happened when he had to autopsy two college students in one week.

"TOD was within the last five to seven hours," Trent interjected.

She looked at the time on her phone. It was ten o'clock. So time of death was likely between three and five AM. Jayne was to meet "Josh" at four, so had she arrived earlier? "I can't imagine many around the campus at that time of day, but that coincides with that text message asking her to meet at four this morning."

"Yep."

"Plenty of time to kill her, clean her, pose her, and get away before the campus got busy." The situation felt even more tragic broken down in stages. Emotion crashed over her from two directions—sadness over the loss of life and fear that Zoe would be taken from her. But when she'd been broken before, she'd thrown herself into her job; it was comfortable, familiar. "Going back to the stab wounds. I was noticing they seem to be placed similarly to Chloe Somner's. Is that correct?"

"I have to get her back to the morgue and check the record to confirm for sure, but I would definitely concur that they're within the same vicinity. Just made using a different approach—from behind versus from the front. I'll confirm that for certain at autopsy."

"Okay, keep us posted on when that will be," she said, and stepped away with Trent. There were a couple of things niggling at her. Jayne's time of death was so early, yet it seemed the killer may have taken a precaution to silence her screams, but who was really around campus between three and five in the morning? And Jayne hadn't been found until seven, so there couldn't be a lot of foot traffic. She was also thinking about the message from Josh's phone number. "Someone went to a lot of trouble to make it look like Josh had lured Chloe and Jayne. Who and why?"

"Wish I knew, but I think it's called spoofing when a call or message shows one number but originates from somewhere else."

"Hmm. Someone is sounding techie, like Detective Briggs."

"Not sure I'm that good, but he might be able to figure out who the real sender is. Is that possible?" He shrugged.

"Not a clue. I'll pop a quick text about that to Briggs now." She pulled out her phone and did just that.

"Luke Hogan and Stephanie Piper seem rather cozy over there." Trent flicked his eyes in their direction.

"They *are* standing rather close to each other, and they could have reason to want Chloe and Jayne dead. Neither girl accepted them. Let's go have a chat."

THIRTY-THREE

Amanda was quite sure Luke and Stephanie had been holding hands when she and Trent started walking toward them. There were some quick movements and a little side shuffle that put some space between them.

"Detectives?" Stephanie said. It was sort of strange the way she'd said *detectives* with the arc of question, as if it was a surprise and odd that they'd be there.

"We'd like to ask you some questions. Please." She gestured to a clearing away from the curious ears around them. It was either there or down at Central.

The four of them moved over to the area Amanda had indicated. So much could be said in the silence. One message was clear: both were uncomfortable. Luke kept adjusting his posture, left leg out, left leg back, right leg out, right leg back. Stephanie's cheeks were flushed, and she was chewing her bottom lip.

"Do you know who it is?" Luke asked.

There was always something telling about the person who chose to speak first—it almost said even more than what was actually verbalized. The need to fill a silence could be seen as an aggressive move or even a sign of guilt. Though it could also be indicative of discomfort or wanting to silence one's nattering conscience. She had strongly considered Luke to be a prime suspect at one time, and his need to talk wasn't helping him right now. "We do."

"Is it Jayne Russell? I mean, that's what everyone's saying," Luke rushed to add.

Whether guilt or nervousness was the cause, Luke was trying to control the narrative.

"It is." She was keeping her responses succinct for a reason. She was playing on Luke's need to fill the void.

"You have any idea who could have done this to her?" Luke shifted his legs again. So uncomfortable. She passed a side-glance at Trent.

"Do you think it's the same person who killed Chloe?" Stephanie asked, either oblivious to the tension and awkwardness coming from Luke or not caring about it.

"Open investigation," Amanda said firmly. She set her gaze on Luke. "Where were you this morning between three and five?"

"With Stephanie." Luke wrapped his left arm around her, the girl's cheeks firing a bright red.

Amanda sought out his right hand, which would presumably be the one that covered Jayne's mouth, but he had that one in a pocket. She set her gaze on Stephanie. "Were the two of you together?"

"We were."

"And where was that?" Amanda countered.

"At my house," Luke said. "In my room."

Amanda didn't care for how Luke seemed to speak for Stephanie, and a look around confirmed their conversation was drawing attention from other students still lingering in the area. "There are some more questions we need to ask the two of you, but here isn't the place to do it."

"We can go inside if that would be better." Luke jacked a thumb over his shoulder to indicate the building behind them—the same one Trent had pointed out earlier.

"What's in that building?" Trent asked.

"Classrooms and labs," Luke replied.

"And is it open all hours?" Amanda jumped in.

"No. It's locked at eleven at night and opens at eight thirty in the morning. Why?" Luke narrowed his eyes.

Amanda gestured for the closest officer to come over, who happened to be Leo Brandt. "We're going to need you both to go to Central—"

"Wait. Does this mean that... that... you think we killed them?" Stephanie's voice was high-pitched, panicked.

"We just have some questions to ask. Procedure." Amanda gave her a pressed-lip smile. "Take them to Central," she directed Officer Brandt when he reached them. "We'll be there as soon as we can."

He left with the two students.

"They have motive, and they could have worked together on this. Just alibiing each other out?"

"Could be." She mulled over the facts of the case. "Putting oneself in Luke's shoes... He wanted Chloe, but she didn't want him. She was dating Josh. It could make sense that Luke couldn't stand seeing them together anymore."

"Except they broke up," Trent inserted.

"Luke might not have known that. We'll need to ask him."

"And the reason for killing Jayne?"

"You've got two girls who have been friends forever. One's not going to give any attention to a guy her friend doesn't approve of."

"You're saying Luke could have blamed Jayne for Chloe not giving him attention?"

"Just one theory."

"It could hold. And we know he has no real alibi for Chloe's murder, and he knows about orchids."

"Yep. Only thing is it *seems* Luke and Stephanie might be a couple. If they are, for how long? Why didn't either of them mention this to us? The first time we heard they were even friends was from Professor McMillan."

"Good question. But Luke being with Stephanie could indicate he'd given up on Chloe."

"Maybe, but I don't think so. I didn't get that feeling from talking with him. He was still hung up on Chloe, and she continued to outshine Stephanie."

"That could have upset Luke on top of his being snubbed by Chloe himself. It may have made him want to put an end to Chloe and Jayne and their demeaning nature toward him and Stephanie."

She hoped that was what had happened. It would mean there wasn't a serial killer stalking these college students and made it more likely that Lauren Bennett was safe. "We definitely need to talk to them again." Her phone chimed with a text message. She read it. "Briggs with a reply. It's called SMS spoofing when it's a text message, and there is a way to track it to the true sender, but it takes time."

"Great. One thing we don't have much of."

Another text filtered in. She scanned it and summarized. "We'll need a signed subpoena to obtain the information from Jayne's cell phone provider. Then Briggs can help us."

"Should be easy enough to get that signed off."

"You on it?"

"The second I find out who her provider is and we get back to the station. Could be something her parents know."

Her parents... Another notification. This week was relentless. Her phone pinged again, and she smiled when she read the message: *Once you have the subpoena, I'll get started tracking the sender right away.*

"Good one?" Trent leaned in, his arm brushing against hers.

She keyed back, *Thanks*. "It's Briggs again, being his usual helpful self. Once we get what we need, he'll handle the tracking."

"Notifying the parents next?"

"Dean Perkins first."

Amanda and Trent found Dean Perkins pacing behind his desk with a rocks glass in hand, amber liquid about a finger's width in the bottom. No ice.

He stopped and looked at them when they entered. "I can't believe this has happened to another student. Will you tell me who it is now? Not sure if the rumors are true. Was it Jayne Russell?"

She and Trent moved across the room, closing the distance between themselves and the associate dean, but still affording him space.

"It was. Did you know her well?" It felt like a sure bet he did and that was the reason for his emotional response this time.

"I do my best to know most of the students who go here, Detective," he said drily and swigged back some of his drink.

"That wasn't exactly an answer to Detective Steele's question," Trent said.

Amanda gave a discreet tug on the back of his shirt, hoping to tone down the aggression. "That's understandable, but you were close to Jayne?"

He nodded wildly and ran a hand under his nose. "She's my friend's kid. I watched her grow up."

Her shoulders and neck tensed. "We're sorry for your loss." The *we* had slipped in there again.

"What am I supposed to tell them?" He met her gaze, his eyes wet and wide.

"You don't need to tell them anything. That's our job. Just be there for them in the days ahead," she said.

"Will you two be informing them?"

"It's our next stop."

He downed the rest of his drink and set the glass on his desk with a thud. "What's going on? Do you have any idea who is doing this?" He dropped into the chair, suddenly, almost as if his legs simply gave out beneath him.

"We're still working on that," she said. "The building that faces the area where she was killed, we understand that it houses classrooms and labs?"

"That's right."

"Are there any surveillance cameras mounted on the exterior that cover where the murder took place?" she asked.

"We have cameras, but you'd need to check with campus security to see if any are on that building."

"Okay. We will. Also, is it normal for anyone to be on campus between three and seven in the morning?"

"I wouldn't say so. Some security and janitorial or support staff—maybe some students or faculty making an early start."

"We're going to need your help," she began.

He straightened his posture. "You name it."

"We need to know the names of everyone—staff and students—who was here this morning between three and seven. Also their purpose for being here. Could you get that list together for us?"

"Consider it done."

She handed him her card, even though she'd already given him one when they'd talked the other day. "My email is on there, along with my phone number, if you come across something else we should know. Thank you for your time and, again, sorry for your loss."

The associate dean closed his eyes and let out a sigh, and Amanda and Trent left.

They hit the campus security office before heading out—no cameras on the building that faced the water. There was one,

however, over the doors that led into the administration building. Amanda told them to expect a warrant for the footage.

"We get the list of students and staff who were there this
morning, and the video should only back that up," she said to
Trent as they walked back to the car.

"Only if they went into the main building."

"It's what we have to work with. But it's also possible
someone will show up on the feed who didn't come forward as
being here in the first place."

"Ah, that's who you're really interested in."

"Yep, and if that person exists, it might very well be our
killer."

"If I were the killer, I'd come forward with a valid reason for
having been on campus, so that I wouldn't stand out."

They got into the car, and she chewed on his words. She
hated to admit Trent could be right. "I have a feeling our killer
is right under our noses."

"Luke and/or Stephanie?"

"Could be. Them or someone else. Either way, this person
blends in and is able to do what they do without being seen." As
she said the words, pressure settled on her shoulders. It was like
they were chasing a ghost. All they truly had was circumstantial
evidence and suspicion paired with a shadowy figure on the
park's security camera. And a twenty-year-old cold case—if it
even factored in. "Stay on top of that Metro PD detective."

"Will do."

"We also need to follow up on the payment history from the
car service app."

"I'll handle that too, once back at the station."

They got into the car, and he clicked on the keyboard for
the onboard computer. "The Russells live in Dumfries."

"Let's get this over with." For the second time in a week,
she'd have to tell parents that their daughter had been
murdered.

THIRTY-FOUR

Connie and Ted Russell took the news about their daughter about as well as could be expected. Not good. At all. Connie had broken down in heaving sobs, and her husband rubbed her back in a circular motion, trying to calm her. They had no idea who could have wanted to do this to their "little girl." Amanda and Trent did walk away with the name of Jayne's cell phone service provider, though. She was attached to her parents' plan.

It was almost one in the afternoon when Trent pulled into the lot at Central. After notifying the Russells, they had stopped by Hannah's Diner for a coffee and a sandwich. Amanda hoped both stayed down.

Now she was seated across from Luke and Stephanie in an interview room while Trent worked on getting a subpoena approved for Jayne's phone records. He'd also received a message from the Metro PD detective with the information he'd requested on the Annie Frasier case.

Luke scowled. "What took you so long? We've been waiting for hours."

"I really shouldn't be here," Stephanie said. "I can't afford to get behind in my classes."

Amanda clasped her hands on the table. "Your cooperation is appreciated. We understand this must be a hard time for both of you." It was difficult to conjure compassion. A fellow student, and one they'd known no less, had been murdered, and Stephanie was concerned about her schooling. "Before we get started, can I get either of you something to eat or drink?"

"You could move us to a nicer room," Luke said. "You've got us in here like we're criminals."

"It's just a standard interview room." There were soft interview rooms that were set up with couches and throw pillows, painted in a soothing color, but Amanda wanted to drill home what was at stake. "Our conversation will be recorded." She pointed a finger to a box mounted in a corner of the room on the ceiling. The light on the unit was green. "What time did you get to campus this morning?"

"Eight," Luke said and took Stephanie's hand. "Together. We're seeing each other. There's no crime in that."

There wasn't, but Amanda noted how Luke liked to control the narrative—and Stephanie. "How long?"

"A few weeks?" Luke glanced at Stephanie, and she nodded.

Around the same time that Chloe and Josh had broken up. Had Luke really moved on? There was one thing niggling at her about that, though—and about them being a couple. "Why didn't you tell us you were seeing each other before now?"

The two of them looked at each other, silent communication passing between them.

"We figured how it might look to you," Luke said.

First Lauren was telling them how things would look. Now Luke. "And how's that?"

"Like we might have teamed up and killed Chloe? It's no secret she didn't return my interest in her, and she tramped all over Stephanie's ambitions."

She didn't miss the strong wording: *tramped all over.* That was quite an accusation. Also brazen to come out and serve up motive in a neat package. There wasn't any evidence of two people killing the girls. If two had, one could have held them while the other stabbed. There was nothing to support that, just as the video showed one mystery figure dropped off. It didn't mean they couldn't have conspired together, though. "Did you team up and kill Chloe and Jayne?"

"No," Stephanie spat. "And I wouldn't hurt anyone. It's just not who I am."

"Everyone is capable of murder given strong enough motive."

Stephanie slumped.

"Is that what being a cop does to your world view?" Luke pushed back.

She didn't care for his challenging attitude. Aggressive, temperamental, angry. "That's reality. Did you know that Chloe and Josh broke up?" She'd change tack to throw him off guard.

He withdrew his hand from Stephanie's. "No."

"They did. Three weeks ago. From the sounds of it, around the time you two started seeing each other." She put that out there but wasn't sure if it was of any consequence. "What were you two doing together this morning from three until you went to campus?" Hopefully the jumping around would serve to set them on edge, and if something incriminating jolted loose, that would be even better. She wanted to press the legitimacy of their relationship too.

Luke looked at Stephanie, and she nodded. He went ahead. "Sleeping. And then we were making out."

"That's all?" She'd expected to be told they were having sex. "Guess we could always ask your parents about your little sleepover, Luke."

"That's enough! We weren't killing Jayne!" Veins bulged in Luke's forehead.

"I never said you were." Cool. Calm. Composed.

"You drag us down here to *talk*"—he attributed finger quotes to the word—"but you think we're somehow involved in the murders."

"Honestly, Luke? We haven't ruled it out."

Stephanie's mouth gaped open, and tears pooled in her eyes.

Luke's expression hardened, his eyes intent, his features shadowed. "We didn't kill either one of them, though they deserved whatever they got."

Amanda drew back. "Whoa. That's quite a thing to say."

Stephanie shifted her chair away from Luke and rubbed her arms.

"What are you doing?" Luke asked her.

"I don't know who you are right now." Her brow furrowed, and her chin quivered.

Amanda stood and opened the door. "Miss Piper, you can leave if you wish."

The girl gave one last glance at Luke and did just that.

"Why does she get to go and I'm stuck here?"

Amanda was slow about returning to her seat and responding. Luke's shoe was tapping out a rhythm under the table.

"What do you know about phone spoofing?" She kept her tone even and relaxed as she sat back in her chair and got comfortable.

"I've heard of it. Not too hard to do."

"You've done it before?"

"Everything's on the internet."

"Not an answer to my question."

"No, I haven't."

"So, you've never sent text messages to someone pretending to be another person?" She leaned forward, inching into his personal space.

"No."

"Not to Chloe?"

"No," he pushed out with more emphasis.

"To Jayne?"

"Again, no," he hissed.

"You said you were familiar with the meaning of the black orchid because of your mother."

"Yeah. So?"

"We spoke to your mother to confirm your alibi for the time of Chloe's murder."

"She told me. And I was at home sleeping."

"That's what she said too."

"Then I don't get the problem."

"I was your age once," Amanda began, feeling a pang for her youth. "It's rather easy to sneak out of the house without parents knowing. Especially if you're determined."

"You think that I... that I..."

"It is possible."

"But I didn't kill her, or Jayne. Stephanie just said she was with me during the time you asked about this morning."

"And this is something your parents could confirm?" She dared bringing them up again, even though the last time had struck a nerve.

"Ah, no. She snuck into my room during the night."

Huh. "She loves you. More than you care about her." It was in the way Stephanie's eyes softened when she looked at him, how she was ready at his defense.

"How could you know—"

"It's in your body language, the way you look at her and talk to her. I think you're still in love with Chloe."

Seconds ticked off in silence. Luke didn't fill the void.

"Where did you get the black orchids, Luke?" She was going at him hard, but she was beyond frustrated with him. And this case. Two young women murdered within days, and she had no answers. On top of it, the cold case felt like it was looming overhead—even if it wasn't hers to solve or in any way related to Chloe's or Jayne's murders.

"I need a lawyer," he mumbled.

"Is that a formal request? If you have something to hide, it's a good idea, though."

He met her gaze, his eyes cold and dark. "I have nothing to hide."

"Could I see your right hand and arm?"

"Why?"

"Just in the name of nothing to hide."

He huffed but rolled up his sleeve and held out his right arm.

She pointed to a bandage on the side of his right index finger. "What caused that?"

"I tend to pet stray cats and one bit me this morning."

"May I see?"

Luke peeled back the bandage and revealed a bright red wound. Not human.

"Looks painful. Where was the cat?"

"In the back garden beneath my bedroom window."

She didn't know what to say to that, but would file it away for now. "You can cover it again if you wish."

Luke did so and pushed his sleeve back down.

"Do you know Ashton Chambers?" She watched him for any tells. His face was blank, as was his body language.

"Who's he?"

"What about the car service app, Pick Me Up? Have you heard of it?"

"Sure."

"Have you used them?"

"No, I have a car."

"Could I have a tech colleague of mine look at your phone?" It was a reach, but if he handed over his phone willingly, a legal warrant would be very easy to obtain. Going this route would also let them know if he'd been behind the spoofed messages faster than going through the cell service provider.

"No." Luke crossed his arms.

"All right. We'll go about it with a warrant, then." She moved to get up.

"Fine, I'll hand it over, but your colleague isn't going to find anything." He gave her his phone and the password to unlock it.

She got up. "Thanks again for your cooperation."

"Am I good to leave?"

She shook her head and left, despite his protests that it wasn't fair he was being held.

Malone stepped into the hall from the observation room next door. "Kid's got a temper."

"Yeah, and motive *and* lack of a solid alibi for Chloe." She held up his phone and said, "At least we got this."

"Uh-huh. Speaking of the whole spoofing thing..."

"Right. I guess you need some updating." She went on to do just that.

"Huh. He could have killed Chloe. This Stephanie girl could be lying about this morning. She might not have been with him."

She nodded, the thought definitely occurring to her. "People who love someone will say a lot of things."

"Well, she's still here. I sent her into the cafeteria to calm down. She was crying and shaking when she left the interview room."

"Great, I'll go talk to her now." She found Stephanie in the cafeteria slumped forward and staring at the table. "Miss Piper," she said quietly as she approached.

Stephanie lifted her head and sniffled, swiped at her cheeks. "He's always going to love her, even if she's a ghost. I'll always be runner-up. Why would I ever expect to come first?"

Amanda sat next to her. "I'm sure he cares about you." Not that she saw evidence of that.

"No, he doesn't. I've been deceiving myself." She faced Amanda and opened her mouth like she was going to say something else, but remained silent.

"Were you together this morning from three AM?" She did her best to ask without aggression or judgment.

Stephanie shook her head, and Amanda's heart sped up. "No?"

"No. I lied. I'm sorry. I just didn't know what to..." Her words disappeared.

Amanda should have put them in separate rooms and questioned them individually from the start. "Why did you lie?"

She wouldn't look at Amanda.

"Do you think he might have killed Jayne and Chloe?" Amanda asked.

She chewed her lip.

"What time did you and Luke meet up this morning?"

"Eight. On campus."

Goosebumps spread on Amanda's arms. "Where?"

"The other side of campus from where Jayne was found."

That meant nothing. Luke would have had plenty of time to dispose of Jayne's clothes and clean up and change himself. "Do you know when he got to campus? Did he arrive before you?"

"I don't know."

"Do you think he killed Jayne Russell?" She'd try the direct route again since it hadn't netted her an answer the last time she'd asked.

"I don't know."

"Stephanie, listen, it's important that you are honest with me. He can't hurt you. I promise you that."

She hesitated again, her mouth opening and closing like a fish breathing. Eventually, she said, "I really don't know what to think. Jayne was dismissive of him—me too, for that matter—but I didn't kill her."

"How was she dismissive?"

"It's pretty much like... well, she wouldn't give us the time of day."

That could have been their perception. "What makes you think he might have killed her? You said you didn't know, so there must be a small part of you that wonders if he did."

"Just his lying and dragging me into it." A few tears snaked down her cheek, and she let them roll off her jaw.

"Okay. You did the right thing by telling me this, Stephanie. Thank you for being honest."

"Do *you* think he killed Chloe and Jayne?" Her eyes wide, expressive.

"It's an open investigation, Stephanie, but he is a person of interest."

That set the girl into a crying jag, and it was several minutes before Amanda could get her calmed down enough to pass her to an officer for a ride home. After that, Amanda dragged herself to her desk, feeling like a damp rag.

Trent popped his head up over the divider. "Subpoena is approved for Jayne's phone records and the request has been made to the provider. I've updated Briggs with a text."

"Great."

"I also have the subpoena approved to get Pick Me Up to provide us with the payment method used from the ride requested Monday morning to the park. We'll have to go to the credit card company after that to get the person's name."

"Still, we're one step closer."

"As you know I received the info from the Metro PD. I took the liberty of seeing if any of the suspects in the Annie Frasier case cross over into our investigations or the university. The answer is none that I could find."

"Okay, well, we tried." It would have been nice to get closure for an old murder case while they were at, but the sad reality was not every homicide was solved. And without a connection to the recent murders, the good news was they probably weren't looking at a serial killer. Chloe's and Jayne's murders were isolated incidents, their lives taken by the same hand, no doubt, but the motive more personal in nature.

"And you? How did you make out?" His eyes went to the phone she held in her hand.

She brought him up to speed, and by the time she'd finished, he was staring at her, mouth agape.

"She lied to give him an alibi, meaning Luke has none for the time of Jayne's murder?"

"That's right. None for Chloe's either. There's nothing to prove he was in bed sleeping."

"We're holding him, then. What about Stephanie Piper?"

She shook her head. "No reason to. She's not involved."

He pointed at Luke's phone. "Should we have a look?"

She sat in her chair and entered the password. Trent joined her in her cubicle.

First, she went to his text messages, and there was nothing but one string of communication with Stephanie, whom was likely Stephanie Piper. Nothing incriminating, but given Luke's dry responses to Stephanie's messages to meet on different occasions, it was clear his heart wasn't in the relationship. It appeared as if he'd settled for Stephanie because he couldn't have Chloe. Amanda shared this observation with Trent.

"I guess it was too much to hope there was something on his phone screaming that he'd spoofed Josh's number?"

"Apparently. But I'm sure Briggs will be able to help us. There's probably something he can see that we can't."

"And it's possible that Luke handed over this phone because he used another number, a burner maybe, to do the spoofing."

"Ah, the intelligent criminal."

"Which we have to assume our killer is," Trent said, "given the thought, detail, and organization he demonstrates."

"True enough." After she backed out of the text messages,

she scanned through the various apps. One was Snap VidPic. "Hmm."

Trent leaned over her shoulder, and she caught a whiff of a pleasant-smelling fragrance.

She pulled her head back. "Are you wearing cologne?"

"Maybe," he dragged out.

"Since when?"

"I dunno. Just felt like splashing some on before work this morning."

"Just felt like it...?"

"Yeah." He pointed at Luke's phone, apparently signaling the end of her inquisition.

"He's on Snap VidPic from the looks of it." She opened the app and had no idea where to go next.

"Hand it over," Trent said, hand extended.

She reluctantly gave it to him.

"See this"—he pointed at a circle in the bottom right-hand corner—"that's the profile for the account. And that's the username." He pointed to the bold text at the top of the screen. The profile picture was a cat. "One minute..." He scurried to his desk, grabbed a piece of paper, and came back. "A list I made of profiles who spoke out against Chloe."

"Thinking Luke's looks familiar?"

"Yep... Ah, here it is. Luke said Chloe should get over herself and be made to feel small."

"Not entirely incriminating, but the guy is a ticking bomb, if you ask me," Amanda said. "He has a crush on her that's not returned. He stalks her online, hiding behind the picture of a cat." *The one that had bit him?*

"*Stalk* might be a strong word."

"Well, that's appropriate in my opinion. And he says to her online what he can't say to her face."

Trent bobbed his head and rolled his hand. "He gets out his frustrations."

"Only it's not enough, and he kills her."

"He very well might have."

"We've got to rip his life apart, Trent, starting with his bedroom." She was on the move, her phone to her ear. She was calling Judge Anderson for a verbal search warrant.

When she and Trent were down the road, she got a call from Malone, who'd noticed them leave the station in a hurry, and she told him what was going on.

"Great. I'll make sure Luke Hogan gets cozy in holding," Malone said, then hung up without another word.

THIRTY-FIVE

Amanda knocked on the Hogans' door, and Judy answered. They informed her of the purpose for their visit and that the search had been authorized by Judge Anderson. The approval came easily with Luke's lack of reliable alibis and the fact he'd had Stephanie Piper lie to cover him. His spewing of hate online was the cherry on top.

Judy didn't put up too much resistance, considering it was her child's freedom on the line, but she expressed her confidence in her son's innocence as she led them to Luke's bedroom on the second level.

Amanda and Trent gloved up and asked Judy to stay in the hall while they worked.

The space was moderate and functional. A bed, a nightstand, a student desk, and task chair. A large window faced the backyard and was situated over a trellis. She pointed that out to Trent and proceeded to lift the window.

"What are you doing?" Judy asked, her voice strained.

Amanda turned and held up a hand at the woman, who had stepped into the room. "Please stay at the door."

Judy returned to the doorway.

The window opened halfway. More than enough space to slip through, and she traced the edges of the screen with her eyes. There were some scuff marks. She gestured toward those. "He snuck in and out this way. No doubt."

"What are you saying over there?"

"Ms. Hogan, if it's easier for you, you can go downstairs."

The woman crossed her arms and jutted out her chin, but otherwise didn't move. "I'm fine right where I am. Thank you very much."

Amanda's phone rang, and she checked caller ID. It was Deb Hibbert. She was torn because she wanted to take the call, but it wasn't a good time. She rejected the call and sent Deb to voicemail.

Trent looked from Amanda to her phone, back up to her eyes, and she subtly shook her head.

"Personal. I'll take care of it later," she said.

They carried on their search of the room, looking for anything that might indicate Luke had killed Chloe and Jayne, but nothing was screaming *guilt* as much as Luke's lack of alibis for both murders. And his asking someone to lie for him. They found a laptop, which the warrant covered, and took it with them. Maybe there would be something on there to confirm guilt.

They saw themselves out, but Amanda told Judy they would be walking around the back of the house.

To Trent, she said, "Luke claims there's a cat that comes around and hangs in the garden outside his window."

"A lie? It's very possible that Jayne bit him."

"I actually think he might be telling the truth about the cat. I saw the wound, and it didn't look like a human had caused it."

They went through a gate and into the yard and caught sight of a rangy, black cat.

"Could be the one Luke was talking about," she said.

"Could also be a scapegoat in cat's clothing," he tossed back with a small chuckle.

"Huh. You just wanted to say that, didn't you?"

He held up his hands. "Guilty."

The existence of a cat only proved that Luke had given his defense some thought. And they could have been wrong about where Jayne's killer had been bit. It was obvious Luke had an escape route from his room. He could have slipped out Monday morning without his parents being aware. Same with that morning. "We need to escalate things with Luke. Get a swab of his DNA and find out his blood type."

Trent nodded. "Rule him in or out for what was found on the snail at the Somner crime scene, and to have something to run against the epithelia pulled from Jayne's teeth. You think a judge will sign off on it?"

"We got this far, and there's a lot stacking up against him." She thought again of the growing list: no alibis, knowledge of black orchid symbolism, the unrequited feelings, and online bullying against Chloe.

"We could always start by asking Luke nicely and go from there?"

"Couldn't hurt," she agreed. "We'll also get approval for his phone records and start digging into that too."

"And we have this." Trent held up Luke's laptop.

They got into the car and headed back to Central. Her phone pinged with a message from Rideout. "Autopsy for Jayne Russell is scheduled for tomorrow morning at nine," she told Trent.

He simply nodded and kept driving.

As she held her phone in her hand, her gaze landed on the voicemail icon in the top left-hand corner. She dialed in and listened to Deb's message, holding her breath the entire time. She hung up and pocketed her phone.

"Everything all right over there?" Trent asked.

"Yeah, why?"

"For one thing, the energy in the car just got weird, and you're quiet. That doesn't happen a lot." He tagged on a small smile to his statement.

"I'll try not to take offense at that."

Full-blown grin, then it faded when she didn't reciprocate. "There *is* something wrong."

She pushed her head against the back of the seat. "You could say that." She pinched the bridge of her nose, a headache blooming behind her eyes.

"Anything I can do?"

Her instinct was to respond that it was none of his business, but she couldn't bring herself to do that for some inexplicable reason. "It's Zoe."

"She's all right. Right?"

"Yeah." *For now*, Amanda thought, but when the girl found out that a stranger was her actual father and the one she'd seen murdered hadn't been... well, that just might screw her up for life. And that wasn't even getting into the fact this stranger could swoop in and take Zoe all the way to California.

"You don't have to talk to me if you don't want to. I understand." He went back to looking out the windshield, but his gentle tone and compassion had her wanting to open up.

"Remember that Mrs. Parker had an affair around the time of Zoe's conception?" He'd worked the Parker case with her and would be aware of that fact, if he remembered.

"Uh-huh— Oh." He twisted his hand on the wheel, then shot her a quick look before facing forward again.

"He's taken a paternity test, and he's her biological father."

"Whoa."

"Yeah."

"So, he's... what? Wanting to come and get her?"

Bless him for struggling to find the right words, but there

was no easy way to ask. "It's looking that way. He's requested to meet her tomorrow after school."

"Sorry to hear that, Amanda. But maybe he just wants to see her, nothing more beyond that."

"I hope you're right, but it's sounding like he wants to pursue his right as her father." As she spoke the words, she felt something inside her break—it was a piece of herself that she'd barely managed to stitch together, and it was being ripped apart again. "I can't lose her."

He awkwardly reached over for her shoulder, but ended up going for her hand in her lap. Their hands barely grazed, and he pulled back.

"Ah, I'm sure it will work out the way it should," he said.

"Her with him." She hated how the pain was swirling in her chest, making it harder and harder to breathe.

"No, with you."

Why do I still feel where his hand touched mine? The thought zapped her and left her confused. It was best to ignore any "feelings" toward Trent. "As always, I appreciate your confidence."

"You'll see." He nodded and smiled.

"Thanks." And for the trace of a second, she allowed herself respite in his calm serenity, a place where happy outcomes existed. The moment was brief, blowing up in the face of reality. Good things didn't last.

THIRTY-SIX

Amanda and Trent were across from Malone in his office, updating him on the search warrant results.

"He's still looking good for this, if you ask me," he said when they'd finished.

She was pleased he felt that way. "Do you think we have enough to request his DNA and blood type through the legal channels? That is, if he doesn't volunteer them?"

"I think it's a dicey situation that could go either way. As we have nothing but conjecture and circumstantial evidence, you struck it lucky with the search warrant, in my opinion."

"You can't be serious?" She never would have expected Malone to be blind to how things were pitted against Luke Hogan. And hadn't he just expressed thinking Luke appeared guilty one second ago?

"I most certainly am. And going back to your question— Yes, ask first and see if you can find out exactly when he got to campus this morning and build a timeline. One murder at a time."

"Will do." Amanda felt the pressure of the ticking clock. They could only hold Luke for so long, and it was four forty-five. Five o'clock marked the end of her shift, and she wanted to leave right on the dot to get home to Zoe. That left her with twenty minutes and a suspect to interview. She still hadn't called Deb Hibbert back, but she had to collect herself before making that call.

She got up quickly and said, "Gotta get a move on."

"Why? Are you in hurry or something?" Malone raised his eyebrows.

"You could definitely say that." She left the office without elaborating.

It took seven minutes to get Luke hauled from holding.

She and Trent went into the room and sat across from him.

"Let me guess, you didn't find anything."

She remained quiet for a few beats, then, "Actually, we found something of interest. You're on Snap VidPic." They'd found that before searching Luke's bedroom but hadn't yet shared that discovery with him.

Luke paled, and his shoulders slumped. "So?"

"*So* you followed Chloe's account and spewed hateful things on there."

He scoffed, "The least of the things I thought."

"All right. Now I'm having a hard time understanding. You loved her, but you hated her?" She faced Trent. "They do say the two emotions lie close together."

"I loved her until she made me hate her," Luke spat.

"You realize you're under suspicion of murdering her," Trent interjected.

"I also know I didn't."

"Then you wouldn't mind letting us swab your mouth for your DNA," she said firmly.

He leaned back. "I don't know about that."

"You have nothing to hide, so why not?" She hitched her shoulders.

He blew out a long, exaggerated breath. "Fine."

Amanda nodded to Trent, who had the swab kit ready to go. He rounded the table, took the sample, placed it in the vial, then sat back down.

"We'll get this to the lab straight away," he said to Luke.

"Good. Clear me."

"What blood type are you, Luke?" she asked him, thinking about the blood spatter on the snail.

"No idea. Why?"

"When did you get to campus this morning?" Amanda ignored his question and resisted the urge to glance at the clock.

"Eight. Stephanie and I told you."

"Only Stephanie said she'd lied for you. That you asked her to."

He dropped his head in his hands and pulled on a chunk of his hair.

"Why ask her to lie?" Trent asked.

Luke cracked his knuckles and stared into space.

"When did you get there, and what were you doing from three until eight this morning?" Amanda bit back the urge to supply him with an answer. *Killing Jayne?*

"I wasn't at the campus early."

"All right, where were you, then?"

He slid his bottom lip through his teeth.

"Where were you?" she asked with heat.

"Leesylvania State Park."

The hairs stood on the back of her neck. "Why were you there?"

"I had to see for myself."

"See what?" She wasn't liking the direction of the conversation.

"Where Chloe died."

"And where was that exactly?" she countered.

He described the precise location in the park.

"How do you know the place where she was murdered?" The specific spot hadn't been made public news.

"I... ah..."

"How did you know?" she repeated coolly.

He wiped his brow and met her eyes. "She loved the snails, and I might have followed her there a couple of times. I... watched her and Josh have sex in the woods before." His lips curled in disgust, and there was something in his gaze that chilled her.

The first time they'd spoken, Luke said he'd just *heard* that Chloe went to the park. Not seen it for himself. "You watched them have sex? Don't you realize how wrong that is?" Her voice was strained, but she was revolted. It was clear Luke lacked a basic sense of right and wrong, on top of his volatile temper.

"It was only wrong that she was with him!" he roared.

Amanda was the first to stand, Trent not far behind.

"Where are you going?" Luke was shaking with anger.

"We're leaving, and you're spending the night in a holding cell." She held the door for Trent, then went through after him.

In the hall, they could still hear Luke's cries and claims of innocence.

"I don't like the way any of this is working out," Trent said.

"Makes two of us." Malone came down the hall, having exited the observation room. His hands were in his pockets. "There's a lot pointing at him, but I still wonder."

She angled her head and leveled her gaze at her boss. His opinion kept flip-flopping. "About...?"

"He was so caught up—it would seem—with Chloe Somner, but there was no evidence of sexual assault?" Malone stopped there and pushed his lips together thoughtfully, and Amanda understood where he was headed.

"You'd think if he was going to kill her, he would have raped her too," Amanda concluded.

"Bingo." Malone snapped his fingers.

"Still, the guy watched Chloe, someone he had a thing for, have sex with someone else and had the strength to stay at a distance. Perverse, and it shows restraint. Just like Chloe's killer," Trent said.

Malone held up his hands. "No argument there."

"Why didn't he rape her, though?" Trent mumbled.

She thought back to the crime scene. "The killer presented Chloe as if she was clean and pure. He left her undefiled. Certainly not how Luke viewed Chloe, it would seem." She faced Trent. "You saw his reaction when he told us he'd watched Chloe having sex with Josh. The act cheapened her in his eyes. Then factor in the bullying on Snap VidPic..."

"I'm not really confident we have enough to hold him," Malone said.

"You must be kidding," Amanda blurted out. "We still have his laptop to look at and we get his blood type and—"

"No. I'm making the call. We're cutting Hogan loose. We get more evidence against him, something on his computer or"—Malone pointed at the protected swab in Trent's hand—"a DNA match. Then we'll discuss our next steps with Hogan."

She didn't respond, simply started walking down the hall. She could feel Malone's and Trent's gazes on her, but she kept moving. If she didn't get the hell out of there, she'd say something she wouldn't be able to take back. Besides, she had to get home for Zoe, and the sooner the better. Amanda wasn't just going to be there for dinner, she was going to prepare it. She keyed a text to Libby to let her know, then peeled out of the lot. Deb Hibbert could wait until tomorrow. From here until home, she had to just breathe and shake the grief, the anger and the frustration that came with this case. The investigation had just hit a wall, and that was tough to accept.

THIRTY-SEVEN

Last night was exactly what Amanda had needed. Instead of cooking, she took Zoe out for a burger and fries at Zoe's favorite place. She and Sir Lucky set up in the booth opposite Amanda. Amanda savored every moment she spent with the sweet girl more than ever, now aware there was the possibility she could be taken away. But Amanda wouldn't let Zoe go without a fight. She owed that much to Zoe and herself. Theirs was a relationship and a future worth defending.

After dinner, they went home and played snakes and ladders, a game Zoe's mother had played with her. When they bored of that, they watched Disney's *Frozen* again. An obvious favorite of Zoe's, as the girl happily watched it any chance she got, but Amanda would graciously accept that if it meant Zoe would stay in her life.

In the time she spent with Zoe, the job melted away. The stress, the exasperation, even the emotional burden that came with notifying next of kin was lessened somewhat. It was never easy seeing the faces of people who were being told their loved one was murdered. Gone. Just like when she had been informed that Kevin and Lindsey hadn't made it. Not murder, but equally devastating and unexpected. It was always hard for her to deliver the news to those left behind because she'd been in their place. Finality. Never to hear a loved one's voice again, see their smiles, warm from their laughter. Nothing left but a void of darkness and despair.

But Zoe had a way of zapping Amanda's personal memories so they hurt less, a soothing balm for the pain from the past while providing a promise for the future. Zoe had saved Amanda, and now Amanda would return the favor. She would be there to help Zoe navigate her own hurdles through life for as long as she could, as long as Zoe would let her.

It seemed all was forgiven from the other night when Amanda hadn't gotten home in time and Zoe had spent the night at Libby's. Ah, the sweet forgiveness of a child. That in itself was a healing ointment.

It was now Friday morning, and Amanda was dropping Zoe off at school.

"I packed your favorite," she said, handing a Dora the Explorer lunch bag to her.

"PB and J?" Zoe was grinning, and her tongue flicked her front lower tooth. Her eyes widened, and she snapped her mouth shut.

Amanda got the feeling it was something more than the sandwich that warranted that reaction. "Let me see..." Amanda moved in and looked in Zoe's mouth.

"It's loose," she garbled, her mouth wide open, tongue pushing the tooth.

Amanda chuckled. Kids could be so dramatic. In all fairness, so were some adults. "Oh, that's exciting. When it goes, you know what that means, right?" She assumed Zoe would; it wasn't her first baby tooth to hit the road. She had one adult bottom tooth already.

"The Tooth Fairy." She clapped her hands and took the lunch bag. "This is the best day ever."

Amanda mussed her hair and kissed her forehead. "Have a good one, sweetheart."

"You too, Mandy."

With that, she was out of the car in a blur of color and excitement. Amanda was left behind in a wake of memories. Lindsey had the Tooth Fairy visit only once before she died.

But, Amanda sat up and took a deep breath, *Zoe is the future.*

An hour and a half later, Amanda stood in front of a cadaver at the Office of the Chief Medical Examiner with Trent and Rideout. Oh, how her life presented such contrasts. One could get whiplash.

Jayne Russell appeared so small under the harsh lighting of the morgue, and her skin was more bluish than Chloe's had been.

"I've conducted the preliminary already. As you know, I suspected epithelia in the victim's front teeth. That's been confirmed and sent to the lab."

"Good." She thought back to Luke's "cat bite," but that was really all it had looked like. His DNA would still be tested for due diligence, but it wasn't a quick process. She still thought they had enough to hold him and get his blood type from his medical records, but once Malone had his mind made up, there was no changing it. And it didn't help their case against Luke that Trent had looked at Luke's laptop last night and found nothing incriminating. Trent arranged for it and Luke's phone to be returned to him.

"She was stabbed seven times. This one"—Rideout indicated an incision on her left clavicle—"is indicative that her attacker did circle from behind. Just as you theorized at the crime scene."

"Is that also the wound that killed her?" she asked, thinking that would have worked effectively to silence her screams.

"No. One to the heart again, but I believe it was inflicted second."

"But why continue with five more blows if he'd already killed her?" Trent asked.

"Does the number seven mean something to him?" she kicked out. Annie Frasier entered her mind, but she'd only been stabbed three times.

"It could be a compulsive thing," Rideout suggested. "Like OCD? Maybe the killer had the *need* to inflict the other wounds."

"Good idea." They could add this to the profile for their killer, but she had to admit she hadn't seen any evidence of this with Luke Hogan. "But what compelled him to kill these girls in the first place?"

"Ah, that's your job to figure out. Me? I stick to the bodies." Rideout grinned at her.

She smiled back. "What else is this one telling you?"

"The killer would have been six foot to six foot four, thereabouts."

"As was the case with Chloe Somner," Trent said.

Rideout nodded. "No sexual assault, as was the case with victim one. Unlike victim one, though, this one doesn't have bruising on her arm. The evidence has supported earlier speculation that she was attacked from behind."

Amanda tried to figure out if that meant anything beyond trying to muffle her screams. It would seem there was another reason as the campus likely would have been deserted. Though the killer probably didn't want to take yet another chance of being exposed. And certainly Jayne would have reacted strongly at the killer's approach, especially after realizing it wasn't Josh coming toward her. Amanda was curious, though— was the killer someone who Chloe would have recognized and let get close, but who would have alarmed Jayne if he'd approached head on? Who could that apply to, or did it even factor in? The chosen location for killing Jayne was certainly a bold and risky one. Yet he'd still gone about laying out the body with meticulous care, like there was no need to hurry. And what motive bridged two friends beyond the people they'd bullied?

"Same type of weapon used?" Trent asked, when she hadn't said anything.

"Appears so. Yes. And there was this in one of the wounds." Rideout turned and plucked a small evidence bag off a wheeled table. He held it up for them, and Amanda took it.

"A piece of metal. Part of the blade?" she asked, hopeful.

"I'd say so."

She wasn't sure why a light of hope even sparked at this discovery. They still had to find a suspect and a murder weapon to compare.

Rideout told them he hadn't gleaned much else and it was time to "dig in," as he'd put it. Amanda and Trent hung around for a while and left at noon. Just before they did, Rideout told them that he'd released Chloe's body on Wednesday. "As far as I know, the family has planned the funeral service for tomorrow."

"Thanks," she told him.

On the way to the car, Trent said, "So, we're looking for left-handed killer with OCD."

"He used his left hand to stab, anyway," she amended, sticking to the technicality. "Just because he stabbed with his left, it doesn't mean it's the killer's dominant hand. He could even be ambidextrous." Her phone rang, and her heart sank at the caller ID. Trent kept walking to the car while she stopped and answered. "Hello, Deb."

"I'm just calling to make sure you got my message yesterday. I haven't heard from you."

Amanda's normal excuse would be her job, but that probably wasn't advisable in a situation where she needed to prove herself readily available to the six-year-old girl she wanted to adopt. "I did. I apologize for not calling back."

"I appreciate this isn't an easy spot to be in, but we need to grant him this meeting."

"When? Ah, where?" Details other than later that day hadn't been part of Deb's voicemail.

"Four o'clock. Here at our office in Woodbridge."

"It might be a little tight with Zoe getting out of school at three thirty, but we'll be there as close to four as we can."

"See you then."

"Yep." Amanda hung up and found Trent milling about outside the car. He was pretending to be absorbed in something on his phone, but he looked up rather quickly as she started to approach.

"The adoption agency?" he asked.

"Yeah." She'd have to tell Malone she'd be cutting out early. She'd also have to let Libby know she'd be picking Zoe up from school.

"Hope it all goes the way you want it to."

She smiled at him. That was the best thing he could have said right then. If he'd gone all positive on her, she'd have lost it on him. She pointed at his phone. "You have something to share?"

"Uh-huh. We have the payment method from the Pick Me Up app. Now we'll get a subpoena for the cardholder and be one step closer to our killer."

Inch by inch... "And while we're waiting on that, we also need to find out the time and location for Chloe Somner's funeral. Her killer may very well show up."

THIRTY-EIGHT

The rest of the workday went far too fast considering what Amanda had ahead of her. She and Trent were able to confirm the details for Chloe Somner's funeral. Four o'clock tomorrow afternoon at a church in Woodbridge. Briggs still hadn't made progress on who was behind the spoofed SMS texts to Chloe and Jayne. But he had uncovered deleted texts on Jayne's phone that indicated she had started seeing Josh romantically in the last week. So whoever the killer was, they must have been aware of Josh and Jayne's shifting relationship to know their text to meet would work. But still, they were no further ahead on suspects. The subpoena on the credit card used to order the ride from the car service was approved and put through to the credit card company. More waiting.

The associate dean at the university sent a list of students and faculty who said they were on campus during the hours of three and seven Thursday morning, and there were only a handful. Officers had interviewed several students, and no one saw or heard anything. The camera feed was sent over from the school too. It showed nothing useful at first glance. But sometimes things clicked from a fresh perspective or with another take.

It didn't help that Amanda was preoccupied with the meeting at the agency. She wanted to be as honest with Zoe as she could, but she didn't think it was a good idea to come out with the fact this man was her biological father. That was unnecessary and would only be confusing. As far as Zoe was concerned, she'd seen her father murdered in front of her eyes. And he was the man who had cared for her and raised her to that point—a father in the most important sense. Would Zoe even have much understanding of what a biological parent was? Amanda spoke with Deb, and they decided the best route was to explain the man to Zoe as being someone who'd been a friend of her mother's. Honest, safe, neutral. For now.

The adoption services building really wasn't much to look at. A dull, redbrick, single-story structure that made Amanda think of a retirement community.

She parked her Honda Civic and turned to Zoe. "You don't have to talk to him for long. Just meet him. Be nice." A silly thing to say as the girl was kind to everyone.

"I will. But I don't understand."

"Like I told you... He was a friend of your mother's."

"But why does he want to meet me?" Her face scrunched up.

"You're kidding me, right? Who wouldn't want to meet you?" Amanda grinned. "Just do it for me. Okay? Five minutes?" *Now I'm petitioning for the guy?*

"Okay." Zoe got out, Lucky clutched under an arm.

Amanda followed and locked the car.

The receptionist sent them right to a conference room where Deb Hibbert was seated next to a forty-something man in a pressed suit. He wore an overpowering cologne that sent Amanda into a brief sneezing fit.

"Oh, here." Deb plucked a tissue from a box and gave it to her.

"Thanks." She took her hand from Zoe, who resisted letting go at first.

Zoe was staring at the man, drawing Amanda's eyes back to him. *Stuffy* could be a good word to sum up the first impression. Back ramrod straight, like he'd been sitting against a ruler his entire life. His black power suit held a fine sheen inherent to expensive fabric and was tailored perfectly to his frame. He paired it with a plain, white, collared shirt and black tie. There wasn't a single wrinkle in sight. His shoes were black and glossy and picked up the light from the overhead fluorescents.

"Amanda Steele, this is Colin Brewster," Deb said.

She held out a hand to him, which he shook. His grip was firm, but the hold brief. When he finished, he wiped his hand on a tissue.

How is this guy ever going to have a kid? But maybe she was being rash and jumping to conclusions too quickly. He wasn't the enemy... Only he was. Or could be.

"And this, of course, is Zoe Parker." Deb added a large grin to that introduction.

The man peeled his eyes from Amanda to land his gaze on Zoe. She had tucked herself behind Amanda's leg, and Amanda put a hand on the girl's shoulder. Colin didn't budge from his chair. He just kept looking at her, studying her, as if she were a specimen in a jar.

"You flew in and called for this meeting," Amanda began. "I'm thinking you have something you want to say to her." Honestly, his behavior was pissing her off. This man came for what purpose? Just to upset things, confuse Zoe? To appease his conscience? To satisfy some curiosity he had about the child?

Deb jumped in with, "Anyone care for water or a coffee? Zoe, can I get you an orange juice?"

"Apple," both Amanda and Zoe said at the same time.

"She prefers apple," Amanda clarified and pinched Zoe's nose. Zoe giggled. Even through all of this, Colin's expression was devoid of emotion, and he just kept staring at Zoe. "I'll take a coffee," Amanda added, and Deb left the room.

The tension in the space was tangible and awkward. Amanda felt the need to make things better—for Zoe's sake. The girl was looking up at Amanda. "Honey, why don't you sit over there and draw?" She nudged her head toward a small table, where blank paper and coloring books were located along with a glass container of crayons.

"Okay." Zoe ambled over, not looking too impressed by the idea but complying nonetheless.

"And I brought these." Amanda pulled a small sandwich bag full of apple fries and a piece of cheese from her pocket.

"Oh." Zoe happily snatched them up.

Once the girl was situated, Amanda sat in a chair facing Colin, and she crossed her legs. They made uncomfortable eye contact just as Deb returned. She handed Amanda her coffee and took the juice over to Zoe.

"Thank you," Zoe said.

"You wanted to meet her. She's here, but you're somewhere else," Amanda said.

He shook his head. "It's just a lot to take in." He tossed out what could be considered the beginning of a smile, but the expression didn't fully form.

Stuffy *and* socially inept.

Deb's attention went to Zoe at the table. "Zoe, Colin was a friend of your mother's. He came a long way to see you."

Zoe didn't say anything but continued crunching on her apple.

"Her eyes look so much like Angela's. It's almost like I'm seeing her again." Colin was apparently in his own world—or *planet*, from the sounds of it. Did he not take any of this seriously? And to think Amanda was stuck here while Chloe and Jayne's killer roamed free.

"Colin was telling me that he has a beautiful house in California," Deb said, as if attempting to smooth out a path for conversation.

"I make good money as an investment banker," Colin added stiffly. He even tugged on his jacket, and Amanda thought of a peacock ruffling its feathers to present a show.

She wasn't impressed. And it would take a lot more than some rigid banker from LA, or wherever he was from in California, to do so. In her career, she'd done a lot of sizing people up— one could say it was a mainstay of the job—and in her opinion, Colin Brewster wasn't father material, let alone *single* father material. "Did your wife not join you for this trip?" She didn't know his life situation, and her question might be insensitive, but she wanted to get more of a feel for him.

"I'm not married."

"Oh. So you'd be..." Amanda glanced at Zoe, realizing she couldn't finish that sentence as intended. Something along the lines of *raising Zoe alone.*

"Yes. Well, I am engaged to be married."

Drying paint could be bored by this guy.

"Ah, Zoe," Colin said.

"Yes?"

"What's your favorite color? Mine is—"

"Blue."

"Red," Colin said, the word dripping from his mouth with disappointment.

Did he actually think he could bond with Zoe over color preferences? He didn't even have the decency to let her answer first. He'd have had a better chance talking about her stuffed dog, but he didn't seem very observant.

"How did you know my mom?" Zoe dropped the crayon from her hand and angled her head, awaiting his answer.

Colin let out a measured sigh, so expertly that Amanda barely noticed. "It was a long time ago," he began. "We used to work together."

"You live here?"

"Well, not anymore. I live in California, where the movie stars do. There's the ocean and palm trees and..." Colin prattled on, infusing his tourist brochure bullet points with enthusiasm, but it petered out as he continued to speak. Probably because Zoe didn't appear impressed. Hard to say if she was even listening. She'd picked up her crayon again and had resumed drawing. "You'd like it there," he added, and Amanda shot him a glare.

"She likes it here too," she pushed out.

Deb fussed with the lay of her shirt.

"You thinking of moving here?" Amanda asked, even though she knew the answer to that already.

"My work is in Cali, so no." His gaze drifted to Zoe, who was focused on some creation.

As far as first meetings went, Amanda had to surmise this one was going horribly. Score that in her favor column. Hopefully. But would a judge care when it could be proven he was Zoe's biological father?

"I do have a huge house, though, and I'll have a live-in nanny to help care for—" He stopped abruptly under Amanda's glare and cleared his throat. "Arrangements are in place."

"Your fiancée must be excited," Amanda said.

His composure slipped at that question. His shoulders lowered incrementally, and he tapped a hand to his brow as if dabbing away sweat, but it appeared dry. "She's coming around to the idea."

"Coming around?" Amanda just wanted to swoop Zoe up and leave this room. They'd never look back. There was no way she could allow this man to take her away. None.

"It will all be fine by the time everything goes through." His voice was tight, but his demeanor was arrogant. He glanced at Deb and smiled. It wasn't returned.

"Well, if there's nothing more you'd like to say to Zoe..." Amanda slapped her hands on her knees. Zoe got up from the table, grabbed Lucky, what was left of her snack, the picture she'd drawn, and walked over to Amanda. The poor girl was just waiting for a reason to leave. *Atta girl!*

"It was nice meeting you," Colin said lamely.

Zoe waved at him and gave him a half-hearted smile.

Deb followed them into the hall. "I'll call you later." She tapped a hand on Amanda's shoulder.

Amanda and Zoe left the building and got into her Civic.

"This is for you." Zoe held up her drawing.

Amanda took the picture, impressed by how fast she'd whipped it up, but it was what it portrayed that had her smiling. Five stick figures: a girl with a dog; two women holding hands; and two women holding a yellow circle—one with blond hair and one with red. She knew from previous pictures the yellow circle was a police badge. Amanda would guess that was her and Becky, and the others were Zoe, Libby, and her girlfriend, Penny. The characters were standing in front of a house, and there was lettering that arched across the top of the page. *My Family xoxo*

Tears pricked Amanda's eyes, but she smiled to suppress the urge to cry. "Yes, we are, sweetheart." She leaned across the console and pulled the girl in for a tight hug and tapped a kiss on the top of her head.

As Amanda drove them home, she thought about the picture and what it revealed. Zoe had an inkling what today's meeting with Colin was about, and she was taking her stand. She wanted to stay with Amanda.

THIRTY-NINE

Amanda admired Zoe's beautiful picture from yesterday that now adorned the fridge door. She'd put it up the moment they got home, but she had an idea of something else she wanted to do with it. That would have to wait, though.

It was Saturday morning, and the original plan had been to take Zoe to the aquarium. But Chloe Somner's funeral this afternoon had ruined that good intention. There was no way she and Trent could skip attending. The suspect pool was shallow—if even existent at this point—but someone might stand out at the service. Maybe even Luke Hogan would do or say something that would have Malone authorizing them to bring him back in. Waiting on his DNA results would take far too long. There were also other results they were waiting on, though. One, who had paid for the drive to the park Monday morning. Two, who had spoofed Josh's phone.

She hated that she had to postpone the fun outing, and it reminded her of the times she'd also missed out on with Lindsey because of some case. If only Amanda had known how short her time would be with her little girl, she would have squeezed every minute dry. If Zoe was taken from her by the doofus,

Colin, Amanda's time with Zoe could also be approaching its end. She should send Trent to the funeral by himself. That was the mother in her. But two sets of eyes were always better than one, and she had a responsibility to be there. After all, she owed it to the two young women who had been murdered—one of whom would be lowered into the ground today, the other to follow soon.

It was the guilt that had her making a humongous batch of pancakes this morning. Zoe was happily munching away on them, but she didn't know their plans for today had fallen through. Amanda had never mentioned them to her. She had only let Lindsey down once due to the job because that was all it had taken to adopt a new strategy. After that first time, she had avoided getting Lindsey psyched up about a trip or outing just in case she couldn't follow through. She became good at surprising her daughter at the last minute, never risking the disappointment. She wanted to do the same with Zoe. Never disappoint her. Too late on the *never* part, but she was determined not to let it happen often.

Zoe's cheeks were puffed out like a chipmunk's full of nuts.

Amanda laughed. "Maybe take smaller bites before you choke." *Or swallow that loose tooth...*

"I'm... okay." Zoe managed to talk around all the pancake in her trap like a pro. Mumbled, garbled, but coherent enough to make out.

"So this afternoon, I'm going to take you to see Kristen and Ava." Maybe one day Zoe would call them her aunt and cousin, but it wasn't that time yet.

Zoe swallowed, then smiled. "Fun."

She and Ava, Amanda's niece, had really bonded in the last couple of months. It probably helped that they both knew Libby. Ava had her as a teacher when she'd attended Dumfries Elementary. Ava was thirteen now, in high school, and was in need of spending money, so sometimes Amanda threw babysitting dollars her way.

"But I need to go to work," Amanda added.

Zoe looked down at her plate and used her fork to push some strawberries through maple syrup. She popped one in her mouth.

"I'd rather be with you, but sometimes—"

"I know. You help people."

The compliment had Amanda sitting back. "I do my best."

"You helped me." She sounded melancholy. "Mommy taught me not to be selfish, to share my toys." She lifted her gaze to meet Amanda's. "I need to share you."

This little girl was an older spirit, and her appreciation and compassion melted Amanda's heart. "Thank you for understanding, sweetie."

"Yes, I'm the best." She grinned, syrup running down her chin. She started laughing and dabbed at the sticky trail. Her fingertips now glistened, and the laughter became more raucous.

Amanda joined in. This was heaven. This right here. As Kevin had once said with Lindsey, the messier the meals the better.

Amanda was still smiling as she and Trent headed to the church where the funeral was taking place for Chloe Somner.

Trent looked over at Amanda. "You seem awful happy to be heading to a funeral."

He probably took her good mood to mean that yesterday's meeting with Colin Brewster had gone well, but she still had no idea what the outcome would be. Deb said she'd call, but she hadn't thus far. Amanda didn't want to worry about what that could mean. "It's just Zoe. She cracks me up."

"What did she do?"

"She loves to wear her food." She chuckled, and it had Trent smiling.

"And that's a good thing?"

"Yeah, it is."

Trent pulled into the church's lot. It was already packed, and it was an hour before the service. "Wow, this place is busy."

"Guess we should have expected this. Chloe was popular and young." Just that latter fact typically drew a crowd.

"And her murder was in the news. Everyone's wanting to gawk at the family."

Trent's view of the human species was cynical but held far more truth than she cared to admit.

He wedged the department car between a Kia and BMW.

They went into the church and stood to the side of the doors, watching everyone coming in. Some faces were familiar—students and faculty from the school and those they'd spoken to throughout the course of the investigation thus far.

From their vantage point, she and Trent could see up the aisle to the front of the church where the casket was. Its lid was open, but someone was standing near it and routing people away for the time being. According to the greeter at the door, attendees could go up and say their goodbyes when the service was over. Those people must have missed receiving that message or were trying to push their luck.

When the time came, the priest said some words. Sitting there and hearing about a God who wrapped Chloe in his loving arms was sickening. Amanda could never reconcile a caring being with someone who took loved ones. All of this was almost too much to handle. She'd been so focused on the case and then distracted by the fun with Zoe before coming here that she hadn't stopped to consider she was going to a funeral.

Images of Kevin's and Lindsey's caskets lowering in the ground flashed over her vision, and she did her best to blink them away.

She had to start living life forward, not back.

When the service ended, those gathered sang hymns and listened to the priest send up a prayer on behalf of Chloe's soul.

People were slow at moving out and many headed to the casket.

Amanda bobbed her head in that direction and said to Trent, "We need to be closer."

They found a place nestled off to the side that still gave them a line of sight to every mourner who came to pay their respects to the young woman.

Josh Ryder could barely keep himself upright as he stumbled toward the casket. He stopped next to it and looked down. He sobbed like a child, pressed a kiss to his fingers, and touched them to her collarbone. He staggered off, stumbling on the leg of a chair, but someone helped him stay upright.

Lauren Bennett was next, dressed in black from head to toe. She repeatedly dabbed at her nose with a tissue and held a clutch purse in the other hand. She spoke to Chloe for long enough that the woman behind her tapped a foot.

Associate Dean Craig Perkins stopped by the casket, looked in, and walked off without a word, but he was crying silently. And the way he staggered, Amanda would guess he had tipped a bottle of amber liquid before coming here. The whole situation was probably too much for the man. While he might not have been as close to Chloe as Jayne, he had to have been thinking that Jayne's funeral was just around the corner. He went over to the Somners and hugged each of them in turn. Then he stood with Connie and Ted Russell, who watched on as mourners lined the aisle. Amanda knew how it must feel knowing their daughter would be next—devastating beyond measure.

Luke Hogan was there with his mother, Judy, and his father, who Amanda recognized from his driver's license photo. Luke palmed his cheeks and looked at Chloe for several moments until his mother tapped his back. Luke didn't look Amanda and Trent's way once.

Several professors from the school said their goodbyes, including William McMillan, who signed the cross and mouthed a prayer over her body.

Eventually, Melissa Somner stepped up and stood over her daughter's casket, tears streaming down her face. She wailed out and clamped a hand over her mouth, rocking back and forth. Her husband, Mitch, came over and lovingly put an arm around her as they walked away.

It was taking all of Amanda's power to hold it together. Her own grief from her losses was palpable amid the pain and heart-break in this church.

As the crowd thinned, Stephanie Piper approached the casket. She gripped the edge of it and looked inside. She was crying, her mouth contorted in anguish.

Amanda nudged Trent in the elbow for him to pay close attention.

Stephanie stood there sobbing for some time. When she turned to leave, she caught Amanda's eye and dipped her head in greeting. She walked toward the entrance of the church to where Professor McMillan was standing next to a woman, perhaps his wife.

Stephanie leaned against him, and he put his arm around her.

Amanda grabbed Trent's arm and whispered, "What's going on there?" She nodded in that direction. Maybe she was judging the situation wrong and seeing something illicit that wasn't there.

"Good question."

The professor swept Stephanie's hair back and kissed her forehead, and the trio walked off.

Swept her hair back and kissed her forehead... Just like Amanda did with Zoe. Her first impression was wrong! "Professor McMillan is Stephanie's father... or a close relative, at least."

"You think so? They have different last names."

"Yeah, but they could be a blended family. Stephanie could be his stepdaughter."

"All right. What does that mean for us?"

"You saw the way that Stephanie reacted today? It's not exactly how she's been with us up until this point." The most emotion she had shown was discomfort with the interview process. When they'd first told her about Chloe, she hadn't shed a tear. But she had been emotional at thinking Luke might have killed Chloe and Jayne. Was that all this was now or was she a brilliant actress calling on emotions when they suited her?

"I agree she seems really upset."

"From guilt?" Amanda was getting this tingling feeling running right through her. "She's tall enough, and she's strong. You just have to look at her athletic frame to know that." Amanda recalled the way the girl had made eye contact with her as she was walking away from the casket. Was it to rub it in? "Right under our noses," Amanda mumbled and tugged Trent's arm. "Come on, we've got to go to Central and do some digging."

FORTY

Amanda rolled closer to her desk and brought up the video from the state park, studying the shadowed figure, angling her head every which way, as if it would better her focus. "Could that be Stephanie?"

Trent bent forward and scrutinized the image. "It could be. But... I don't know."

Amanda played the video and watched the movements of the person on the screen. She wasn't an expert on gait to know whether this was a man or woman just by the way they walked. "Shoot."

"Okay, well, we know Stephanie has no alibi for the mornings of the murders either. Just that she was home sleeping. She had reason to hate Chloe and Jayne. Chloe always outshone her. Jayne rubbed that fact in."

She mulled both facts over. Had it been enough to move the girl to murder? But it was hard to ignore the complete change in her demeanor from when they spoke to her previously and today at the funeral. At the church, she had appeared quite shaken and affected by Chloe's death. Then again, funerals had a way of reaching in, grabbing one's heart, and squeezing so hard there was no redemption. The finality couldn't be ignored any longer.

Amanda keyed in Stephanie's name to pull her background again. Something she'd seen earlier in the investigation, but at that time nothing had popped. She wanted to do some more digging before they headed over to question Stephanie once again. "Her father is listed as Max Piper, fifty-one, and the mother as Leah McMillan, forty-two."

"So the professor is her stepfather. And no one mentioned that at all before now?"

She gave it some thought. "Really, there was no need for it come up, but look"—she pointed to Leah's maiden name—"Turnbull. Holy shit."

"And that name is a big deal because...?"

"Black orchids."

Trent smiled. "I'll need more than that."

"When we were at Lee's Flowers in Woodbridge, Lee took out the order book..."

"I remember."

"The name of the person who ordered black orchids was Leah Turnbull. Why she'd used her maiden name, I don't know. Maybe she hadn't married McMillan yet?"

"Well, that was three years ago when the flowers were ordered," he pointed out.

She looked in the system. "Looks like they've been married a couple of years. Ah, so that's why she used Turnbull. But as you said before, the killer could have access to a private stock of the flower."

"Okay, well, if she ordered the orchids to grow and breed herself, then she might need to have some sort of greenhouse." He raced around to his cubicle, and his chair squeaked as he sat down. He started typing.

Curious, she went to his desk to see what he was doing.

"Look." He pointed to the screen, which showed a satellite's view of an impressive house. "This is the McMillan property. That there, I'd say, is a greenhouse."

There was a part of the house that jutted out, and it was clearly a greenhouse given its ceiling of windows.

"We just connected Stephanie Piper to black orchids, but let's take a step back and talk this out a minute. From the looks of the report I pulled, Stephanie lives in Woodbridge with her parents," she said.

"I can see that. Stephanie was focused on her studies. By living at home, she'd have less distractions."

"All that hard work, and Chloe could have made her feel like her efforts were insignificant. Maybe Stephanie couldn't take it anymore and snapped. Though, if she's our killer, she still took her time to think about the execution of the murders."

He shrugged. "She's a smart girl."

The more they spoke, the more plausible it was that Stephanie Piper was the killer—right under their noses. She didn't have an alibi for either murder. But how did she connect with Ashton Chambers, if she did at all? Was it just a coincidence that he was the one who drove the killer to the park *and* had a past with Chloe?

Then Amanda remembered something. "Stephanie told us she was a nervous driver and that she took public transportation..."

"Right. So she could have ordered the car from the Pick Me Up app."

"I wonder if there isn't more to it. Maybe she went to high school with Chloe and the rest of them. If so, she would have known what Chloe had put Ashton through. She could have found out what Ashton did for money and exploited that, knowing there would be a possibility that the investigation would lead back to him."

"Very smart, if so. We're busy looking at Ashton and who he could have teamed up with, all the while not looking at her."

"Where did Stephanie go to high school?" She jogged back to her cubicle where the report was still on the screen.

Trent leaned in, beating her to the answer. "Looks like Leah has always lived in Woodbridge so it could be assumed Stephanie has too."

"Just like the Somners. It would be plausible Stephanie went to the same high school as Chloe, Jayne... Ashton. It's time to brief Malone and move on this."

"Just go in there from a calm perspective, have a talk with her, feel her out," Malone said from the other end of the line. He wasn't in the best of moods, but she had interrupted an early dinner.

Back in her cubicle, Amanda had him on speaker so Trent could be part of the conversation too. "You heard what we have on her, right? The connection to—"

"The black orchids. Yes. I heard everything you said. But we just can't go running in there on another assumption."

Sure, she could admit that the track record with this case hadn't been that great. There had been a lot of leads that didn't pan out, but they all served as stepping stones to get them to the true killer. That, Amanda knew in her bones. And in her and Trent's defense, they'd had valid reasons for bringing in each suspect when they had. "We're moving forward based on evidence," she seethed, taking a tone she didn't very often pull on Malone.

"Don't get smart with me, Amanda. Do you have information back yet from the credit card company on who ordered the car? What about DNA evidence or... or... that spoofing angle?"

She glanced at Trent, who nodded—her silent message that she needed some privacy received. She took Malone off speaker and walked with her phone to a small conference room and closed the door.

"Are you still there?" he prompted.

"I'm here, but I'm wondering what happened to Sergeant Malone."

There was a stretch of silence. One he didn't fill.

"Stephanie Piper had motive, as well as access to black orchids."

"Josh had motive, Luke had motive, Ashton—"

"Fine, I concede. Yes, they all did, but Trent and I had valid reason to pull them in for questioning and to hold them." Luke would have still been in lockup if she'd had her way.

"And you say Piper has access to black orchids, but do you know that for sure? You're basing it on an order her mother—or someone with the same name—made three years ago and a greenhouse on the property. She could be growing hydrangeas, for all you know."

She clamped her mouth shut. He had a point. Had she gotten so wound up in trying to close the case she was making leaps now? She could appreciate if it was her alone, but Trent had his suspicions about Stephanie Piper too. That had to mean something.

"Detective?"

By using her title, he was reminding her that at this moment he was her boss, not her friend. Still, she had to push—a little. "Sarge," she began, going with his formal address, "usually you'd be backing me up. 'Always have your back,' isn't that what you say?"

There were a few beats of silence.

"Is there something you want to tell me?" She voiced the question with respect.

"There is."

She'd suspected there was something, but hearing confirmation of that had her pulling out a chair at the table in the room and sitting down. "What is it?"

"I've been trying to figure out a way to tell you, *when* to tell you."

"Just tell me. You should know that about me by now." The part left unsaid was that she preferred people speak their truth, to hit her with it straight-up, even if it was cold, brutal, and paralyzing.

"I've been recommended to be the next police chief."

If she hadn't been sitting, she'd be on the floor. Not because Malone didn't deserve the post—he more than did. The appointment would catapult him to the top of the command structure without the need to climb all the ranks to get there. It was rare when this sort of offering came along but not completely unheard of. But if Malone accepted the position, where would that leave her? Who would take his place as her sergeant, and what kind of person would they be to work under? All these were selfish thoughts, but still... "I didn't know you wanted to be chief." Those words tumbled out in place of "congratulations," and remorse fluttered through her.

"It wasn't something I set out to do, but it's holding some appeal the older I get."

Malone was in his fifties—quickly approaching geriatric in law enforcement. "So you're taking the job?" She swallowed roughly. She'd miss him.

"I'm giving it some serious thought."

"And that's why you've been coming down a little hard on us lately?"

"Hard on you? Pfft. I'm never hard enough when it comes to you. But, yeah, it's why I'm watching the investigation a little more closely. To make sure everything that happens is above reproach."

"I understand." His words reminded her of how she'd disappointed Malone by running off to pursue a killer in the past without notifying him or taking proper backup.

"Anyway, now you know."

"Keep me posted on what you end up deciding, okay?"

"I will. And you keep me posted on what comes of your interview with Stephanie Piper."

"Yep." Amanda hung up, and she had this sick feeling in the pit of her stomach. She had dreaded that they were making the wrong call approaching the McMillan household without backup. Her and Trent's lives could be on the line if things went sideways—along with Malone's judgment for his refusal to take his detectives' suspicions seriously. But she had her orders, and she would follow them.

FORTY-ONE

The McMillans lived in a stately home with a large front yard, wide driveway, and a double-car garage. The Mercedes was in the lane, but the couple's BMW could be in the garage.

Amanda rang the doorbell, Trent by her side. A trickle ran down her spine, telling her it was a horrible idea to come here with no other backup.

The door was opened by the woman who had been standing next to the professor at the church. A face Amanda now recognized from the background they'd pulled on Leah McMillan and her driver's license photo. Amanda and Trent held up their badges.

Amanda introduced them and asked, "Is Stephanie home?"

"She is, but now really isn't a good time."

"We won't be long."

Leah's gaze flitted about, landing briefly on Amanda, then Trent, then behind them to the street. "Fine. Come in." She opened the door wider.

The home was open concept from the front door, and there was a large, circular table in the middle of the entry beneath a teardrop chandelier. A staircase swept up the right wall, and there was a small landing that overlooked the entry. But in spite of the grand opulence—something that didn't really impress Amanda at any time—the vase of flowers on the table had her attention. Black orchids.

"You have a beautiful home," Amanda said, moving farther inside the house.

"Thank you." Leah's body language was stiff and awkward. She clasped her hands in front of herself, then let them fall free. "Let me get Steph. I'll be right back." She took off up the staircase.

Amanda and Trent stared at the orchids and then each other. "Black orchids in plain sight," she whispered.

Trent nodded.

She thought about calling Malone right then and there, but given his current mood, he would likely say a few in a vase hardly constituted a smoking gun.

Footsteps padded overhead, toward the back of the home. Then low voices.

Amanda immediately moved deeper into the house, working in the direction of where the greenhouse had been on the satellite image.

"What are you doing?" Trent hissed from the foyer.

"Greenhouse," she said over her shoulder.

He shook his head. She kept moving.

She had a backup plan if she got caught snooping. She kept her steps light and slinked down a corridor. Trent would no longer have a line of sight to her, and it was possibly risky doing this, but Stephanie, their suspected killer, was upstairs. Amanda would be fine.

Light spilled into the hallway straight ahead. Her target was just a few feet away.

She picked up her pace. Stopped cold.

More movement above her, footsteps headed for the front of the house.

Frick!

She hustled, giving quick looks around her. She reached the door for the greenhouse and held her breath as she turned the handle. It was unlocked. She went inside, and stepped into a space overrun with different varieties of orchids in assorted colors, along with roses and other flowers Amanda couldn't name. She found the black orchids in the far corner of the greenhouse, farthest from the house. Why were they tucked away back there, or was it where Leah always kept them?

Amanda picked up her pace. She needed to look at the plants and search for any evidence that stems had been cut recently.

Her heart was racing, and her mind was screaming at her to hurry the hell up and get out of there.

She reached the plants and inspected them. Then she spotted what she was searching for—several, in fact. Would any of these cuts match up with the stems left on the girls' bodies? She pulled out her phone and took a few pictures.

"Detective Steele, is it?" A man's voice from behind her.

She pinched her eyes shut briefly, trying to calm herself, and slowly put her phone away. She faced him and smiled. Professor McMillan, and he was still dressed in the suit he'd worn to the funeral.

"Oh, hello, Professor." She did her best to hide the fact that she'd been busted where she had no right being.

"Is there something I can help you with?"

"I was looking for the bathroom when I noticed all these beautiful flowers. I got distracted. But I really need to go." She winced and bounced in place.

He was scowling. "Well, you're not going to find a bathroom in here."

"As I said, I got distracted, and it's been one of those days. I must have gotten turned around." She went to pass him, but he remained immovable.

"First door on the right. You would have had to go by it to get here. Why are you in my house?"

"We just wanted to speak to Stephanie. My partner's at the entrance waiting for her."

He still hadn't shuffled aside to let her by, and she had this sickening feeling of dread. Someone right under their nose. Someone at the school... They'd been focused on the students, but what if— No, what motive could he possibly have?

"Why do you want to see Stephanie?"

"She seemed quite upset today. We wanted to check on her." She put it out there nonchalantly, as if this were just a social visit.

He stiffened. "Well, she did lose a classmate in a horrible way. That's bound to do it."

"Very true. Two classmates, in fact."

"Right. So I'm not sure why you'd want to bother her now. Her mother and I can take care of her." He pinned her with his gaze, and she didn't like how it sent shivers slicing through her. He was also still blocking her path.

What motive? The question repeated in her head with the rhythm of a repetitive—and annoying—bass beat.

"Detective Steele?" Stephanie was in the doorway of the greenhouse with Trent and Leah. "Mom said you wanted to talk?"

The best way to describe Stephanie's expression would be *distraught*, plain and simple. Her hair was frizzy, and her face was blotchy. Her eyes were bloodshot and shadowed with dark rings.

"We would like to, yes," Amanda said, stepping around William.

"Thought you were in desperate need of using the bathroom?" William asked, now behind her.

She looked over a shoulder at him. "Oh, I've held it this long. A bit more shouldn't hurt." There was something strange to the energy in the room. It felt entirely *off*. But she still needed to get a grip on the situation and what it was telling her. The professor was acting suspicious. Had he acted alone or were the murders a family affair?

Stephanie was looking at her as if waiting for Amanda to speak.

Amanda looked around, and saw no place to sit. She positioned herself so she was at the side of the greenhouse—to her right was the house, Trent, Stephanie, and Leah, and to her left was the professor. "It might be easier if we sat down," she said, directing this to Stephanie, but she saw the mother's face.

It was just a glimmer of a glance, so minuscule it would have been easy to miss, but Leah appeared to be looking in her husband's direction. Amanda turned to him, to Leah, back to him. Their eyes were locked on each other's, and something had been communicated between them.

She turned again to Leah and watched in horror as the woman snatched Trent's service weapon from his holster. It all happened so quickly.

Leah nudged Trent into the greenhouse. He met Amanda's gaze, and his face was pale, his features shadowed with fear. Leah held the gun on him, but Amanda had drawn her gun too. She kept it pointed on Leah and glanced back at the professor.

He was holding a knife on her—in his left hand—and the tip was missing. Had he killed Chloe Somner and Jayne Russell with this blade?

"Mom! Bill! What are you doing?" Stephanie was screaming hysterically.

"Get out of here, Steph! Go to your room!" William barked.

Stephanie jumped at his voice but stayed put. "What are you doing?" she wailed.

"We're not letting you accuse my little girl of murder." Leah ignored her daughter's question, and her hold on the gun was uneasy, her hand shaking.

Amanda met Trent's concerned gaze as she tried to piece it all together. Had Leah conspired with her husband or was she simply aware of what he'd done and was determined to protect him? There was also the matter of motive—something that could wait considering the weapons in her and Trent's faces.

"We're not accusing any—" The blunt end of the blade pressed to her neck had her shutting up.

"Of course you are. That's why you're here. The police don't stop by for friendly chitchat. Not without an agenda." Considering he was holding one cop at knifepoint, and his wife across the room was holding a service weapon on them, he was speaking in a level tone, calm, surrendered.

Motive? She was screaming the question in her head now, hoping it would net an answer. "We just wanted to talk with her." Amanda grunted as the blade dug into her flesh enough that she felt the warmth of blood trickle down her neck. Her gun was still in her hand, but she might as well be unarmed for its current usefulness.

"Bullshit. I'm not going to let you hurt her and put her through more grief," he spat and tapped his hand against his leg seven times.

The same number of stab wounds. Rideout had mentioned the killer might have OCD.

"You're hurting her this minute by your actions."

"I'm—*we're*—protecting her. That's a father's job."

She'd have done almost anything to protect Lindsey, and now Zoe. Had he seen Chloe and Jayne as a threat to his stepdaughter? Had that been all it took to push the professor to murder—twice? "But you couldn't, could you?" she challenged him. "You couldn't protect her. Not from the kids at school. Not from Chloe or Jayne. You were powerless to do anything about them. Until you came up with an idea."

"Shut up. Now."

"Bill, is that true?" Stephanie was crying as she spoke.

The professor was trembling beside Amanda.

"Did you kill them?" The question tore from Stephanie as a piercing, high-pitched squeal.

"I... I didn't have a choice, sweetheart." His voice was gravelly. Again, he tapped a hand to his thigh seven times. "Chloe treated you like shit! She took everything from you! I saw how hard you worked, and she just stepped all over you."

"It wasn't like that," Stephanie snapped. "Yes, she beat me at a lot of things, but she only made me want to do better. She challenged me."

"But the way you'd go to your room and cry over her."

It sounded like he was trying to get his stepdaughter to understand why he had to murder Chloe and to accept his reasons, but Stephanie was shaking her head as angry tears fell. The professor had also underplayed Stephanie's reaction when they'd interviewed him. He'd said that she sulked but got over it.

"Did you kill Jayne too?" Stephanie asked.

"She was just as bad, always making you feel like you were nothing. Both of them were mean girls, honey. And Jayne couldn't even be loyal to her best friend, Chloe. I saw her kissing Josh."

"They broke up. And don't call me honey!"

William must have sent the text! If he'd seen Jayne and Josh together, that explained his gamble that Jayne would respond favorably to Josh's text. His observations would also have meant he knew Jayne liked being next to the river on campus.

"And maybe they couldn't help it. Chloe anyway. Her dad is a corporate asshole."

"So what?" Stephanie pulled on her hair and stepped back, regarded her mother. "And, Mom... did you know he did this? That he killed them?"

"He did it for you, Steph."

"Mom." One word, a strangled expression. Life as

Stephanie had known it was shattered. She pulled out her phone. "I'm calling nine-one-one."

"Don't." William's firm tone had Stephanie's attention. The blade had Amanda's. He'd pushed it in a little deeper. "If you do, I'll kill her. And your mom... well, she'll kill him."

Stephanie's eyes widened. "Stop. Leave them alone."

"Go to your room," Leah barked at her daughter.

"I'm not going anywhere." She crossed her arms.

During this time, Amanda and Trent kept catching each other's eyes, trying to silently communicate their next move and how to deescalate the situation. They needed just the crack of an opening.

Amanda considered her next words carefully. If she asked them what sort of outcome they expected here, it could help the McMillans see there would be no positive one for them. The flipside was it would encourage—and challenge—them to think about just how they would get away with murder... again. "Why the black orchid?" Maybe something unexpected could buy her and Trent an opportunity. So far, she still had her gun, but the odds were against her unless something changed the dynamics.

"Why not? What does it matter?" William scrunched up his face.

Amanda tilted her head toward Leah and said, "She knows what it represents."

Leah spoke, monotone, devoid of emotion. "Light and dark. Good and evil. Perfect for those girls."

Goosebumps laced Amanda's arms. "You really do know the flower."

"So what?"

There was no evidence of a partnership at the crime scenes, and it would have been tricky to pull off as a team. But it was obvious that Leah was aware of what her husband had done and condoned it—maybe even helped in the planning. "The black orchid was *your* touch."

"Smart as you are pretty, Detective," Leah said.

"Mom!" Stephanie screamed.

"Those girls were evil, Stephanie. You are so good, light. They were taking your future from you. And now they'll also be exposed for the type of people they really were."

Why they were posed naked...

"They made me better." Stephanie folded into herself and sobbed.

"Enough talk. Let's get this over with." The professor nudged his head toward Leah, then spoke in Amanda's ear. "Put your gun down."

"I will. Nice and slow." She held up one hand and leaned forward to put the Glock on the table in front of her next to pots of yellow orchids. Her gaze drifted briefly to the red roses climbing up a trellis in the corner. Something clicked at the edge of her consciousness, something just out of reach.

William had given a little space between her and his blade. It was the opening she needed. Making eye contact with Trent, she nodded slightly.

She tucked her gun into her chest and lowered to the ground, placing more distance between her and the professor as she did so. He lunged toward her, and Amanda prepared herself to pull the trigger. But she didn't need to.

A thundering boom.

William dropped the knife, and it clattered to the ground. He grabbed his chest as red bloomed across the fabric of his shirt. Then he crumpled into a heap.

Amanda kicked the knife out of his reach and turned around.

Trent had his gun back, and it was trained on Leah. In the time Amanda had made her move, he must have made his, regained control of his weapon and taken the shot. Brilliant.

Leah was wailing out her husband's name.

She tried to get to William, but Trent held her back.

Stephanie was standing in the doorway, shaking, pretty much paralyzed from everything she had just witnessed.

As Amanda placed the call for responders, she took in the carnage around her.

Leah and William would be going to prison—if he survived the bullet to his chest.

And all of this had been for the love of a child—a warped perception of love. And maybe that was the best anyone could settle for. Love was unique to every individual and yet a glue that held societies together. Amanda was prepared to do all she could to fight for Zoe, but at what cost? Maybe the girl's biological father was the best thing for her. Maybe a fresh start in a new city and state was what Zoe needed. Sometimes true, unconditional love meant letting those you love the most go.

EPILOGUE

TWO DAYS LATER

Monday

"Everything will be okay in the end; if it's not okay, it's not the end." Maybe there was some merit to that saying, after all. Before Zoe, she wouldn't have agreed. But Zoe had her imagining that a bright future was possible, and every moment she spent with her, she was enraptured by her innocent curiosity and zest for life. For however long she and Zoe had together, Amanda was going to make the most of it.

She'd taken the day off work and pulled Zoe from school. One day here or there wouldn't hurt anything. Besides, Zoe *was* getting an education today, even if it wasn't in a classroom. They were at the aquarium in Washington, standing in front of a large tank watching stingrays put on a performance. Zoe kept giggling and pointing to each one as it swam close. Her fingerprints smeared the glass, making Amanda happy that cleaning it wasn't her job. There would be millions of little hand impressions by the end of the day.

As they wandered the aquarium, she kept thinking about how blessed she was to have Zoe in her life. She even dared to dream what awaited them in the future. But intermixed in her thoughts were ones about the investigation, about how everything had shaken out.

William McMillan was going to survive the bullet wound. He and Leah were facing two charges of conspiracy to commit murder and two murder charges in the first degree. Leah was remaining tight-lipped about her role with the black orchids, but there was damning evidence against her. The sprigs left with Chloe Somner and Jayne Russell tied back to two plants in Leah's greenhouse collection.

The knife that William had pulled on Amanda was also a match for the one used to kill both girls, and the tip recovered from one of the wounds in Jayne's body clinched it as the murder weapon.

While they still waited on DNA, William was the right blood type for what had been left on the snail. Amanda loved how that small bit of evidence played out to help them put a killer behind bars. It was like Chloe's dedication and interest in them had paid off.

The search of Chloe's car hadn't revealed any implicating evidence, and Amanda didn't hold out much hope her belongings or Jayne's would ever be found. The McMillans weren't talking about where or how they'd disposed of them. All the investigation turned up was that blue coral necklace and the running shoe found in the forest, which also ended up being Chloe's. Amanda would have liked to be able to return Chloe's laptop and all the information on it to her parents, but that wasn't looking promising.

The credit card information from Pick Me Up linked back to William.

After talking with Stephanie, they learned that Ashton Chambers had given her a ride home a few weeks ago when she'd requested one from the app. She'd mentioned running into him to her mother and what his life currently looked like.

Leah must have blamed that high school prank for his less-than-stellar career path, and it served as the last push she and William needed to kill Chloe and Jayne. But they'd also needed someone to cast suspicion away from themselves and had targeted Ashton Chambers. He'd been victimized again.

Detective Jacob Briggs was able to find out who had spoofed Josh's phone number and that had led to a burner in Leah's possession. When questioned about it, she had said, "It wasn't hard, and why not try to frame the boy? He wasn't any better to my girl and had no loyalty. He should just be happy that William didn't kill him too."

Just thinking about Leah McMillan sent shivers running through Amanda. She was one cold-hearted, homicidal bitch. But, as it turned out, William McMillan wasn't much better. He'd conspired and schemed with her and carried out the actual murders.

"Look at that fish! He looks like he's on fire!" Zoe was tugging on Amanda's arm.

"Wow, would you look at that?" *Bright red...* Just like the rose left with Annie Frasier. Leah... *cold-hearted, homicidal.* She had red roses in her greenhouse. A common flower, a mere coincidence? Twenty years ago, Leah would have been twenty-two—college age. Stephanie had mentioned that her mother had a rival in college the first time they'd spoken with the girl. Her mother had tried to convince Stephanie that it only pushed her to work harder—but what if it pushed her to do something else?

Amanda shook her head. She'd taken the day off work, one measly day, and murder was still on her mind. She pulled out her phone and called Trent. The moment he answered, she rushed out, "What university did Annie Frasier go to twenty years ago?"

"Georgetown."

"What university did Leah attend?"

"One minute..." Fingers clicking on a keyboard. "Same."

"There's something about Leah that isn't sitting with me. She's cold and calculating and doesn't seem fazed by any of this."

"I agree."

"Can we connect her to Frasier from years ago? Apart from them going to the same college?"

"Let me call the Metro PD detective and see what he says."

"Call me the second you hear anything." She pocketed her phone and put a hand on Zoe's shoulder. She was just getting comfortable when her phone rang. "Just going to get this, sweetie." Zoe was busy staring into the tank.

Deb Hibbert was calling. Amanda took a deep breath and answered. Whatever she had to say, she and Zoe would weather the storm and get through it. Somehow.

"Amanda," Deb said. Just her name, and it had Amanda breathing easier. There was good news coming. She could feel it. She reached for Zoe's hand. The girl smiled up at her.

"Colin isn't going to pursue custody. He saw how good you and Zoe are together, and he admits he's really not in the position to take her on in his life."

She could breathe fully now, her lungs expanded. "That's such great news."

"I'm very happy for you two. There are just some more boxes to tick off, but I suspect that it may be possible for the two of you to officially be a family by Christmastime."

"Oh, we're already that." She smiled and swung Zoe's arm. The child giggled and yanked her hand free.

"Oooh." She was pointing at another fish. This one tall and thin, and the brightest blue Amanda had ever seen.

"Legally, I should say. Overall, the process has gone smoothly for you two. Like you're meant to be. Have a great day," Deb said.

"Thanks." Amanda ended the call. *Meant to be.* Say that again! She'd taken that picture Zoe had drawn during their meeting with Colin and had bought a frame for it. She'd placed it inside and gifted it to Zoe before they left home that morning. They'd decided the perfect spot was next to the front door and hung it before leaving the house. It would mean even more now. In just a matter of weeks, it would be official. Zoe would be hers, and she Zoe's.

Her phone rang again. This time it was Malone.

"Thought you'd want to be one of the first to know," he said. "I've decided to put off being chief for now. Not the right move just yet."

She knew he'd harbored some guilt and regret over not taking her and Trent's suspicions as seriously as the situation ended up warranting. But he didn't have a crystal ball, let alone the ability to read one. If he hadn't been concerned about impressing the Board of County Supervisors, who appointed the police chief, maybe he would have sent them with backup. "I'm supposed to encourage you to take the post, but..."

"Not at all." He was smiling, the expression traveling the line. "Besides, now I'll be around longer to mold you and Trent into respectable detectives."

"Hey." She laughed.

"I'm proud to be your sergeant."

"We're proud to have you."

"And to think you fought me like hell when I first tried to pair you with Trent."

She rolled her eyes. "Is this where you say 'I told you so'?"

"Why not? I did tell you so." He said goodbye and ended the call.

She couldn't stop grinning, and that lasted all day. They were getting their coats from the coat check around four thirty when her phone rang.

"It's always ringing," Zoe said to her.

"It is," Amanda agreed and answered.

"Got in touch with the detective. Leah was a classmate of

Annie Frasier's, and the two of them were apparently seeing each other."

"Ooh, the reason for the red rose is becoming clearer—if Leah did kill her." Not that Amanda had any doubts that she had. And red roses symbolized passion and romance, which was a well-known representation of the flower and something Leah would be very familiar with. She'd have chosen it because it was how she'd felt about Annie Frasier, though it would seem at some point Annie had let her down. "Competitors and lovers? It must have worked for them."

"Until it didn't? Anyway, the detective had interviewed Leah but never really considered her a suspect, so she wasn't on that list they'd sent over."

"She's a good actress. The detective needs to question her again. Did you tell him she's under arrest for her involvement with two murders?"

"Yep, and he's going to revisit the cold case."

"Good news."

"Yeah, it is."

The line went silent, but it was one of those voids that felt electric. Trent had something else to say, but she broke the silence.

"I have more good news." She became aware of Zoe beside her again, and she couldn't say what she was going to. "I'll text you. I can't say it right now."

"Okay. Well, I'll look for it."

They ended the call, and she texted Trent, *Colin not going for custody. Zoe may officially be mine by Christmas!*

Not five seconds later, she received his response.

I knew it! Congratulations. X

Her heart paused beating. X? Did he mean to send her a kiss? No, it had to be a finger slip.

She shook her head and tried to laugh it off. Yep. Surely it had just been a mistake. She silenced her phone and put it in her pocket. No more interruptions. Whatever happened in the world today could wait for her until tomorrow.

She looked at Zoe, who had her head tilted back, her mouth open in a wide grin, showing off the gap where she'd lost that tooth. The Tooth Fairy had visited on Sunday. "Want to get some ice cream now?" It didn't matter it was pretty much dinnertime.

"Yes, please!" she squealed.

They left the aquarium and stepped outside. Amanda took in a deep breath of the cool fall air. She supposed this would be considered "the end" in that old adage, but everything was far more than okay. It was absolutely fantastic.

A LETTER FROM CAROLYN

Dear reader,

I want to say a huge thank you for choosing to read *Black Orchid Girls*. If you enjoyed it and would like to hear about new releases in the Amanda Steele series, just sign up at the following link. Your email address will never be shared, and you can unsubscribe at any time.

www.bookouture.com/carolyn-arnold

If you loved *Black Orchid Girls*, I would be incredibly grateful if you would write a brief, honest review. Also, if you'd like to continue investigating murder, you'll be happy to know there will be more Detective Amanda Steele books. I also offer several other international bestselling series and have over thirty published books for you to savor, everything from crime fiction, to cozy mysteries, to thrillers and action adventures. One of these series features Detective Madison Knight, another kick-ass female detective, who will risk her life, her badge—whatever it takes—to find justice for murder victims.

Also, if you enjoyed being in the Prince William County, Virginia area, you might want to return in my Brandon Fisher FBI series. Brandon is Becky Tulson's boyfriend—we didn't see much of him in this book, but you'll be able to be there when they meet in *Silent Graves* (book two in the series). This series is perfect for readers who love heart-pounding thrillers and are fascinated with the psychology of serial killers. Each installment is a new case with a fresh bloody trail to follow. Hunt with the FBI's Behavioral Analysis Unit and profile some of the most devious and darkest minds on the planet.

And if you're familiar with the Prince William County, Virginia area, or have done some internet searching, you'll realize some differences between reality and my book. That's me taking creative liberties.

Last but certainly not least, I love hearing from my readers! You can get in touch on my Facebook page, through Twitter, Goodreads, or my website. This is also a good way to stay notified of my new releases. You can also reach out to me via email at Carolyn@CarolynArnold.net.

Wishing you a thrill a word!

Carolyn Arnold

Connect with CAROLYN ARNOLD online:

carolynarnold.net

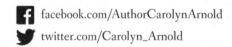
facebook.com/AuthorCarolynArnold
twitter.com/Carolyn_Arnold